THE LAST MUSIC BEARER

NEIL MACH

The Last Music Bearer

Neil Mach

© Copyright March 23rd 2015

The right of Neil Mach to be identified as author of this work has been asserted by him in accordance with the Copyright, Designs and Patents Act 1988.

All Rights Reserved

No reproduction, copy or transmission of this publication may be made without written permission. No paragraph of this publication may be reproduced, copied, or transmitted save with the written permission of the publisher, or in accordance with the provisions of the Copyright Act 1956 (as amended.)

Any person who does any unauthorised act in relation to this publication may be liable to criminal prosecution and civil claims for damage. A CIP catalogue record for this title is available from the British Library.

- First Published 2015
- Second edition 2016
- Third edition 2022

The eBook is licensed for personal enjoyment only. The eBook may not be re-sold or given away to other people. If you would like to share this book with another person, please purchase an additional copy for each recipient. If you're reading this book and you did not purchase it, or it was not purchased for your use only, please purchase your *own* copy. Thank you for respecting the hard work of this author.

Sketches by the author. Cover art by Mat Yan

❊ Created with Vellum

"Qui cantare volunt, semper carmen inveniunt..."

Those who want to sing will always find a song

— Brother Florian

1
THE CANTICLE OF THE FOUNDLING CHILD

Landgrave Grassus called for a male offspring. He required a male heir to perpetuate his royal succession. When his first child was born — a girl — he went through the covert handling of leaving the female baby out for 'a taking.' The father arranged that his daughter was surrendered by the wayside, a baby-in-a-bundle, so the monks would take her *elsewhere*. And the monks *did* take her away because they assumed she must be an orphan. Although, as we now know, she *was not*.

The Landgrave decided they should address the issue in this way, because it was a simple and definitive end to the matter. He did not consult the girl's mother. A man need not consult a woman about such complications, especially if the man is the kinglet of a minor kingdom. This was the way of all things.

The girl's mother, Landgravine Sophia, became outraged that her daughter had been snatched from her breast in such a callous way. She never thoroughly recovered from the shock of separation. Sophia retained the bitterness deep in her bosom. She confessed that *one day*, she would seek revenge upon the husband. She likewise prayed she would meet her stolen daughter again. Though the experience left her sterile.

Landgrave Grassus gained the son he demanded, a year after

forsaking his legitimate daughter. Voices inside the walls whispered that this young boy's mother must be a servant with no name or consequence. Not that a mother is important. A mother is never relevant in such things. The father, the male, passes on the name, the birth right, and the title. So only the man is necessary.

When Landgravine Sophia heard the news of the birth of the boy, she sent out her spies to locate the child. Once she discovered that the child lived beyond walls, with the family of a benevolent woodsman, the Landgravine had the boy forcibly removed. Then she determined, through the same spies, to have the child left outside, on the by-way — so traveling monks would remove him in the night too, just as they had taken her cherished daughter. And so the monks took the boy orphan away in the night, as they had taken away his half-sister. And with this mirror-act of revenge, the Landgravine thought it would lessen the pain that clasped her core and made her spirit furious with resentment. She thought that the removal of the Landgrave's son — his only true and living heir — would be an appropriate punishment for the pain and torment he had caused her. Yet, she continued to burn with bitterness, rage, and madness. Soon the Landgravine required more retribution.

∽

The venerable monks, known as the 'Music Bearers,' hired traveling-consuls to do their bidding. One of the consul's tasks was to 'take away' orphan-children. Constantly moving, a traveling-consul could never get not learn the true circumstances that linked a rejected child to a community. For example, on this occasion, the consul could not suppose the link between the child and the Landgrave. Nor could the consul suppose there was a link between the two babies taken from the same place the girl first and, later, the boy. Though, it surprised the traveling-consul, a consul named Temenos, that one of these babes showed no obvious sign of what they called the 'harmonic root.' Thus, the consul thought it highly irregular that a community would abandon a non-harmonic child for 'taking.' Such a thing was exceptionally rare. The circumstances of this abandonment did not altogether make sense. So, quite unusually, consul Temenos did a little private research into this child's background. The research allowed the consul to gain a better understanding about who the babe's parents had been.

The other child that Temenos took away, however, possessed amazing harmonic gifts and was a genuine treasure. One child was musical. The other was not.

The monks named the girl child Atalanta. Their secret order transformed her. They trained the girl to someday become their most valuable asset and they hoped she would provide a lifetime of service and help them achieve their most secret missions.

But this is a story about another child. This is a story about a boy named Elis. A boy abandoned by a parent. A boy whose mentally anguished mother left him to die.

2

THE CANTICLE OF MATTY

The two women had chosen a sloping side of the plot where the terrain was flinty, and the wind was cruel. The thorny windbreaks were on the other side of the incline, and lower down. But they had chosen a point on the slope that was higher, and which offered little shelter from icy gusts that penetrated the air.

The lower slope became kinder, with the landscape less craggy — they had chosen a higher point for a purpose. They favoured an uncomfortable place so they would not be disturbed.

From their position, at the top of the steep slope, the women viewed across several furlongs. It was to be a secret meeting. They wanted to see the early approach of any strangers.

The frosty rain penetrated their patchy shawls as they worked on the wet and grey afternoon. They harvested a few dirty roots — they collected them in a basket. But their minds were on other issues. They spoke about a child.

'Matty refuses to speak to other children. The others of his age use many words. They can recognise animals, objects, and faces. Matty just looks at me. He knows no words.'

The other woman gazed in understanding but did not want to interrupt. She knew it was important that the wife could explain her problem without interruption. The woman needed the freedom to express herself.

'Two of the sisters came from the convent on the hill to look at him—' the older woman continued. 'They asked questions. They brought him a straw dolly. The sisters smiled and played with Matty. They gave him the dolly. He did not react...' She wiped dirt from her fingertips. 'Later, they told me they had seen this type of thing before. They said that his head was not right... he will always be voiceless. He is impossibly mute.' The mother had moisture in her eyes. It may have been from the squall, or it may have been from growing tears. She pulled at her shawl to protect her neck. 'They said there's nothing they could do for him. He would grow that way. Never talking. He cannot notice things. He lives inside his head, do you see? That's what they told me. He does not share with the rest of the world...' The woman shuddered. The cold on the hill enclosed them. 'He will never be a real man. He will never father children. He will never fulfil destiny. It is heart-breaking—'

The mother was distraught. Her sobs were all used-up. A year of sobbing had exhausted her. Now the mother was out of ideas. That was the reason she had arranged this dangerous encounter.

The other woman finally spoke: 'He can never expect to become a trader or merchant. He may never be a parent — that much is true. But Matty might make an excellent farmer. He has a strong heart. He has healthy bones. He can use his fingers. He might become a useful craftsman —'

The other woman interrupted, 'That is what the sisters said too, when they visited. That's what the other mothers say when I chat with them at the market. It's why I came to you. Are you saying you cannot help me?'

The mood on the hill became chilled. The air seemed frosty. Even the wind silenced itself, as if an angel tried to eavesdrop on their hushed conversation. The younger woman took the mother by the hand and squeezed it tight, as if she were taking hold of a child's hand: 'Did your mother give you the gift of a cradle-song?'

'No! She was strict like that,' the older woman replied.

'And you?' This challenge was direct. It showed there was still mistrust between them.

'I just want what is best for Matty. If there's a chance... even if there's half-a-chance...'

Then the younger woman did something extraordinary. Quite unexpected. She moved her body closer to the mother and delicately turned her around, so the back of the older woman's neck now faced her young lips. She looped both her arms around the woman's waist, and she gently rocked her. It was as if the older woman were an infant and she, the younger female, became the parent. And while she cradled the mother this way, she pressed youthful lips close to the sides of the woman's temples. And she sang.

At first, the song was a minuscule sound. Too distant to hear. Like a feather fluttering. The smallest of tones. The trilling did not scare the older woman. In fact, it became ever-calming. The most luxurious feeling she had ever experienced.

And while she made the sweet sound, the younger girl swayed to another hidden rhythm. The woman experienced a wonderful moment of love. It seemed to go on for much longer than it did. After a short while, the swaying ceased. But the younger woman continued to embrace the mother with warmness.

'I know the Warrener...' The younger woman blurted: 'Take the child to see him. Go to his old house. Out by the glebe lands. Tell him I sent you to him. Find an excuse. Tell the others you are going for a walk. Say you are looking for new soil.' The two women sat in silence for a while. The rain became heavy. Both checked their basket. They regarded their miserable collection of roots. 'A Friar named Florian will see your boy at the Warren. I will make preparations. I will contact you when it is time to see visit it,' the younger girl explained. The older woman turned to look into the girl's eyes. She seemed so inexperienced. So sweet. Yet she seemed wiser and more sympathetic than any other woman in the world.

'That song that you sang to me, was that your cradle song?' the mother asked. The girl nodded.

3

THE CANTICLE OF THE MUTE BOY

The music bearer known as Brother Florian arrived at the next quarter moon, as scheduled. By then, the mother of the boy had already been to visit the Warrener, as advised. The warrener had expected her. He befriended both her and the sick son. He led her to an old building at the furthest edge of the fields. He explained the building had once been a chapel. A hermit had formerly used it. It had a musty, damp smell and toadstools grew in a ring around an entrance that had been veiled by spider webs. 'This is a good sign...' the Warrener had told her, as he wiped away the sticky threads with enormous hands. 'It means no one has been here for a long while.'

All these arrangements had to be put into place so that, when Brother Florian arrived, he had an entirely safe place to meet mother and boy. The old chapel was remote and secure.

On the allotted day, they sent the mother a message telling her to attend the Warren. By late afternoon, the light had already dimmed in a washed-out sky. The mother wrapped a chunk of barley bread in a leaf and placed it into a willow basket. Then she made sure a linen rag protected her boy from the chilly wind and wrapped his shawl tight around his bare little shoulders till only his pink face looked out. Then she hurried, with the lad, to the pre-defined location.

Instead of going through the main entrance at the Warren, though, she made her way into warrener's lands via the side — traveling through a small copse. This was so that she arrived at the deserted chapel by a curious route and could not easily be followed. She arrived in good time and waited inside the damp building for the music bearer to appear.

Soon she heard footsteps. Leaving her boy seated on the wet shawl, she peered out. A tall man approached. He had tousled black hair. She noticed he carried a leather bag. He had an elliptical face with dark eyebrows and brown eyes. He had a reddish complexion. Weather-stained, she assumed. She figured he might be about twenty summers old. He walked boldly toward the chapel. When he saw her, the man returned a generous smile. A beam that seemed to extend across his entire face, causing his eyes to glisten. 'Call me Florian,' he said as he greeted her with the sign of the cross.

Florian had sinewy arms and generous hands. The mother did not know if she ought to bow or curtsy. She felt confused by the man's unexpected friendliness. So she managed to do both. 'There is no need for awkwardness,' Florian said, with a grin. 'I'm just a working man.' He blessed her and blessed himself, before entering the chapel darkness. Once inside the deserted shrine, Florian went straight to the baby boy. As expected, the lad said nothing. The lad simply regarded his mother with a look of alarm on his face.

The mother reassured her son by saying, 'Hush, sweet boy. There is nothing to fear. The friar wants to look at you and ask some questions...'

Brother Florian seemed happy with this explanation, and a laughsome smile spread across his face: 'Right, let's see what I have in my bag for you, young man—' As he said this, the friar took a leather bag from around his neck. The mother made movements to go outside. 'There's no need to leave,' Florian told her. 'The boy will feel safer if you stay.'

Brother Florian found a handmade rattle in his bag. He pulled it out. It had been produced from a hollow root and had peas or beans hidden inside empty sections. As he revealed the thing, he shook it near the boy's ears. The boy gazed at the rattle. Neither mother nor son had ever encountered such a strange thing before. Then the friar started a song. The song was loud and uneven. With a lot of oohs! and aaahs!

The plainsong had a trotting rhythm. The mother thought it sounded like a lucky horse. The friar clattered the rattle with the rhythm of the verse. The song was about a pig. A big fat pig who slept all day in mud. Every time Brother Florian said the word 'pig' — he puffed-out his cheeks. His eyes protruded, too. He proclaimed every word with a big breath. As if he coughed-up the word. He rattled the root after saying each word. The mother guessed this was to reinforce the strength of the beat. Brother Florian went through the song again. It was a song cycle. It never stopped. It kept rolling. The mother thought the song sounded like a waterwheel she once saw. She wondered if it became a twirl of sound. She had never heard a song before, let alone a song-cycle!

Each time Brother Florian sang the word 'pig' — the boy burbled and smiled. The boy held out his little arm to grab for the rattle. This went on for a long time. The monk never tired, and the boy seemed to be thoroughly beguiled by the activity. The lad loved the silly song. Then something extraordinary happened. At first the mother could not believe it. Perhaps she had imagined it. But no, undoubtedly it actually happened. Each time the monk arrived at the word 'pig,' the boy said it too! He spoke! Just one word, but even so, it was extraordinary.

Later, the friar started a new song. This different song was about a moocow. It had the same rhythm as before. The same pattern too. This time, the monk emphasized the word 'moo.' The boy caught-on much faster this time. In two rounds of the song, he said 'moo' with the monk, at the required point.

Florian gave the boy the rattle. So the child might continue to sing alone. The boy used incomprehensible words, chiefly, but shouted 'pig' and 'moo' at all the relevant places.

'See —' said Brother Florian. 'Your boy talks.'

By then, the mother found herself in tears. She knew something amazing had happened. It was nothing less than a miracle. 'We must thank God,' she said.

'Let us thank him now in prayer —' Florian offered. 'We should thank him for the miracle of music.'

4
THE CANTICLE OF FLORIAN

This was one of many 'miracles' performed by the Music Bearers. They travelled the kingdom, helping those who required music therapy. But Black Hounds were invariably close-by. Black Hounds always sniffed close at their heels.

Sooner-or-later all the Music Bearers, even Brother Florian, became seized. Just a few months after his successful intervention with the boy who would not talk, Florian was caught in a town not far away. A talented 'heretic hunter' — a member of the dreaded Black Hounds, seized him.

The authorities soon began their interrogation. The outcome was pre-arranged. As expected, they found the Music Bearer guilty of all charges. He awaited his fate.

The supreme authority, across all known lands, was The Church. The Church decreed that all music was wrongful. Bells, whistles, drums, and gongs — all these things were illegal. The steady tap of a hammer on an anvil was the closest anyone got to commonplace man-made rhythm. And indeed such tapping had to be strictly regulated by The Church in case someone misconstrued it as music. The steady beat of a lover's heart, the simple voice of waves crashing on a pebble beach, the regular pulse of water at a cascade, all these were natural sounds, provided by God, so might be experienced without guilt. But nobody could perform music. Nobody could appreciate music. Not in any form. The Church detested man-made vibrations. The Church proclaimed that music was immoral because it devoured the soul. Music caused man to stray from the true path of righteousness.

Some elders of The Church suggested that music was pulled from ether by wizards. Or that it had been demoniacally provided by a fearsome spirit known as the muse. The Church concluded that music was wicked. And it had to be brutally suppressed.

When the authorities captured a practicing musician, they treated him as if he were a magician or a satanist. They made an example of a sorcerer. So when they finally caught up with Brother Florian, he knew he could expect an appalling fate. The Church believed that if they created enough terror in the hearts of music supporters, they might stamp out depraved practices. Church leaders concluded that followers of music were a 'sect,' and that sect-members would be intimidated and demoralised if their false-priests were tracked down, later punished. The Church believed a clearer lesson was taught if the inflicted punishment was both imaginative and memorable.

But vicious punishments were not invariably effective deterrents. The practices of the Music Bearers never stopped. People continued to seek the power, the peace, and the nourishment that they could only find in music. The growth of a complicated music-network flourished. So, The Church reasoned they needed to inflict more punishments. They struggled to be inventive with the punishments, too. The Church reasoned that effective penalty should contain three elements: suffering, pain, and humiliation. In this way, a punishment would achieve the greatest disincentive to the wider population.

So, when Brother Florian was delivered into the crowded marketplace on his execution day, the last thing he saw before he succumbed, was a torturer wielding an exceedingly sharp knife. The torturer sliced off his ears. After mutilation, Brother Florian was blind-folded. The Black Hounds forced the captive audience to stand and watch. The audience winced, and many tried to look elsewhere, but were forced to look back at the awful sight. The Hounds broke the knees of the musician with a blacksmith's hammer. This was the penalty for 'flying from justice.' Florian dropped to the ground. But even though his legs had been broken, the Music Bearer did not fall unconscious or even cry-out in pain. He was hauled back onto his shattered legs and tied naked to a post. His head was pulled high, tied hard, then his back was brutally lashed against the stake. The friar was further restrained with leather laces. They forced his mouth open using the painful metal claws of the torturer's tongs. Then the Church Executioner poured pre-prepared molten metal into his wide-open mouth. This was a symbolic act, devised to 'cleanse the violating tongue' so his wickedness and heresy would not spread into the world. Yet, even then, the victim beheld the sky, in a state of bliss. But the torturer ensured he endured a prolonged death. The tormentor continued scourging the victim long after life expired. There was no coup de grace   no final death-cut.

They devised the finish of a Music Bearer to be long and painful.

5
THE CANTICLE OF THE MARGRAVE

'You need to get a grip.' The Military Commander of the State, also known as the Margrave, addressed the highest-ranking man in the land, the Landgrave. He was not talking about the Landgrave's grip on politics. Or the man's leadership ability. Neither was he criticising the power base. No, the Margrave was commenting on something that was much more difficult for either of them to come to terms with. He was talking about the Landgrave's family. 'For months now, you have been fretting about your son. We lost him. We must now deal with this matter with some finality. You have got to move on. You must face the fact that your son is forever gone...' The Landgrave winced at these words. 'And your wife–' The Margrave continued, but now in hushed tones, 'She is remote to you. She plots and schemes against you. I fear the moonstone touches her heart...'

It was true, thought Landgrave Grassus, his wife certainly became more mentally disturbed by the dy.

As the military ruler of the province, the Margrave could speak to the illustrious Landgrave in this plain and truthful fashion. The Margrave was used to speaking to his men in the same no-nonsense manner. He liked to spell out the truths as he saw them, in simple but effective language. The Margrave was the only man in the land brave enough to speak to His Highness the Landgrave in this manner and that's because he spoke as an equal, although he was not. He spoke as if he were a brother. This was somewhat true. The Margrave was the half-brother of the Landgrave, so had a duty, as he reasoned, anyhow, to speak with his closest kin with the candour that others might not dare.

The Landgrave bit the inner skin of his cheek and picked at a fingernail. He felt an uncomfortable pain in the pit of his stomach. He had kept the secret of the removal of his daughter to himself. He had not even shared the story of her 'desertion' with his half-brother. And that was because, after he had completed the wicked act, he had felt a terrible sin of disgrace and shame. He felt regretful about bringing her ending. He also recalled, however, that when he first saw his baby girl, freshly born, he cried bitter tears because he felt that fate had dealt him a cruel blow. Who wants a girl-child? How was he supposed to pass on a grand title to a female offspring? So he decided they should poison the girl at their first opportunity. He even considered administering the nightshade himself. But he installed a false nurse (taken into his retinue so she could spy upon his wife), and it was she that suggested they could leave the girl at the wayside for 'taking.' He'd persuaded himself that this was a better proposition than poisoning. Also, it would not be a crime, technically. So he had asked the false nurse to make the arrangements. He didn't actually need to get involved in the shadier aspects of the nasty business. And so, when the babe was eight months old, they calmly left her outside to become 'disappeared.' And that was the end of the matter.

Except that it wasn't. Because one year after that sin, his true heir and only son had also been 'taken' by monks. After that tragedy, the Landgrave thought more-and-more about his baby girl. What happened to her? Would God blame him in the next world? Should he confess his sins? He often questioned his own behaviour, especially in the dark hours of night. So, when he asked his half-brother the next question, he had both his lost children on his mind: 'Don't you have spies in the Black Hounds? Someone who might learn if my child is alive or dead?'

The Margrave listened, but a furrow of impatience widened across his bald forehead: 'I could put out feelers,' he replied. He scrutinised the eyes of his half-brother with a mixture of exasperation and affection. 'Though I warn you, the Black Hounds are more difficult to penetrate than the Music Bearers. They take great care in keeping secrets unto themselves. Even if I could place one of my secret agents anywhere near the Black Hounds, it would doubtless prove useless. They will know about as much as us about your boy's fate as we do, maybe less...' The Margrave took a deep breath. 'When your son was taken away, the monks will have provided them him with a new identity. They would have started him on an alternative path. That's if he survived at all! Being left by the wayside is frequently fatal. But if he survived, his mind would have been indoctrinated. His past would have been brushed clean. The monks would have re-moulded him to become one of their filthy instruments of evil. They would have forced him to follow their wicked ways. He is as good as dead anyway.'

'But I need to know if my child is alive,' murmured the Landgrave.

'Assume he is dead,' said the Margrave. The military man made a decisive gesture by thumping a clenched fist onto the campaign table.

'And if he is not?' enquired the Landgrave, with a meek flicker visible on his top lip.

'He died the day they took him. If he is alive, he lives as a heretic. The Black Hounds will discover his whereabouts. You know they seek their prey to the ends of the world...' The Margrave glanced at his half-brother, and then continued. 'Someday they will seize your son. And when they do, they will burn him at the stake. Heresy carries the death penalty. You know all these things.' The Margrave paused for a breath. 'So, now or in the future, your son will be dead — his soul will be sent to Hades, no redemption. You know that. You know all these things. You know them very well, but you want me to spell such things out in plain words, I suppose...'

'There is no hope!' the Landgrave exclaimed.

'Look...' continued his half-brother, in a more conciliatory tone. 'I possess lands in the south. I have a wealthy a home there, with vineyards, fruit, and honey. Butter and cream. Fountains of fresh water. Even hot baths.' He looked at his half-brother to check he had lured him with enticing details. 'Why don't you take a trip to my winter lands? Make excuses. Invent a conference, or something. Take a few courtiers with you. While you're there, away from your wife's constant machinations — well, you might find comfort from Southern women. You may find that our girls are pink-lipped and very generous.' The Margrave winked. 'Our girls in the South have wide, childbearing hips...' The Margrave stood. 'Go down to my large house in the green fields. Tell Her Highness that you have an urgent conference to attend. Spend a few days, weeks even, in our verdant valleys and woods of blue. I'm sure you'll find a luscious girl in the south. A girl of your liking. I am sure that in the Southlands you will sow your royal seed. You need to rest. You need to have fun. Hence, all the things that God wants for you; they will come. I am sure of it.'

The Landgrave sighed. The idea seemed pleasant. To get away from the Landgravine would be agreeable. And it was true that he needed to put his lost children far from his mind. So the Landgrave nodded approval. He rose to leave.

'Leave all the arrangements to me...' the Margrave told him. 'I will take considerable pride in ensuring you have a long and healthy holiday.'

The two powerful men stood eye-to-eye. The Landgrave moved forward to kiss his half-brother on the cheek. The Margrave responded by providing a deep bow.

6

THE CANTICLE OF THE CONSUL

They had trained Atalanta to be a consul for the Music Bearers.

They had chosen her for her holy heart. A consul was an agent who worked for the Music Bearers inside a town or village. The most important thing about the secret and essential role of a town-consul was that she had to be trusted by the common folk. To gain that trust promptly, the consul needed to become integrated into the strange community as effectively as possible.

Atalanta would take over from an experienced and well-respected town-consul. The qualified girl that she was to replace was moving to another role — that of a travelling consul. This older consul had just a few available days to introduce Atalanta to her new family and to provide her with any guidance.

The older consul had already made all the arrangements. She had chosen a home for Atalanta. And Atalanta's role would also involve working as a handmaiden to one of the younger ladies in this rich house. They would then expect Atalanta to work her way up from a humble position, progressively earning confidence and promotion. If she performed well, then she would rise to a place where her loyalty would not be called for. Then she could work more productively as one of the Music Bearer's secret town-consuls. Her 'secret job' would be to help visiting monks (who would bring their valuable musical therapies to town.) And also directing the Music Bearers to those individuals who most needed their 'magical' healing powers.

Because the Church outlawed music, the role of town-consul was dangerous. However, the work was essential. The strategy of incorporating consuls within communities had worked well for Music Bearers for one hundred years. It seemed almost impossible to break the system they had developed. It seemed unlikely that the Black Hounds could ever infiltrate the network. And although the Hounds sent out many spies and used their own secret-agents, and these reported back suspicions, it was often the harbouring townsfolk who protected and saved the Music Bearer's consuls. Their 'families' and their new friends defended them, and often sheltered the town-consuls, even at their own considerable risk. And that was because they increasingly gained the townsfolk's trust. Once trust became secured, the Music Bearer's consul became a valuable member of her community.

The initial inclusion process might take a while. The household did not expect Atalanta to perform any demanding duties at first. This meant her position in the community was insecure to begin with. She had to be assured she was beyond any suspicion.

The new family interviewed Atalanta. After a short meeting, going through formalities, they took Atalanta to face the family members she would serve. They took her to greet the young lady for whom she would serve. When Atalanta was presented to this little lady of the house — a spotty, plump, and indifferent teenager — it surprised her they were both about the same age. While Atalanta had spent years studying, travelling, and working, this pampered young lady had spent the intervening years indulging herself. But despite this, the little lady was compassionate and easy-going. So soon accepted Atalanta as her maidservant, and the house took Atalanta on and she started duties at once.

Atalanta helped the little lady dress and to bathe. She also helped in the kitchens and assisted at meal tables. She performed small errands for the entire family. Once or twice a week, she was dispatched to the market to seek provisions. She even went with the women of the family to choose rich fabrics brought into the city walls by travelling merchants. After a short while, the family positively accepted Atalanta, and she became a recognised and trusted citizen of the town.

∼

Several weeks passed before Atalanta had her first Music Bearer's task to perform. While chatting with another servant-girl in the marketplace, she was told about a beautiful little baby-girl named May had become desperately sick. Evidently, this girl was a few months old and suffered from what they described as 'sleeping sickness.' The girl's mother was the wife of the Verderer. Atalanta made a mental note of this information and planned an encounter with the child's mother. The opportunity presented itself a few days later when Atalanta was charged with fetching fresh provisions from the market. At the market, Atalanta worked her way around the vegetable stalls until she got nearer the wife of the Verderer. She got so close that their shoulders briefly rubbed. This caused the wife to spin around suddenly — to see who banged into her. When she saw the clear eyes of Atalanta, she recognised a simple girl. The simple girl beamed back a smile of pure gold. The smile illuminated the whole market.

But the Verderer's wife seemed exhausted. She had tired eyes. She had spent many hours of sadness, so could not respond accordingly, not even to offer back a smile. The Verderer's wife had been fretting about her poor sick child. Sleepless nights had taken their toll. So she ignored the girl who rubbed against her, and she continued with her shopping.

'Do you have a cradle-song?' Atalanta asked, with no other introduction. The moment seemed precarious. If the Verderer's wife had reported Atalanta at that stage, weeks of careful preparation would have been wasted. Atalanta's mission would be cut short. Doubtless, she'd have to flee town.

But the woman looked into the smiling face of the younger female. She concentrated on those graceful eyes. She focused on the delicate lashes. Then her vision became blurred because her eyes moistened. 'My daughter is ill. She cannot last another week. I'm in pain...' she said in a whisper.

There. She opened her heart to a stranger. What would happen next?

Atalanta felt genuine compassion. Nature was cruel. Purposely, she placed an arm around the waist of the older woman and hugged her tenderly: 'I can help...' Atalanta said.

The woman looked away, and far into the distance, perhaps so her tears would not betray her true thoughts. After a few minutes of silence, the wife composed herself. Then she gazed back into the face of the younger girl, 'If you come to my house after dark, I can meet you in the yard. I'll take you to my daughter. Will you come?'

Atalanta nodded. She squeezed the hand of the mother, but then quickly disappeared into the crowd.

∼

Atalanta expected the next Music Bearer would attend on the cusp of the half moon. But he never arrived. She waited another day, but still he did not attend. Time was running short for the Verderer's wife and her sickly child.

It surprised Atalanta that the Music Bearer had not arrived in the city at the appointed time. She did not know, at that stage, that the authorities had already hunted him down, like they had done all the others. The Black Hounds had tracked him and taken him. The Music Bearer had been on his way to see her when they seized him. She did not know it was Brother Florian who had been due to attend.

But now Florian was dead — they had filled his throat with liquid iron. They had tortured and flogged the friar. These were dangerous times.

After some thought, Atalanta went to see the wife, but without the friar. She decided this was the only thing that could be achieved in the circumstances. She got a message to the Verderer's wife explaining that she would attend her home that night.

After sunset, Atalanta wrapped herself in a cloak, before undertaking the long walk to the Verderer's house. She hid her face under the brim of a wide hat that he had borrowed from her rich employer. When Atalanta arrived to see the wife, she knew she was too late. She felt a sudden pain of apprehension. It shot instantaneously through her heart. This was going to be difficult. Atalanta was taken, hastily, to see the sick child. The mother had bedded the child on a mattress of gold straw inside a cosy barn. Stacks of fragrant grasses surrounded the baby. The place had been lit by beeswax candles. The poor babe was white as snow. She breathed long gasps that Atalanta knew would not last much longer. The infant's skin felt damp, but cool. Her eyes were sealed.

Atalanta motioned for the mother to join her by the temporary straw bed. She put one arm around the woman's waist, then gestured for the woman to take hold of her baby. To cradle the body. The woman did not protest. She did precisely as she was told. It was as if she already knew what was going to happen. The mother had rehearsed this moment over-and-over in her mind. Once the baby had been cradled, Atalanta began her sweet song. It was a caring and kind lullaby. As Atalanta sang, she swayed gently. Her rocking action meant the mother swayed too. Soon all three of them swayed to the rhythm of soft melody. The mother felt her agony slip away. She felt panic dissolve. She felt a special harmony. It was harmony with this strange girl. And it was harmony with her beloved child.

As they swayed together, as they gently rocked to the wonderful lullaby Atalanta sung from pure heart, the child died. It might have been a moment of bitter grief. It should have been a sting to the heart. But, in reality when the mother remembered that sad evening, she recalled that it was a blessed moment. It felt as if the gates of heaven opened and that an Angel beckoned her child inside. Into heaven, almost unnoticed.

Subsequently, the mother sobbed. She cried until she could cry no more. But her tears were not tears of sadness or grief. No, they were tears of release and deliverance..

7

THE CANTICLE OF ELIS

From his earliest memories, Elis knew nothing but love. His 'sisters' surrounded him, and they lavished care and attention on him. Elis was raised in a 'home' — actually a remote chapel-house — with some uncommonly gentle, matriarchal figures. They assigned him two 'sisters.' One was roughly a year older, and they allocated her to be his companion. Invariably by his side, this girl, named Cinnamon, was educated seamlessly alongside. Elis also had an older 'sister' who was four years his senior. Her name was Eshta. Her role was to be his mentor and to protect him in his early years. Since he had been just four summers old, Elis spent long hours in a kind, yet effective, classroom. This was where boys and their protective and somewhat older sisters would sit and learn lessons. The boys were trained to be Music Bearers. The girls were there for some other purpose.

The boy's lessons included languages, arts, history, and the basics of song. There was invariably a religious significance in everything that was taught. At this stage, all their teachers were female. The lady of the class could deftly connect issues such as history or politics with musical ideas — so that music, rhythms, and rhymes, were picked up alongside the other topics. They taught each subject as a 'memory game' because this was an important part of the learning cycle. These rhymes also reminded Elis and the other children of the dangers that lurked in the outside world. There could be unseen hazards and those more obvious.

~

When he was young, Elis and his beloved companion, Cinnamon, made an early-morning unscheduled trip. This was the first of three hazardous journeys that they forced him to make during his childhood. Although he did not realise it — they required he made these journeys because of changing circumstances. Black Hounds were closing in. So Music Bearers were compelled to keep moving, or they would be identified and slaughtered.

On the first of these three trips, Elis had to be packaged into a basket. Once in the basket, he was bundled into a warm bag to wiggle and giggle next to Cinnamon. Then they were trundled into the darkness and placed on the back of a covered wagon.

Eshta, his older 'sister,' also travelled with the two younger children, but could sit at the front of the wagon with the male driver. The trip was long, but Elis never felt fear. In fact, he enjoyed the journey. It was a pleasant adventure. They instructed him to remain silent, so he spent his time judiciously, repeating over-and-over the rhymes they had taught him in class. And by going through Bible stories in his head and repeating wonderful prayers and psalms, he could create sounds and rhythms in his heart.

After almost two days of travel, the group arrived at a small agricultural community. They permitted the children to sneak out of their hiding places. Elis thought it was brilliant to be allowed to help feed goats and collect eggs. He watched young ducklings learning to swim in a millpond. And he helped to clean up pigeon mess and milk ewes. He and Cinnamon learned how to draw water from a well. They brought water into the roundhouse using wooden buckets. The water splashed over the edges and onto their feet as they skipped and giggled. In the kitchen, an old housekeeper taught the children how to boil water in a pot and how to make a soup on a pot above the fire. The children were never cold or hungry — the adults never mistreated them. After a morning of fun spent playing around the farm, they filled afternoons with classroom activity. The 'classroom' at the farm was simply an old barn. They had stacked bales of hay to form benches and chairs. And the barn had a swallow nest in a corner. Elis loved to see the birds zoom in and across the barn — then flit through a hole between roof beams and suddenly out into bright sky.

At the farm, Elis met his first adult men. Until then had been blanketed by women. The two men were farm labourers who kept themselves-to-themselves. But they seemed friendly and were forever larking. They were rougher than women. Elis noted they would do things like spit on the floor, or punch and slap each other. They told bawdy jokes and whispered mischievous secrets. Often, shared remarks caused loud eruptions of uncontrollable laughter. The classmistress would scold them, telling them they were 'shocking' the children. So the men tried to behave.

While he stayed at the farm, Elis had his first meeting with danger. One morning, they sent him off to find mushrooms. They directed him to a small, wooded area on the outskirts of the community. Elis rushed to the woods, happy to be free. At the village, he felt liberated. Elis was proud to be given such an essential task. Cinnamon ran alongside and Eshta could barely keep up. Their little knees brought them promptly to the heart of the thickest woodland, where they might be sure to find the choicest mushrooms.

When they arrived at a glade, Elis knelt so he could see the earth easier. He looked around, close to the roots. This was the type of place where he might find the mysterious and succulent fungus-fruits. Cinnamon stayed close, kneeling in muddy compost too. She pawed at the mulch with dirty hands. Both looking for the elusive mushrooms. Eshta looked on. She was not bored, because she enjoyed her time with the younger children. She loved this place.

While the two younger kids scurried about the forest floor, a crashing sound surprised them. It came from a nearby thicket. The two kneeling children shrieked in surprise. A huge wild boar burst noisily from the undergrowth. It stared at them with hate in its eyes. The beast was the evillest thing Elis had ever seen. The boar's nose was long and dark. It snorted in annoyance. It had ragged ears, torn and fluttering. And it had an enormous mouth that drooled. The boar's eyes were deep in its colossal head. It stared at Elis with undisguised malevolence. The children could see muscle swaying through the beast's thick fur — as the creature prepared to attack the children.

Elis acted promptly and unconsciously. He stood full height. He rushed to Cinnamon right away — and hauled her to her feet. Then he pushed her back towards Eshta, so he might position himself between the savage creature and his 'sisters.' Elis then stared at the ferocious looking animal. The pig gazed back at the boy, assessing the situation. Then the pig made a small but costly mistake. It focussed on a beetle that it saw crawling across the forest floor. This gave Elis the time he needed to pick up a big piece of stick that he glimpsed at his own feet. He threw the wood at the wild boar and as he did this, he screamed and ran forward. He made out he was about to attack the animal. The boar squealed in alarm, turned and it ran. The beast crashed through branches, where it disappeared. Elis turned to the girls, to confirm they were well. They looked astounded. Elis didn't fully comprehend what he had done. He did not feel bold or even especially victorious. He felt as if he had done the right thing. That's all.

'We should go to a different part of the forest to collect mushrooms.' Elis blurted. The girls agreed with quick nods.

~

Back at the farm, the girls told their story about Elis. They described how he boldly he had protected them from the wild beast. If they had known that the wild boar was merely a piglet, they might not have been so proud. But they did not know that. Nor did any of them know that the mother of the piglet Elis chased-off had seen the whole incident. The sow observed the whole episode from behind a curtain of thorns. And might have attacked and killed them all if her baby had not run back into her protective custody. Luckily, for all of them, it did.

Elis had performed a very brave act. Though he didn't know quite how brave.

During these days at the village, they introduced Elis to his first Music Bearer. He did not know what to expect. It thrilled everyone to learn that a Friar would come during the next weekend. In his mind, and informed by the Bible stories he had heard, Elis expected the friar would be ancient. He expected him to be a cross between Moses and Abraham.

In fact, the monk who attended, named Brother Ed, was younger than the agricultural labourers. He had nutty brown hair and was thin as a barn rake. His eyes shone like sharp flints. All the women at the farm behaved curiously around him. They presented him with hot drinks when he did not need them and gave him sweet cakes that were pointedly made for him even though he'd told them he was stuffed-full. The younger girls gave him bouquets of wildflowers and the older women took away his cloak for repair. They zealously worked on his sleeves and re-stitched his fraying edges.

Brother Ed taught the children in the barn-house schoolroom how to make a pipe-whistle out of a reed. First, they had to find a reed in the duck pond. It took all morning for him to explain how to measure out the holes they needed — using a thumb as a guide. Then Brother Ed spent the entire afternoon explaining how to blow down the tube. All the children got some notes out of their own home-made pipes by supper time.

When Brother Ed played his reedpipe, the sound that came out-of-the-end was amazing. It sounded like ripples on a mill pond, or trills of birds in the orchard. It sounded like the wind as it rushed through a straw roof. Or the rain in a gully. It seemed as if a man could harness the sweet sounds of nature. If Brother Ed could harness the sound of nature, all of them could possess and control those sounds in the same way. That's as long as they concentrated hard enough.

The children looked forward to the day when they could play the reedpipe as energetically as Brother Ed.

8
THE CANTICLE OF THE JOURNEY

The next place that Elis was to be taken was a fortress by the sea.

The trip was not as much fun as the trip he had made a year earlier to the farm. Then he had Cinnamon squeezed next to him as a travelling companion. But when he left behind the farm on the sad day of moving on, hidden into the back of a wagon, squashed between bags of rotting carrots — Cinnamon didn't travel with him. They could not say goodbyes. Adults rarely need to explain to children what is going on.

Cinnamon was to become a mentor for another boy. That was her destiny. She had a separate path to follow. This path was planned out by the elders of the community. But Elis did not know the plan. Why should he? He was still a child and adults decided on such matters. Elis was approaching the age when he needed to be separated from female partners. At this age, he needed to enter a more male-dominated society. They required Elis to take the first steps towards a life of celibacy. All this was unknown to him. So he sobbed a little, curled inside the bag, next to stinking carrots. He had a nervousness in his stomach — a feeling he could not altogether understand — a sick feeling. He knew he would never see Cinnamon again.

The journey he undertook was longer than Elis had ever made before. It included overnight stays in dark forest clearings.

Once at a forest, the driver of the wagon lit a fire and the other man asked Elis to help find twigs for a blaze. Elis was glad to be given this job because he needed a distraction. The trees of the forest watched him as he gathered firewood. The shadowy branches were in constant motion and made strange noises. It was as if a wild boar were about to charge out of the darkness at any moment. Just like the board did in his dreams.

When Elis looked around for tinder, he saw virtually nothing worth collecting. But he quickly became accustomed to the silvery light, and, in a brief time, he found a few sticks. He assessed them for dryness with his hands. Though he was sure never to venture far from the moving, stooping shape of the other man.

After a while, the other man made his silent way back to the wagon, so Elis duly followed — holding as many sticks as he could. He felt stupid when he returned to the sparkling fire, because he saw the other man had taken a bag with him to collect more wood. Elis had tried grabbing the sticks with his bare hands. He held a miserable offering for the fire. But the older men seemed satisfied. They sat around, watching the flames dance. The driver of the wagon took out a leather pouch and from this he offered the others hard-boiled eggs, chunks of crust and roots to nibble. Though this was not a party, it felt like a mini-feast — to celebrate their success! The success of getting this far without attracting attention. The men said grace before they ate — the driver of the wagon took charge of the prayers. Then, after the simple meal, the men coiled into their bags and laid their heads onto soft leaf-mulch. They kept close to the dying embers of the fire, so felt saved from the darkness.

Elis found that, when sleeping outdoors, days started early. With the first glimpse of weak sun, the morning came alive. There was too much noise from the woods to ignore. All the little creatures heated and started their daily lives early on. So it was early when Elis and the other men stretched and yawned. They stood and checked around. Elis had a strange feeling in his stomach. But the wagon driver pointed to a nearby tree. 'Go over there. Behind the tree. Use green leaves,' he pointed out some ferns. 'Later, when you come back, we'll have water for you.'

Elis felt his bones creak as he walked toward the tree. It was only when he got to the tree did he realise what the wagon driver had meant. He gathered ferns and 'did his business' before returning to the wagon. He washed his hands carefully before he took a sip of water. The other men also went elsewhere to prepare for the next leg of the journey. Soon they were on their way, anew, heading for their final destination.

At midnight, Elis smelled an aroma unfamiliar to him. It fizzed in his nostrils and get inside his head. The aroma made him feel alive — more awake than he should have been feeling, especially after several long hours of cramped travel. The smell got stronger. And soon the wagon slowed, and the wheels stopped creaking altogether. They rolled along something smooth.

When the wagon stopped altogether, Elis heard an unfamiliar male voice nearby. He had been told to stay still and quiet when the cart stops. He strained to hear what was being said — but everything seemed all right. He heard the wagon driver laughing and then the sound of other men coming towards the cart. Soon he was found in the back of the wagon, and they freed Elis from the confines of his narrow space. They encouraged him to 'undress' from the bag and, after pulling down the sack, he appeared in the tight circle of men. They surrounded him. And all grinned.

Elis realised he was a prized commodity. he felt like the champion billy-goat at the town fair. He was for protecting and admiring. Not for slaughter. The men observed the boy with a mixture of admiration and pride. It was as if he was the most precious stone or the most expensive gift they had ever seen. They were proud to be entrusted with transporting him and keeping him safe. At that moment — with all those strange and adoring eyes peering at him — Elis knew he had a destiny. He had been given a distinct role to play.

They took him by the hand, so he could get out of the bag. Then the biggest man of all, as tall as a horse with broad shoulders and dry hands, lifted Elis high onto his shoulders, carrying him piggyback style towards a high walled building. From this point of view, Elis could see everything around. In the distance there was something flat, and grey, and blue. He stared at the surface through his half-closed eyes, then realised that the flat-grey surface moved like the back of a donkey. It was sort-of bobbling. Small bubble-like tufts flickered upon it. He guessed, with a shudder of excitement, it must be the sea. He had been smelling seawater. The grey surface went all the way to the horizon. Then he figured the wagon had been travelling on a causeway of sand. And the building in front was some kind of fortress. In the distance were twinkling lights. The glitters were lanterns and candles in a far town. The tiny town seemed crushed into the tiniest of spaces, like the swallow's nest in his school-room barn. The town seemed insignificant when compared to the vast horizon and an infinite sky.

∼

Elis learned that the sand-fort would be his new home. It would be his new school for the foreseeable future. The 'school' contained Music Bearer brothers, members of the teaching staff. The school also contained other young lads like Elis. They were there for learning. The fort must have once housed over a hundred soldiers, perhaps more. But now the place seemed mysteriously empty, with merely a few men and boys rattling around inside. The dilapidated shell had holes in the walls, rats running along hallways and doors were too warped to shut properly. Rainwater fell through gaps in the roof, and the biggest of these pourings were collected in terracotta pots to use for cleaning. But although the fort was dilapidated, Elis admired it. It was the first enormous building he had ever seen.

The other lads were about the same age as Elis. And likewise at about the same point in their education. Elis noticed that there were no girls or women at the fort. Elis joined the other boys to study — much more sincerely than he did before — and it was the study of the craft of making music. The pupils concentrated on their mastery of the many technical skills they needed to conduct their music missions. They would require them to express spiritual elements — and to master techniques that would move a listener's minds and elevate a listener's thinking to an emotional level.

Skills included instruction on how to fashion simple instruments from products that might be found readily as they travelled. The Music Bearers taught the boys how to create meaningful song patterns that could be entirely improvised. Elis and the others in the fort-school learned that music was a kind of language — a variety of nonverbal communication. And the teachers encouraged them to use this language of music in the classroom. They reproved them when they did not do so. The students also learned about the power of constant rhythms. And how and when to break the regularity of a song, so it would surprise and excite a listener.

When these skills had been polished, the teachers expected the boys to become proficient at creating a sense of harmony between the soul of a listener and the music. So they practiced this on each other, and at various times of the day. Most of the music they practiced — whether it was plainsong or played on simple instruments — became smooth and relaxing. They carefully designed such songs to eliminate anxiety in a listener, to achieve lasting peace in the heart.

The novices also learned the most important lesson of all. How to create a cradlesong. Their teachers taught them that a cradlesong should be peaceful and hypnotic. They expressly created a cradle song to help young children eat and sleep. It needed to be modest. It needed to be pure. So it might be easily taught to a young mother — so she could use it herself before a new baby was born to the world. It would later become an important 'key' for the Music Bearers because it would stay locked inside the child through his or her development and they could use it in afterward to 'unlock' memories and help bring inner peace.

Most accepted that the cradlesong was the most powerful 'musical' tool the Music Bearers had at their disposal..

9

THE CANTICLE OF TELSON

The members of the Order of the Black Hounds specialised in assimilating and digesting information. They collected 'evidence' about secret communities, and they concentrated their activities on the monks known as the Music Bearers.

Pope Honorius founded the Black Hounds to combat heresy. The brotherhood prided themselves on their tireless work. They studied the behaviours and movements of those stained by heresy. In particular, the Black Hounds hated the notion of music. Music, they considered, was a sinful thing. It was hedonistic, it was sexual, and it was licentious.

Most alarmingly, though, they thought music was an uncontrollable force — it had mysterious power — it was almost unstoppable. The Black Hounds believed that music practitioners invoked magical spiritual beings, or Muses, drawn from another dimension as mysterious metaphysical beings, to help make their music. Therefore, music was an act of sorcery.

The concealment and clandestine behaviours of the community called the *Fraternitati Sancta Ordinis et Caecilia* — better known as 'The Music Bearers' could be considered as further evidence that music-making was a sin. Why would they perform it secretly if music were righteous? Why conceal such a good thing? Though that was twisted logic. But the same logic helped the Hounds recruit their spies and put pressure on those that protected the Bearers.

So the Black Hounds studied the Music Bearers from afar. And carefully evaluated everything they saw.

The Hounds worked conscientiously, so they might nip any errant behaviour in the bud. And they would act swift, and ruthless, if music were ever detected. When they were ready to pounce, they sent a Black Hound to grasp at the problem. The Hounds were excellent at playing this game. They saw it as an achievement of God's work on earth. They had performed the service for years.

Telson was a member of the Order of the Black Hounds, raised and schooled at St Hubert's Abbey.

The extensive grounds of the *Ordo Fratrum Hubertus* — otherwise known as the Order of the Black Hounds — were located in a verdant valley. The valley had abundant natural resources and a temperate climate. Many other abbeys, of this sort, were located in high places, often in remote locations. This was so members of the Religious Order might find solitude and peace. Perhaps so monks of an Order would escape the influences of an evil outside world. But St. Hubert's Abbey was quite different. Yes, it was remote. But it was also intrinsically hooked up to the outside world. It had to be. And that's because the Abbey, dedicated to founding father St. Hubert, was not like any other Abbey in the known world. Strategically, and because of the work the clerics performed inside the walls, the Abbey required reliable and efficient transport links. Their holy community required strong connections with the outside world. So they had cleared away space for the Abbey lands and adjoining meads, while the principal buildings stood beside a winding river. This connection allowed trade to move freely back and forth. There was also a well-trod path on top of a wooded ridge — this allowed the Abbey monks a quick and safe land connection. They needed such routes if they desired to get to their enemy, those evil music-makers, in a hurry.

The countryside around the Abbey was fertile. The community employed more than half of all its members on the grounds or in the fishing lakes. These members also prepared drinks and medicines from aromatic lavenders that grew in plots around grey-stone walls.

They cultivated seed-oils, which they milled themselves. They collected oils into jars, then sold them at markets, as medicinal anointments. These worker-monks also propagated cherries and peaches, pumpkins, beet roots, and many other salad and vegetable items.

But they did not create the Abbey of the Black Hounds for pleasure. Nor for sanctuary. Not even prayer. No, they founded the Abbey as a seat of learning, and as an epicentre — the world headquarters — for anti-music missions.

∼

The Black Hounds organised their Abbey as a nerve centre for these activities. It was the principal place where all records were stored. Such records went back hundreds of years. These perfectly maintained reports listed and referenced many individuals that the Order had investigated and assessed over the years. Here, clerics managed a centralised database of wrongdoing. St. Hubert famously asked God, 'Lord, what would you like me to do for you?' And he received his answer from heaven: 'Go, seek.' And, from that moment onward, the Black Hounds had been doing just that. They had been seeking their prey. They had been doing it for decades. They found that God's work involved a great deal of preparation. It involved gathering knowledge. It involved collecting and filing reports. Thus, over the years, their Abbey became a storehouse of data. And most of that data was about one group: The Music Bearers.

∼

Like other adherents at the Abbey, the Order of the Black Hounds collected Telson from the wayside. They had taken him to their place as an orphan. Few members of their Order were volunteers. They were typically 'foundlings' or ragamuffin children who had been reduced to protective custody by the Friars of St. Hubert.

Telson was not even sure how old he was when he had been picked up by the Black Hounds. They had never told him. And he never thought to ask. He guessed he must have been less than a year. He felt grateful that the friars fed and clothed him. They also provided him with an excellent education.

They taught Telson Latin, the language of The Church; and they lectured him in ancient Greek, the natural sciences, mathematics, history, and geography. They taught all these subjects to the foundling children from an early age. The lessons took place in extremely dull classrooms. Strict masters instructed the children. There was an emphasis on studying the scriptures. The Bible stories.

They achieved all this knowledge using a system the Abbey called learning by rote. Learning by rote meant memorising lists. Awfully long lists. All pupils, Telson included, continually repeated, and practiced these lists. So, for example, Telson recited his Latin vocabulary each day in front of the entire class. Teachers punished minor errors or hesitations with a quick hit from a cane. The scholars called this method 'learning by cut.' Serious errors might draw a pupil twelve strokes on the bare buttocks — or indeed a 'birching.' Birching required the recipient to be tied to a wooden pony — really a specially prepared block of wood — where a Master would thrash him. The Master used a bundle of wetted birch twigs for the thrashing. Often, a boy was flogged so hard his rump became red-raw. After a birching, a lad could not sit for two days. The boys said that the punishment was the standing. A birched boy would need to stand for all lessons and for meals. He could not even find comfort in his crib at night. It was part of the punishment. The indignity and the pain. The pain of standing. There was invariably someone standing in the classroom. Some days, though seldom, it was Telson that stood.

A typical school day at the Abbey ran from dawn to dusk. So, in winter, school days were shorter. But they were often more painful. That was because students had less time to study lessons and achieve best results in their memory tests. In winter, birching was common.

In summer, school days started when the first cock cried. And would go through to midnight. These were agonizingly long days. So long, in fact, that the boys looked forward to the darkness, misery, and birched pain of winter months.

At the end of his studies in the schoolroom, after about twelve summers, Telson started his period of training in preparation to become a novice. If he became a successful novice, he might one day be a fully-fledged Black Hound.

They did not choose all boys for this vocation. They did not call some boys to higher religious life. Those boys who botched their lessons, for example, or those who could not pay full attention in class, or those who failed to learn from the frequent corporal punishments — these boys were spurred to leave the Abbey. The Abbot expected failed students to look for work in the wider community. Some lads, it's true, left the Abbey and were never heard from again. But most did not want to leave. They had nowhere to go, so the Abbey offered suitable employment — working in the fields. Toiling on the land, growing, and gathering food was preferential to being cast out.

Telson was a talented student, so he didn't have to become a farmer or a labourer. He was a careful and serious learner. He tried hard to please his Masters, and to avoid a birching. So Telson passed on to the next stage of his learning. At the next level of training, they expected a junior novice such as Telson to collaborate readily with a Director of Study. The Director would help the novice deepen a closer relationship with God and the Order.

This Director would explain the missions of the community. He would divulge their innermost secrets. Through prayer, self-denial and rigorous disciplined study, the junior novices steadily gained an introduction to their divine secret vocation.

As a novice at the next level, a promising student, such as Telson, would learn about the history and life of the institution. He would learn about how Black Hounds worked in the wider community, how they hunted down heretics.

Telson worked steadily to achieve 'full tonsure.' This was full induction into the Black Hounds and would mean the end of novitiate training. He was told it would take about three years of commitment and humility to get to such a point. If he ever did. Full tonsure was far from guaranteed.

Telson had studied attentively for two years. Although it's true he became bored and frustrated by the novitiate system. All the feedback — that was bad enough. But he also had to perform hours of tedious analysis and lots of archive-work. He especially hated the endless filing of reports. Telson also assumed that all the others in his Order — even those boys who were far less competent than he — rose above him in the rankings.

He watched as many of his 'brothers,' including those who started out after him, gained advancement long before he did. He grew angrier by the day.

Telson did not know who to turn to for advice or guidance. He wanted to talk about the sense of anger and frustration that grew inside him. He was agitated when he discovered his own Director of Study, his trusted teacher, had once more recommended a member of his peer-group for advancement — again overlooking Telson. On this occasion, instead of stewing on the injustice of it, Telson did something about it.

10

THE CANTICLE OF THE BREAD

Directly after the hour of Morning Prayer, when all the others crept back to their workplaces, Telson loped towards the bakehouse. He was about to commit an offence for which, if he were spotted, would mean imprisonment and harsh corporal punishment.

He entered the bakery and found what he was looking for near the pantry area. He stuffed two scabs of barley bread into one of his capacious pockets and a fist-sized portion of cheese into the other. These will do admirably, he thought. Telson slipped from the kitchen, his sandal-leather creaking on the paving stones. He made his way to his workplace.

But instead of stopping off at his workplace, Telson made a sudden left turn down a dark hallway. Then he furtively entered the office of his Director of Study. He was about to put the second stage of his plan into effect. He felt pleased to be at last getting revenge. Telson reasoned he had spent too long being mistreated by the injustices of an antiquated 'system.'

He sniffed decisively, holding his nose high in the slate air, as he tried to detect how far away the old man was. Satisfied his director was not nearby, Telson promptly made his way around his supervisor's private room, before heading behind an enormous oak desk. This was where the old man sat every day, recording and checking infinite notes. The oak desk had a large, unlatched softwood box upon it. Telson viewed this box and decided it was a suitable place to set-up his trap. He took the bread and cheese from his pockets, then squeezed the items of food into narrow spaces he discovered between the texts in the box.

After this, Telson checked the office again, and delicately stepped back into the dark corridor.

∽

Later that same day, Telson found an excuse to visit his Master, the Director of Study. This would be the materialisation of his plan. He had a wonderful sense of excitement rumbling in the base of his stomach. He knocked with unusual gentleness onto the door of his director. Then he waited for the old man to cough before asking to enter. After the cough, Telson entered the room with all the confidence he could muster. He paused before being asked to come forward. He held a rose-coloured document in his hands: 'I wonder, Master, if you might help with this problem?'

He waited for the Master to answer. After a while, the older man beckoned him over.

Telson moved towards the enormous desk and offered-up the rose-coloured paper. He then waited, trying to remain as patient as possible. The Director of Study seemed flustered. He waved his hands, signalling the novice to come forward — to move closer, so he could see the document in illuminating light. 'I still cannot see it...' the Master complained. 'Come closer.' He pointed to a spot alongside his desk, where a pool of soft light spilled from a notch window.

As Telson complied with the gruff instruction, his elbow jogged at the softwood stationery box on the Director's desk — toppling it somewhat.

Telson reacted spontaneously, grabbing the box in an over-exaggerated way, as if it were likely to fall from the desk. As he took hold of the box, he jerked it — imperceptibly. As expected, and of course as planned, out rolled two lumps of crusty bread, followed, dutifully, by a great knob of cheese.

Both monks seemed startled by the food. The secret stash rolled efficiently onto the tabletop. Before his Master could say anything, Telson grabbed a nugget of bread. He held his fingers over the chunk, cupping it, as if trapping the thing beneath skinny fingers. He compared the bread to a frightened mouse. He felt the softness of the body under his bones. Then he pushed down hard on the crust, as if he were breaking the back of the creature. He felt a satisfying crunch. Especially rewarding was the last breath of air as it became pinched out.

During all this, Telson gazed straight into the eyes of the fool. And for the first time, really, he understood how timeworn the old man indeed had become. Telson, the young monk, stared directly into those pale old watery eyes, then he spoke: 'Why do you not break bread with others of the congregation, Master?' He waited for an answer. The brotherhood considered the sin of gluttony to be the worst of all imaginable sins, especially for monks in Holy Orders. It was a worse sin, even, than theft and cheat. The Abbot might even excuse sexual corruption. But he'd never excuse gluttony. All the brothers at the Abbey ate one simple meal a day — two meals during winter months. These meals were always received together. The only exception to this strict rule was that the sick, those who could not leave their beds, would suck soup through a straw on their sick bed. And the community even frowned upon that unless the patient was dying. Only the Abbot himself could take meals in the privacy of private rooms.

The old man seemed surprised and confused. He stared at the incriminating evidence on his desk. The knob of cheese and crumbs of bread were plain evidence. He could not ignore the proof. The old man could not find a voice that might explain what had happened, so instead, he cleared his throat with a choking sound.

The young monk continued to probe: 'This is luxury, isn't it? To keep bread in your room is a sin, isn't it? To consume it at your own leisure...' Telson's words faded as he removed his hand from the bones of the bread on the table. The morsels fell away like lumps of meat. Telson gazed, wide-eyed, at the broken form. Then he slowly turned his head to look candidly into the eyes of the old man. His manner was soft and calmer than ought to be expected. He pretended to be non-accusing, and he 'put on' his best expression of understanding: 'Are you unwell, Master? Why haven't you gone to the apothecary to ask for help or remedy? Is there anything I can do?'

The ancient Director of Study examined the eyes of his young pupil. He shook his head in weary acceptance. 'There is nothing I can say.. I'm afraid you have outdone me...' He pointed towards the door and gestured that the young man should leave his presence.

When Telson was outside the room, he smiled with satisfaction. His eyes darted from side to side, and he allowed his tongue to lick all the way along his upper lip.

∽

Telson waited several days before he met with the Formation Director.

The Formation Director was the most senior member of the Black Hounds community. His rank was second only to Abbot. The Formation Director was in charge of all trainee monks. He was also the line-manager of the Directors of Study.

At around noon, on the last day before Sabbath, Telson asked permission, from the Formation Director's elderly Scribe, for a talk with the Formation Director himself. They informally knew the Formation Director as the blessed 'Superior of Superiors.' The Formation Director was typically gruff when Telson entered his office. He was settled at the far end of a large room, reading notes by a warming fire. He permitted Telson to approach. The Master gestured the novice ought to come forward — waving for him to make his way to one side of the fire — but to stay out of the warmth and light.

Telson provided the Formation Director with an account of what he had seen in the office of his Director of Study. He explained how he discovered that his old teacher had been surreptitiously storing bread and cheese. He added a dramatically gigantic sigh at the end of the story, before pointing out how he had asked the Master if there was anything he could have done to help him, adding: 'Because I was worried about his well-being.'

The Formation Director did not respond immediately. Neither did he seem shocked by the outrageous behaviour of one of his most senior members of staff. The Superior of Superiors simply took it in. After that, Telson could tell by the look of concentration upon the Superior's face that he mulled over the problem. The Superior narrowed his eyes for a moment before he nodded in silence. He collected his thoughts: 'It is good you came to me with this, Telson,' the Formation Director offered. 'Your conduct is worthy, and your discretion is wise. Exposed, as you were, to disturbing proclivity, I might have expected you to have told your story to the entire community. But, sensibly, you grappled with the problem in your heart. And took the sensible step of bringing the matter straight to me...' He paused for a second, then recollected his thoughts. 'I would be most grateful if you would continue to employ wisdom and prudence in this matter; and to guarantee to me that this information will never be played-out around the community, from voice-to-voice, as it were—'

'Yes, Master, you can trust — '

But the Superior-of-Superiors cut his words short. 'Instead, I wish you to divert attention from that sad matter and onto another. I would like you to employ your undeniable curiosity and inquisitiveness elsewhere...' He glanced at Telson, checking he had the young man's full attention. 'I have received other reports that concern me... I would like you to investigate more lapses...'

Telson tried not to smile. This was exactly what he wanted to hear from the Formation Director. He was at last getting the recognition he deserved. He waited for the next words to emerge — with an awareness of mounting excitement.

'I have received reports...' the Formation Director continued 'That some of those working in the Library of Transgressors do not attend meticulously to their occupation. It is essential we always maintain logical processes. And that we all work with definite objectives.' He put his bony finger to his chin. 'You have my authority to switch from the direct control of your Director of Study and to act separately as my eyes-and-ears in the Library of Transgressors. I will find an excuse for you to work in the background. I will tell the Library Master that I have given you important research to carry out, into some vague area...' The Superior slouched a little in his chair. Then he continued. 'I will tell him to leave you alone...'

Telson shuffled his feet as if he were eager to start his new work right away. But the Formation Director had not finished: 'I would like you to study the activity of those who work in the library and report any misgivings promptly to me. Do you understand? Your new role will start the day after Sabbath.'

Telson thanked the Director. He was about to speak again but was cut off by the Superior, who raised his hand to silence him. 'That is all, Telson. Leave now.' He waved the novice away.

11

THE CANTICLE OF THE LEDGER

Telson began his new investigation with an eager heart. They employed five brothers to do clerical work in the Library of Transgressors. The Library Master kept himself to himself in his anteroom. Every so often he came out of the darkness to bark commands at the monks in the primary area, but otherwise, Telson seldom saw him.

The chief work of those who worked in the Library of Transgressors seemed to be cross-checking and cross-referencing files. These were the records kept on the Music Bearers. There was not any actual written work to do. Essentially, the job of a librarian involved checking facts and archiving. At the Abbey, they maintained a complicated type of record-keeping. Each piece of data had to be recorded and re-recorded more than once — they had placed each fact into many elaborate categories and sub-categories.

Telson soon figured that the library provided a name for each Music Bearer. This name was the title of the file. Under the file name, they kept information about the character of the Music Bearer. The information included his current whereabouts, any descriptions or sightings that had been recently registered, and any other useful information. This file contained all known information about the Transgressor.

As additional facts came in about each Transgressor, a file would be located — checked thoroughly — then they would place any fresh information neatly into the file, under the correct category.

Occasionally, other Friars would appear in the library to gather information for their own studies. Sometimes these visiting monks might just refer to a file. Or sometimes they might take a file away. If this happened, the workers at the library entered the name of the inquiring monk into a large ledger. This ledger entry included the filename and the date upon which they had taken the file. They left the date the borrower returned it blank — so it could be filled-in once they had returned the precious file safely back into the store-cabinet. After the file was back in its place, the process could be 'signed off' by the Library Master. They hastily returned most of the files after they had taken them. But sometimes a file went missing. And when a file went missing, the Tipstaff Office had to be informed.

Monks could not remove any files from the confines of the Abbey. Brothers who failed to return a file by the agreed date were reported to the Library Master. One of his primary duties was to chase-up missing files. To enable him to do this forcefully, the Library Master had two Tipstaves from the Tipstaff Office permanently assigned to him.

The appointed Tipstave Friars carried short, stout, wooden clubs of office. These wooden clubs, or the 'staves' associated with their title, had been tipped with a large bronze pommel — lending each staff some hefty weight. Tipstaves could deliver a nasty blow. The Tipstaves at the Abbey used these clubs — hitting monks on bare limbs — if needed. They were not to be argued with.

They gave all Tipstaves special assignments. Senior staff used some to retrieve lost information or issue lesser punishments for minor infractions. Others assisted senior brethren with personal tasks that might need the extra weight of authority.

Telson noted that they kept the two Tipstaves permanently attached to the Library of Transgressors, and both seemed fully occupied. When one was dispatched on a quest, typically to 'remind' a brother that they must return a file, the other one would be checking the ledger to see when the next file was due. When a Tipstaff returned to the library, the other one trudged off. So there was always one 'armed' official hanging about near the library entrance. Telson wondered if some decree from the Abbot himself had reinforced this system.

The monks in the library did not interact with each other. They did not pay any attention to Telson. Once or twice he squeezed past — and perhaps they noticed him — but if they did, they never gave the courtesy of a nod or a smile. Most of the time, the library monks ignored the world around them. They even avoided making eye contact with each other. No one ever talked in the library. Telson noted that when Tipstaves wanted to exchange any communication, they slipped into the corridor for a chat. If a senior brother came to ask a question, they would invite him into an anteroom for hushed conversation.

～

Telson found that the information stored on the Music Bearers was fascinating.

It included testimonies from many sources. Peasants, town-folk, city guards, mole-catchers, farmhands, fishwives. Even Lords and Ladies. They all sent in reports about The Music Bearers. They all wanted to keep 'on the good side' of the Black Hounds.

The Hounds had their spies everywhere. And they collected huge piles of information. Each file in the Library of Transgressors was a riveting collection of daring stories and amazing exploits. Each file was a bulk of rare sightings, false leads, missed opportunities and defiant getaways. The file name of each nonconformist might only be 'supposed' because there was never any certainty about the exact identity of any individual.

The Music Bearers were as enigmatic as they were irritating, thought Telson. But he fostered a grudging admiration for the slippery characters. And, although he never forgot that his sworn mission was to track down every criminal, he appreciated their courage and boldness.

～

Telson spent a week watching, waiting, listening, and learning before he developed his next plan of action. He noticed that a round-faced brother, one of many tailors who worked at the Abbey, visited the Library of Transgressors more frequently than others. This round-faced tailor-monk stitched cassocks and cowls. So, as far as Telson could reason anyway, he had no business to be in the library. His frequent visits seemed suspicious. Maybe the tailor-monk was designing a disguise for a spy to wear. Or perhaps he worked on a special pattern for a new cloak with secret pockets. Who knows? Perhaps the round-faced monk had a good excuse to visit the library. But that was not Telson's concern.

Telson kept a note of the round-faced monk's frequent visits. Recording how long the clothier spent in the room and noting what time he arrived and left. Six days into this secret survey, Telson noted with some pleasure that the clothier had exited the room with a plump file in his scrubbed hands.

One worker at the library offered to make a note of this transaction in the big ledger before he left with the file. Telson realised he would have to bide his time before his next move — maybe wait a week or more — but in this timeless place, a week would not seem long at all.

∽

Precisely six days after the round-faced monk had taken the file from the library, Telson left his cell. He decided it was time to spring the next trap. It was a few minutes before dinner, but Telson didn't go for a meal. Instead, he headed stealthily for the stitchery. This was where the round-faced tailoring monk worked. Telson waited by a wash-bowl built into the wall, figuring correctly that the round-faced monk would surely be the first of many to make his way to the refectory to feed his face. As predicted, the round-faced monk and his colleagues passed by. Telson had pushed deep into the little alcove, almost disappearing, so could not be seen. Telson heard the round-faced monk's sandals slapping down the corridor with the others.

Telson then slipped to the tailor's workshop. They latched the door to the craft area — kept safe with a simple knot of thin rope. Telson studied this rope and ran his finger around it. He worked out the best way to replicate the knot when he had finished. He then undid the knot, slid open the bolt, and slipped into the room. He quickly scanned the entire workshop before he could see what he came in for. On one side of the cold, drab room were some drawers. These were situated underneath a cutting table. Telson thought that this must be where the tailor's patterns and plans were kept. He opened the top drawer, and saw some roughly made patterns, so pulled these out with care. Under the papers, he found the file he required. It was the file that had been taken from the Library of Transgressors by the round-faced monk.

The Transgressor named in the file was a Music Bearer described as 'Mickleham.' According to up-to-date information, this heretic had been active for the last 28 days.

Telson glanced at the file, running his eye across the words, then slipped the file under his cassock. After that, he prudently replaced the tailor's patterns back into their drawer. Then he slid it closed before he softly left the workshop. On the threshold, he stopped, making sure he heard no footsteps on the cold hard slabs before he proceeded. When sure the hallway was empty, Telson re-attached the rope knot on the door, and latched it shut. Telson made his way to the refectory. He slipped into the back of the dining room without being noticed. Most of the other brothers were already at the big table, greedily slurping their food.

Things were about to get interesting, Telson thought.

~

Telson waited for the fun to begin in the library. By mid-week, things got genuinely exciting. They sent two Tipstaves from the Tipstaff Central Office to look for the missing file. The round-faced monk got summoned to the Library Master's anteroom. Telson reasoned that the soppy fat monk was being grilled about where and when he last saw the missing file. But Telson had retrieved it, furtively.

They summoned the Head Tipstaff to the Library area too. It

seemed he was about to explode with rage. They organised a thorough search of the whole Abbey — more Tipstaves had to be called to handle this wider search.

They were all stupid, believed Telson. Nobody thought logically. It was typical of this place. They were out of touch. None of them possessed common sense. All they needed to do was look in the most obvious place. Because, on the same night he had 'liberated' the file, Telson had surreptitiously returned it to the library. He slipped it into the cabinet, exactly where it belonged. He put it in its correct place. He smiled at the simplicity of his plan and the idiotic nature of his brethren.

Another 24 hours passed before one of the library monks shouted out in surprise. He had made an unexpected and happy discovery. 'I found it, I found it,' shouted the monk, with eagerness. 'It has been here all along.' His cry caused a ripple of commotion around the library, and several monks went to him. Followed by the Tipstaves assigned to the library.

Telson needed to hasten if he were to preserve the evidence. While events and commotion distracted people, he deftly slipped out of the library and went promptly to the office of the Formation Director. The Formation Director's Scribe was sitting at his usual desk, outside of the Superior of Superiors office, checking notes. Telson asked the Scribe if he would go down to the Library of Transgressors with him — at once. The cleric seemed stunned by this sudden demand on his time. He was unaccustomed to taking orders from junior novices. But Telson seemed insistent. He used assertive body language.

The Scribe said that he would need to allow this 'unusual' activity with the Formation Director, perhaps to wrong-foot the young monk. Telson nodded and accepted that this was the correct course of action. So the Scribe went into the office of the Superior of Superiors and returned a few moments later with wide eyes. 'Yes!' he said. The Formation Director had told him to go with the young monk to the library.

The curmudgeonly old Scribe was slow, and he took carefully slow steps. He had problems with his hips, and this meant that he walked pointedly, almost over-cautiously. He seemed to growl under his breath with each agonised step.

'Come on, come on...' Telson muttered under his breath. 'Hurry up, old man, or we'll be late...'

Finally, the two men arrived at the Library of Transgressors. By now, Telson rattled with nerves. He was sure they had taken much too much time to get to the place. He was certain that, by now, someone would have tampered with the evidence. So, when they arrived at the Library, Telson went straight to the big ledger book. This was where all the transactions on the movements of precious files had been recorded. Telson ran a finger down the lined page until he found what he was looking for. He located the note made about the file the round-faced monk took when he removed the file. He felt a pang of pleasure ripple through him. Good! The idiots hadn't been quick enough.

He pointed at one particular item in the big old ledger. He invited the old Scribe to inspect it. Telson said nothing — he simply pointed out the space at the end of the entry, underlining it with his fingernail. This made it easier for the old man to focus upon the mistake. The old man glared, so Telson backed off. Now the old Scribe would see all the other entries in the ledger and compare them. Then he would notice that all 'blank' spaces filled-in with return-dates. But one was not. The entry that Telson had pointed out.

The truth seemed self-evident — someone had removed the file and had not returned it within the agreed time.

The Scribe peered at the inadequate entry for a long time. He studied many other entries in the ledger, too — his whiskery old eyelashes fluttering. He tried to make sense of what he could see. All the while he muttered unintelligible words. Then the Scribe straightened his back in time for the Library Master to appear from his anteroom.

The Library Master examined the two men standing by the ledger. One, the young and arrogant novice, the other, the crinkly septuagenarian from the Superior of Superiors office. He walked towards them with an artificial smile. 'Excuse me, can I help you with something? Is there anything you need?'

The old Scribe scanned the Library Master with scarcely disguised contempt. They must have fallen out in the past, thought Telson.

'Yes,' the old Scribe said, 'The Formation Director asked me to check this ledger for errors. It seems I found one. This sensible young man alerted me to a record that is incomplete. A file has been removed from the library yet not returned within the agreed time-scale—'

'Oh, that...' the library master mumbled, dismissively. He waved his hand. 'Is that all? Yes. I know about it. The matter has been sorted out now — the file arrived — there was an oversight. Nothing more.'

'If it was an oversight...' interrupted the old Scribe, 'Then why has the ledger not been amended with the fact? Why hasn't the return date been documented?'

The Library Master sighed and shook his head with a weary, yet fake smile. 'These things happen, Brother. It's a simple mistake. The file came back in suitable time, but the ledger was not updated correctly. The fault was a simple administrative error. Nothing more. And nothing to worry yourself about. Please don't tell the Superior of Superiors.'

But, indeed, the Scribe was not concerned. He couldn't care less about the error. He eyed the Library Master and gave him a hazy smile. The Master took the ledger away from the scrutinising eyes, but, just as he was about to slap the pages shut, thus putting the entire issue properly at an end, there was a sudden interruption. The interruption came from the Head Tipstaff who strode into the room with the sourest expression imaginable on an ever-reddening face: 'What is the meaning of this?' he blustered.

Telson and the elderly Scribe observed the angry man — but realised he directed the question to the innocent-looking Library Master. As he spoke, he brandished his silver-tipped stick. The Library Master stared with widened eyes, waiting for him to continue. So he did. The Head Tipstaff was livid: 'My men have told me you had them looking high and low for a missing file. Yet it was here all the time—' The Head Tipstaff shouted the last words, to get the point across.

'Yes, an oversight, I assure you, dear chap. An admin mistake. I am sorry,' responded the Library Master.

'Excuse me? Are you dullards having a joke? A joke on me? Because, if you are, I am not laughing. Oh, no! I am not the laughing type. Before you call us to clear-up your mess in future, I expect you to do your job efficiently. Why didn't anyone check to see if the file was indeed missing in the first place before you got us launched on a wild-goose chase?'

It stumped the Library Master. So he gawked blankly at the enraged man.

'Idiots...' shouted the leader of the Tipstaves. He marched away in anger.

~

The next day the story of the incident spread around the Abbey. People exchanged whispers in private corners and shared the story in fields. They even murmured about the scandal during prayers. The scandal of the 'file and the ledger' cost the Library Master his job. The Formation Director removed him from office. They allocated him a job that was considered more suitable for a man of his limited abilities; they reassigned him to the pigsty. There, he was given the task of cleaning out the muck.

~

Things settled down to a normal routine after a few days. It became a lot calmer in the library. Then Telson was relayed word that the Formation Director wanted to see him.

Telson arrived at the Director's office, where he was acknowledged by the curmudgeonly old scribe, the gatekeeper. But, since the incident at the library, the scribe had a twinkle in his eyes. It was as if he looked upon Telson with less exasperation and even a speck of affection.

Telson got ushered into the large office: 'Your work in this matter will not go unrewarded,' said the Superior of Superiors. 'I am referring to your investigations into how apathetically the Library of Transgressors has been, thus far, managed.' The Director checked to see that Telson paid full attention. When he nodded understanding, the Superior continued: 'Therefore, I have named you my new Library Master. You will perform the role for as long as I see fit...' He fixed his eyes firmly on Telson. 'I have yet to make the declaration formal. But, nevertheless, you will assume the responsibility directly.'

Telson was shocked to hear this news. He expected the plan to go well, but not this well. He felt slightly light-headed. What an honour!

The Formation Director continued: 'Well done Telson. This is a significant promotion, but you earned it.'

Telson stepped out of the Formation Director's office feeling giddy with excitement.

He was on his way now.

12

THE CANTICLE OF CYRUS

Telson settled into the role of Master of the Library of Transgressors very well.

On the first day of his new job, he called in all the library monks — they now worked for him. He issued new instructions: The first was that no one, emphatically nobody, could take a file away from the library.

Telson could not afford to let things slide again — especially since his name was now linked to the place.

His second instruction was that they should use the ledger to record the names of any visitor who might arrive. This meant that Telson would have a promising idea of who was to blame if things went awry. It would also give him a clue of who was looking into what. This would provide him with an early warning of any other ongoing investigations he should know.

After briefing his personal library staff, Telson called in the two Tipstaves that were attached to the library. He thanked them for their loyalty and their devotion to duty, and he explained the new system to them as well. He reinforced the notion that no one was to remove any files from the library. They nodded their approval. He thought they would prefer his new instructions, since the old system meant that they were continuously on the move, looking around for missing files and issuing warnings. This new system meant they could hang around the library — notably near the entrance — providing a visible deterrent to any monks who might think of taking a file away. He told the Tipstaves to look out for any monk who might attempt to hide files, or otherwise behave abnormally.

When all of his staff had been informed of what they needed to do, Telson felt he could get on with his chief function. And that was to find patterns in all the data. He needed to search his way through vast piles. Because, like everyone here, they employed him to sniff out Music Bearers. He already had a notion he wanted to satisfy. And now he had unrestricted access to all the files, plus a little group of workers to help him, he realised there would be no better time to work on his hypothesis.

He figured out that they gathered reports of some Music Bearers being seen, on more than occasion, in specific cities or at certain settlements. He put effort into collecting information about these sightings, because he thought he might establish a pattern. And from a pattern he might predict when and where a Music Bearer would show up next.

Telson found it difficult to establish any patterns because the Music Bearers were such slippery animals. They were forever changing the way they appeared. They altered their clothes and their haircuts. Beards were cultivated, then cropped back. Hair was developed into ponytails, then lopped off. Moustaches came and went over the period of one day. The Music Bearers often altered their fake names too and falsified their occupations. So Telson had to look for something in particular.

He searched for recognisable traits or, better still, obvious facial features that could never be altered. He was not interested in spots, unusual skin patterns, or worry lines. All these could be added, obliterated, or altered. A person could use a dab of cream or fleck of mud to hide a spot or change a dimple. No, what Telson searched for was something rather unusual. An extraordinary physical imperfection that could not be conveniently hidden, perhaps, for example, distinctly shaped lips, cuts or tears in ears, or noses flattened. That type of thing. A characteristic that even a lazy gatekeeper in a darkened room would notice and probably recall.

He set to work, and after a week of intensive study, Telson tracked down three targets: the first target had a noticeable scar on his neck, below his right ear. Telson supposed this Music Bearer might pull-up his scarf, or grow a beard, to hide it the feature. The next had obvious protuberances on his head. These bumps were just above his eyebrows. But, Telson reasoned, a hood or a cowl could cover up bulges effectively. The last target he found had high cheekbones — these would be difficult to hide in any circumstances — and in any light.

So Telson concentrated all of his efforts on this one. His filename was Brother Chad. He pulled together all the files he had on this Brother Chad and he discovered that a person meeting the same description, high cheekbones, had visited three walled-cities within the last year — Castle Acre, Yernemuth and Lynn.

In each case, the visitor had entered the city and purported to be a general merchant or 'Mercer,' as suppliers were frequently described. Telson searched back through all the old files, and he found that a Mercer, one of a similar appearance, with high cheekbones, had also visited the city of Castle Acre several times before. If Telson calculated things correctly, it would seem that this Brother Chad was likely to visit Castle Acre again in the next few months.

Telson felt pleased with this discovery. At first, he supposed he should alert the Gate Keepers at the town of Castle Acre. And also warn their friends at a nearby Priory. But then he thought better of this course of action. He didn't want some local Burgess to screw things up. Or worse still, take all the credit for himself.

No, Telson reckoned, he would need to handle this one by himself.

∼

There was one other line of enquiry that Telson was eager to work on. A matter that had always intrigued him, so he looked into it now while he had the time, the staff, and the authority to do so.

It had always intrigued him to consider the method the Music Bearers must use to connect and communicate with fellow heretics. How did they do things without being detected? Telson reasoned they must have their own secret agents. Presumably like the ones who hired the Black Hounds. He also thought that they must embed these agents in the cities.

However, it seemed impossible for the Black Hounds to trace any of these secret agents. They had still not unlocked the secret methods used by the Music Bearers to communicate with each other across their network.

∽

St Hubert's Abbey possessed several libraries. The Superior had appointed Telson as the temporary Library Master of one of many library rooms. To find out about the secret agents used by the Music Bearers, Telson would need to contact the Master of the Library of Violators Associates.

So, early one morning, he visited that library to introduce himself to Brother Cyrus. It surprised Telson to discover that the Library Master at the Library of Violators Associates was of similar youthful age to him. They had other things in common, too: both had manipulated matters in a way that had greatly advanced their careers through scheming and deceit. And, though neither were yet entirely tonsured, they had already earned themselves considerable influence and power over other monks at the Abbey. They achieved all this without being thoroughly inducted into the brotherhood.

'I come from the Library of Transgressors. I seek some advice about the files you keep,' Telson said, by introduction.

'I have heard of your temporary promotion,' replied Cyrus. 'And I congratulate you on your skills as a tactician and strategist.'

'Thank you, brother. And you too have been advanced rapidly. That is also meritorious. You are to be congratulated.'

'How can I help you?'

'I have been able to locate a Transgressor...' explained Telson. 'The individual I have found has distinctive and perhaps unique physical features about him. I think I can predict, with some accuracy, where he might turn up next. But I want to get an idea of how this Music Bearer arranges contacts with his handler. How does he get messages to his superiors? I am ignorant of this information.'

'Yes, I understand. You have come to the right place for answers,' offered Cyrus. 'This is where we keep files on accomplices and their cohorts.' Cyrus took Telson into the main body of the library and chose a random file. 'This girl — they always use girls for this work, by the way...' he showed the file to Telson. The file described a female subject, given the name Sister Editha. There had been various descriptions of her, and notes made about her fate: 'Believed deceased. Not seen for eight seasons.' But it was a flimsy file, not as bloated as the files found in Telson's Library of Transgressors. 'This girl is one of their spies.' continued Cyrus. 'She hides in plain sight. Within the community. She is activated when required. We do not really understand how they do this. But we know they do. She helps the Music Bearers get into the city. She arranges for them to leave as well. She provides them with passwords, safe routes, and secure passage. She gives them secret messages and instructions. He leaves. She stays—'

'Why is there so little information recorded here?' Telson interrupted.

'She is a secretive little miss. That's why. They all are. She lives inside the city walls. So we never get information about her travels. We seldom get sightings reported to us. The city-folk protect her. They surround her. They safeguard her. They provide many obstacles that hinder our best efforts to find out more.'

'How did you achieve this information, then?'

'We paid for facts and material. We have spies in every town. Porters and gatekeepers will keep an eye out for lone girls. Sometimes a parent will be upset by one and will run to us with a story. More often than not, though, it's a rejected lover. A spurned suitor will come to us with a tale. We call this the jealousy angle. We get our best information from such sources.' Cyrus grinned when he said this. 'Sometimes it is the only way we can take out these girls.'

'What do you have on their girl at Castle Acre?' Telson asked.

'I will have a look for you. We can try to track down the information for you, brother. But it might take a day or two.'

So now Telson had a better understanding about how the Music Bearer's agents worked in the cities and the towns. He inched ever closer to what he actually needed to find out.

But at this point, he thought it wise to keep his cards close to his chest.

∼

Telson spent many hours in the Library of Violators Associates with his new friend, Brother Cyrus. They got on well. Cyrus helped Telson in his efforts to track down information on the agent at Castle Acre. Telson, meanwhile, collected information on the Bearer with high cheekbones.

Telson also worked on his own, on a far more sensitive, intelligence gathering project. The facts about Castle Acre superficially interested Telson. Although, and, it was true, he did plan to go to the walled-town and capture the Music Bearer known as the Brother Chad. But he already possessed all the information he required that particular mission. The trapping of Brother Chad could wait until Telson finished his other project. This was a private venture. And it was the principal reason for his hunt through the files of the Library of Violators Associates. After days of fruitless search, and with freshly developed eye strain, Telson figured he needed help from his new friend, brother Cyrus. Especially if he was ever going to find what he actually looked for.

'I'm seeking more information,' Telson told Cyrus. He was bleary eyed with fatigue. And he offered a weak smile. 'I'm sorry I did not reveal this to you before,' he added.

Brother Cyrus did not seem upset by the revelation. In fact, he expected it: 'Yes, I know that you have been inspecting files outside our hunt for the agent at Castle Acre.'

'I am puzzled. I wonder if I could ask for help?' whispered Telson.

'I'm sure I can help. What do you need?'

'I confess I'm looking for another type of agent.' Telson chose his words deliberately. 'She must be an uncommonly special agent because the agent I seek does not stay in one place. The agent I hunt may fly from town-to-town as a free bird. She must be one of their most independent, strong, and experienced agents. I imagine she is rather like a hacked-back falcon.'

'Yes, there are such agents, though very few. I am aware of the sort you describe,' replied Cyrus. 'But may I ask… what made you assume that they existed?'

'Well, I meditated on the problem.' Telson replied. 'How do their girls turn up in towns and cities? Someone must bring them to city walls. Someone must introduce them. I suspected that the Music Bearers have some kind of 'travelling' agent too.'

'You do not tell all, though, do you, brother? You wonder if there is something else, perhaps?' Cyrus raised an eyebrow.

'You are right.' Telson realised he must now be honest. 'I wish to know this: who takes away the foundlings? Who takes away the flawed and faulted babies from the wayside? Who takes away offspring for adoption? That must be the work of those 'independent flyers' too—'

'You are right in your assumption…' Brother Cyrus offered. He led Telson to a small side cabinet. It contained a few dozen files. 'This is what you look for. I wish you had come to me earlier with clear intentions…' Cyrus handed Telson a dossier of notes. 'We packed this dossier with sightings, facts, and rumours about one particular free-running agent. Her file name is Sister Temenos. She collects babies left by the wayside. This is the one who introduces new agents into the towns…' Telson eagerly read each page about the free-bird named Temenos. Where she had been, how she appeared, what disguises she had used. Dates, times, places. He committed all these facts to memory. Evidently, she was one of their most important agents. She was free to move all over the kingdom, possibly with impunity. No one seemed able to stop her. This free agent named Temenos seemed untouchable.

Now, if Telson could trap this little hen… well, it would make him the most famous Black Hound for decades, wouldn't it? A culmination of his life's work..

13

THE CANTICLE OF THE BLACK HOUND

'Tell me — who is the Warden of the fortress?'

He addressed the question to the landlord of the Waverside Inn. The innkeeper moved a cask across a stony floor, so did not look up. The crunch meant he could not hear the words with any clarity. And, anyway, he was not accustomed to such plain-speak from the towns-folk. The voice he heard indicated a forceful personality. It wore authority like a Prince wore a breastplate. Although the voice was obviously not noble. The innkeeper figured it did not belong to one of high birth. As a result, and since he was busy with his barrels — but largely because he was not being addressed by a Lord — the innkeeper ignored the question. He continued with his demanding job and rolled the next tub into place.

'Tell me who is the Warden of the fortress, and I shall reward you,' insisted the voice.

This time the innkeeper became interested. What reward might a peasant could conceivably grant? To reinforce his authority in his own tavern, the innkeeper ignored the second question and also the veiled threat behind the approach. He kept his head by the barrel, though made a pretence of wiping a cloth across the top of the cask. This was to clear away unseen smears and so he could shrewdly glance over the counter-top to take stock of this stranger. He scratched his chin, curious about the prospect of a reward.

The stranger remained uncommonly still. He was undoubtedly a very self-composed individual. In fact, the landlord could not even hear him breathe. Or see his feet shuffle. He might not be a Lord, thought the innkeeper, but might be someone interesting. Perhaps a visiting mercer. Or a future investor. So, the landlord decided he ought to be nice to the stranger... well, somewhat more sociable, anyway, so he put his cloth down, straightened his back, and twisted his body to look at the man.

The strange character stood in the half-light. He was thin, positively gaunt. The stranger had a mat of wispy, fine hair upon a skeletal head. Sea spray and wind had encrusted his face with salt; green snot ran along his jowls. The man possessed emaciated cheekbones and an upturned nose. His dominant feature were sticky eyes. They were a limpid, cornflower, blue. Glued by rain and grime, the eyes darted attentively, observing everything but focussing on nothing.

The innkeeper took in all these details — examining what he saw — like he had done a thousand times before. Because every visitor to a village inn is a viable threat. He'd learned that long ago. Involuntarily, like all landlords, he made swift judgments based on appearances. Those judgements were generally correct, and often lifesaving. This client was not a noble man, for sure. Noble men didn't have snot on their faces. Neither was this stranger a mercer. Mercers don't have salt in their hair. No, this creature appeared to be a wild man. Some kind of wretch who lived, most probably, in a hole. If that was the case, how come he was so self-assured? A vagrant who couldn't even feed himself well should not go about town making demands.

So the innkeeper beheld the skinny visitor with a mixture of pity and contempt. He was about to shoo him out of his place, but a pang of conscience bolted through him. He decided he should at least be charitable. Compassion doesn't cost much, does it? He decided that after offering food, he would tell the snotty faced stranger, in no uncertain terms, to move on.

'Would you like bread and broth? I have some bubbling in my pot if you want. You look cold and tired. Do you want a warm place to stay?'

'I do not want a room or soup. I want information,' the stranger said. 'Just tell me who the Warden of the fortress is, so I can be on my way.'

'Now, look here...' returned the innkeeper. He was not familiar with the concept of charity being rejected. Frankly, the arrogance of the stranger became tiresome. He determined to tell him to clear off. 'If you don't want soup or a bed of straw than you ought to bluebottle-buzz off,' he said. 'I do not have time to help every travelling pilgrim. Especially not wretched skeletons like you. It doesn't look like you have a silver-penny to your name. So, how dare you suggest that you'd reward me for information?'

The stranger seemed curiously composed. Even though he wore the clothes of a ruffian, he remained remarkably confident. The landlord expected the bag-of-bones to turn around and step out, but the stranger did no such thing: he remained motionless. The strange vagrant seemed as proud and imperious as a King. A small smile trickled across his dirty, dry-cracked lips. All the while, his glazed blue-grey eyes flickered-this-way-and-that; never stopping to focus on any one thing in particular. Perhaps the stranger probed for weaknesses, examined vulnerabilities, and envisaged controlling probabilities? For the first time during the full encounter, the innkeeper felt uncomfortable: 'Like I said, stranger — get out of my face. Leave before you come to regret it.' But the bedraggled stranger was not going anywhere. He stood motionless like a church cross, except for those blue eyes. They were always on the move.

The sun was low, and two prongs of light spilled through the shutter. The landlord saw something he had not noticed before. Something gleamed. It glinted readily on the front of the stranger's dark cloak. The landlord could not appreciate the thing at first. He was in the darkness, down by barrels, and the stranger had positioned himself between pale sunlight and the darker recesses of the backroom. But, as the light grew weak, the innkeeper realised that the stranger wore a tattered monk's habit. He hadn't noticed this garb before. The innkeeper tried his best to make sense of what he could see. But the key to the puzzle was the burnished object pinned on the pilgrim's cloak. It was out-of-place. A gleaming bright jewel on an otherwise shabby uniform. That object was extraordinary.

The stranger moved forward just one step. It was as if he could read the mind of the innkeeper. He wanted to show the man what they had pinned to his habit. As the monk stepped into the pale light, the innkeeper immediately recognised the glinting ornament. As he acknowledged the object, he felt a deep pain of anxiety rise into his stomach. Pain bubbled in his belly while bile rose into his throat. Dread gripped the innkeeper. He hastily thought of ways in which he could appease the stranger. *God! At least I offered him food and lodging!*

The badge became unmistakable in the light. It was a symbol. A symbol that everyone dreaded. They had mounted the emblem on a pin. It was the notorious emblem of 'Four Fangs' — the sign of the Order of Black Hounds. The badge was a cross of white metal. Although no ordinary cross, it resembled four sharp dog's teeth. The innkeeper felt wildly around him — as he struggled to locate the cloth he had formerly dropped. Now he needed to wipe away drops of sweat that formed on his forehead.

'Come outside...' the thin stranger directed.

'What?' said the landlord with startled eyes.

'Come outside. I will pray for you.'

The innkeeper decided he had better not to question the wild man again.

The monk beckoned towards the door. A weak sun filtered through gaps in the panels. The stranger made his way to the entranceway, followed by the cautious innkeeper.

The innkeeper found he had even more reason to be dismayed when he emerged into the light of afternoon. Because not only was the stranger, hoisted full-height now in glimmering sun, wearing the habit of the Black Hounds, with the dogs-fang cross boldly visible — but the innkeeper saw two other menacing men with him. These men watched and waited. Both were manifestly soldiers, and it was clear they were Palatine guards. Papal protectors who travelled with

Black Hounds on their hunting sprees. The landlord assessed these two guards: One wore a sword. He also had a large knife scabbarded on a leather belt. It seemed as if the blade on the knife had seen a lot of recent hacking. He wore another side-knife attached to his leg. The landlord guessed this knife had a long and horribly cruel blade. The soldier's hair was unkempt. He doubtless had been travelling for days without washing. The guard wore a breastplate of leather and chaps to protect his legs. He had tatty, fingerless gloves worn on ruthless hands. He was wiry and intelligent. But this soldier was not the more dangerous of the two guards. When the innkeeper regarded them both, he knew that the other man was far dodgier. This other soldier slumped on a post by the village mounting block. Also a Palatine guard, he did not possess a sword or even a hacking knife. He did not wear a breastplate. He had no need of protection because he was not a combatant. He had one weapon, and he held it in his right hand. His weapon of choice was the scourge; a nine-tongued black whip. The 'flagella' symbol had been stitched onto the breast of this man's doublet. It meant he was their torturer. This man's job was to gain confessions. The torturer was a head taller than his brother soldier. He had a bruised face, scarred from recent fighting. He looked skinnier than the other, manifestly under-nourished. He had an especially wild look about him. In fact, all three foreigners gave the notion of being untamed. They were windswept, dirty, and they each smelled like pigs. They were predators who'd spent too much time on the hunt. Loaded with menace, they seemed ready to burst with uncontrolled rage at any moment. The innkeeper guessed that, like a group of cornered badgers — these hunters were inclined to scratch, bite, or snarl at anything that moved.

'Kneel!' demanded the Black Hound. The landlord peered into a muddy mess of urine and dung. But he thought better of arguing with a man who wore a black habit and the emblem of the fanged-cross. 'Kneel and I will pray for you.'

The innkeeper did as he was told. He knelt in the stinking sludge. He bowed his head — ready for the blessing. Or worse. He sensed that a soldier came towards him. He felt his heartbeat increase. He panted. He tried not to show fear. The innkeeper concentrated hard, stopping his bones from shaking. He guessed the monk made a sign of the cross above his forehead. He followed this sign by muttering obscure words, perhaps in Latin. The blessing was not pleasant. Other blessings had provided the innkeeper with a sense of hope and peace. This blessing was different. It left him with a sense of anxiety and apprehension.

'Look up,' the Black Hound commanded with a snarl.

The innkeeper glanced upward, though he dared not look into the eyes of the Black Hound. Nor did he wish to stare at the two Palatine guards. They stood close-by, enjoying the show. The innkeeper gazed over the shoulder of the monk, to focus on something in the distance. Up on the hill side. He looked towards the disused fort.

'Who is the Warden of that fortress on the hill?' The Black Hound snapped. 'Be warned, this is your last chance to earn redemption...'

'Brother! There is no Warden at that fortress. The place is absolutely deserted.' The innkeeper gave his answer in nervous, jerky puffs. 'This village is not a castle district. There are no castle-guards or a castellan. Either in that fortress or in this town. We are vassals to no high person. We are freemen. We live in a free community. We elected our own Port-Reeve. He pays taxes on our behalf to the County Reeve.'

The Black Hound sniffed, perhaps satisfied with the information. He nodded. 'Right, get up!' My men will stay at your inn tonight. You will provide them with shelter and food. You will provide drink for their bellies. I will pay you, in coin, for your trouble.'

'Thank you, brother. Thank you.' The innkeeper knew that he thanked the Black Hound for his life. 'And you, brother? Where will you stay?'

'I will stay there...' the Hound indicated to large cobbles near the village water trough. Two corners of an adjacent building offered some kind of shelter from wicked coastal winds. It seemed an odd place to stay. But with those words, the monk made his way towards the trough. He collapsed hard onto the rocky cobbles, then pulled his cowl above his head and dropped his chin. The monk closed his eyes soundly, and he resembled a simple beggarman. How could anyone fear such a character?

The innkeeper was going to offer the monk a bowl of warm-up soup. But the Palatine guards shook their heads. They implied no one should dare disturb the cleric. Not now. Not ever.

The guards followed the innkeeper into the warmth of the hostelry. To leave their master in the cold.

14

THE CANTICLE OF THE PORT REEVE

The fishing village of Waverside included about thirty buildings. Most were modest structures — with floors and walls built from clay, covered in sand. The villagers had thatched each rooftop with galingale, a stringy plant that had a fresh smell when cut. The herb was plentiful in these parts. Along with dwellings and fishing huts, most community buildings in Waverside were situated around a town square. These buildings included the village inn where the Palatine guards rested their heads during their first night at Waverside. Other shared buildings included a small brewery, a roper's workshop, stores, a smokehouse, and a small chapel. The meeting house was the biggest construction. It even had a back room. The elected Port-Reeve exploited this room as his official residence.

The Black Hound stopped there.

∽

The pudgy-faced Port-Reeve was entertaining the young daughter of a fisherman in his back room. He smiled like a juvenile. A silly grin filled his face, while his yellow teeth matched the straw-coloured hair on his bare chest. He allowed his pinkish hands to explore the girl's waist — his pudgy fingers sought to sneak their way towards soft white skin that lay beneath her bodice. She laughed too — because his hands tickled her stomach, and the sensation caused her legs to squeeze together. His breath smelled of stale beer and pickled fish. But she did not mind the smell, or that he was at least twice as old. He was the most important person she had ever had.

They rolled and played on the straw-sack pillows. They each took deep breaths and laughed so much that they did not notice a thin, dangerous looking man who entered the room in silence.

For a while, this dangerous man watched playful the lovers. He scrutinised them as they fumbled. A wry smile twisted across his lips. Finally, the Port-Reeve squeezed the backside of the maiden — and this pinch caused her to turn around and to squeal in mock-alarm. Then she faced the Port Reeve — allowing his stinking breath to blast her in the face.

From this perspective, she could see right over his shoulder. A silhouetted figure seemed to emerge from the darkness at the other end of the room. She did not really scream, although her mouth gaped open as if she were about to. Instead, she burped. The burp was indeed emphatic. She clawed the Reeve's shoulder to get his attention. But he continued to guffaw and thought the clawing was part of their lovemaking. The Port-Reeve imagined the girl became livelier, so he rubbed her neck before giving a playful pat on the bottom. Yet she was unyielding now; just glaring at the dark shape she saw at the far end of the room.

∼

The Port-Reeve stopped his pat-a-cake and turned his neck to see what was going on. He dropped his lower jaw in surprise, too. He saw where she gazed: a thin shadow, a lurker, had invaded his private chamber. 'What the hell are you doing here?' the Reeve shouted. He rose, adjusted his clothing, to ensure it exposed nothing, though his cheeks flushed red in exasperation. The Port-Reeve no longer smiled. He seemed angry as hell. How dare someone enter his private chamber? He thought about the consequences of being found out: he was married. If the tale was told, a about how he frolicked with a village harlot, his good name might become damaged. 'What is the purpose of this? How dare you come into my room? Who the hell are you?'

The stranger did not respond. He took a step closer: 'Are you the Reeve for this town?' The stranger seemed authoritative and over-confident.

'I *am*. Though, I ask the questions. Who are you? How did you get in? By what authority do you disturb me?'

By now, the fisherman's daughter hid herself behind a pile of straw pillows. She sought to make herself disappear. The Reeve glanced at her hiding place, behind paddings, and surmised that, perhaps, this intruder was a spurned lover — or maybe an older brother. If that were the case, the Reeve could pay him off. He'd provide gold to guarantee confidentiality. He'd learnt, over time, that a pouch of gold helps pew fellows keep lips closed. Gold stops blabbing.

But the stranger did not seem local. He seemed wild. 'I am Zadock,' he said. 'From the Order of the Black Hounds. 'I came to see the Town Reeve. I came through that doorway there...' The monk flicked his wrist in the general direction of the entrance.

'But... erm? How did you get past my guards?' He did not intend to ask aloud. He blurted it.

'Your guards are *distracted*, I'm afraid.' The Black Hound smiled. His blue-grey eyes scanned the room. 'Who is that woman who hides behind you?'

The Port-Reeve had been expeditiously processing all the information. He thought hard. The monk was a member of the Black Hounds. That meant he travelled with armed guards. Palatines, presumably. This whole situation might have unfortunate outcomes, especially if he failed to negotiate his way out of things with his usual political cunning. He reminded himself that he became the Port Reeve because he could talk himself out of a problem. That's what made him an adroit leader. He could apply himself in such circumstances. Folk said he could talk his way out of a leather bag if he wanted to. So, instead of answering the direct question that had been postulated, the Port-Reeve changed his demeanour and attitude. He put on a deliberately wide smile and extended both arms forwards, to offer a warm welcome to the wild man who intruded into his private space. The Reeve stepped into the open, so he might greet the visiting stranger properly, and also so that the monk could see that he 'meant business' and offered no resistance.

Zadock, the Black Hound, watched as the overweight, sweaty man approached. He saw the foolish man's fat arms and watched how they outstretched in an ugly display of false welcome. He noticed the idiotic smile on the man's pigface. The taste of bile rose in the monk's throat. He shook his head in disappointment. The Reeve was a grotesque and flatulent lump of pork fat. He did not deserve to be of notable rank. The man was a disorderly slob.

So, when the Port-Reeve was within bear-hugging distance of Zadock, the monk side-stepped him calmly. Diverting around his bad-breath, Zadock headed to the fisherman's daughter who, by now, crouched low. Sensibly, she had ducked under the bales, intent on staying out-of-sight. She kept her body as small as possible as a precaution. But Zadock stepped to the girl. He used all his physical strength to pull her to her feet. He used her own armpit to hold her upright and lever her body into position. Then he spun her around, so she faced the Port-Reeve. As he did this, Zadock held her flabby cheek with his left hand. She flinched because the monk hurt her. But he responded by grasping tighter: 'I asked you before. I ask you again. Who is this woman?'

The Port-Reeve stood gasping, like an upright fish. His mouth opened and his tongue fell forward. Sweat glistened on his neck. His heart thumped, and his knees shook.

'Is she your wife?' the Hound asked.

The Port-Reeve shook his head.

'Is she your daughter? Your niece? Your goddaughter? Is she a servant? Is she a pupil in need of tutoring?'

The Port-Reeve continued to shake his head.

'Is she the village harlot?'

'I... *uh*.' The Port-Reeve stumbled over his words. 'I sincerely do not know who she is. Just a local girl. Just a girl, she means nothing to me. She is just a... just a...'

'Harlot,' the monk said, harshly. Zadock's blue eyes gave nothing away. But rapidly, and furtively, he took a thin-bladed knife from a secret sheath at his back. Promptly, he slid the icy blade into the girl's heart. The deed was conducted so powerfully, so pragmatically, that she did not even realise what happened. She looked at the spot of dark-red blood that now spread prettily across her bodice. Then glanced at the Port-Reeve. He had a perplexed look on his fat-face. The girl could not comprehend what happened. The monk let her body slide gradually to the floor.

The Reeve stood still, frozen to the spot. Shock turned him into a statue. Zadock moved to him and place the knife into his right hand. The fat man looked closely at the knife.

Zadock smiled. 'Guards!' he cried.

The Reeve heard the plodding noises outside, so looked up to see two men appear at his door. These were the village guards. The Port-Reeve's *own men*. One man was young; he had a fresh, enthusiastic face. The other guy was a lot older, with wrinkled hands and a wonky eye. Zadock examined the two village guards and made a rapid and correct assumption: the older man was the senior officer, so he addressed him first: 'This man attacked the girl. He threatened me with a knife when I attempted to intervene—' Zadock gestured to the knife that the Reeve now held in his right hand. 'I am Zadock, from the Order of the Black Hounds.'

The Port-Reeve appeared confounded by the accusation. He dared not speak. The situation rendered him dumb with horror. He concentrated long and hard at the knife that now lay in his own hands. The blade dripped darkened blood onto his knuckles. The guards gazed at the Port-Reeve, their master, with a mixture of surprise, disgust, and resignation. They knew this was bound to happen, sooner-or-later. The older guard approached the young woman. Her body now flopped on the floor-slabs, motionless and cold. 'What did you do?' he asked. The question was directed at the Port-Reeve. Because no one in the world would expect a man-of-the-cloth to carry-out such a brutal act.

Zadock, the Black Hound, took charge of events. 'Well, I suppose you're the senior person now...' he proposed, as he gazed at the older guard. Zadock turned his attention to the younger one. 'You there, get sturdy rope — bind the arms of the prisoner.' The younger guard guessed he referred to the Reeve. This murderer must be delivered to the High Sherriff. He will pay for this crime. Make sure he is properly secured and place him in a cell. Then get word to the primary authority for your region.' Zadock checked back with the older guard: 'If you need any help tonight, my personal guards are at your disposal. I will stay near the inn if you need me...'

The older guard nodded.

'Tell me, how many men do you command?' Zadock asked.

The guardsman appeared confused by the question. 'Me, brother? I don't command any men, *um*—'

Zadock made a dismissive gesture with his hand. 'You function as the Port Reeve now. You are the most senior person in the village, so, I ask, again — how many men do you command?'

The full weight of the monk's words sunk into the older man's thick skull: 'Oh, I see. I have taken over! In that case... there are ten men on my watch.'

Zadock seemed satisfied with the answer. 'Good, get messages to all of them. I need them tomorrow night at the Inn. After sundown...'

The new commander of the town-guard nodded his understanding.

15

THE CANTICLE OF SEBASTIAN

"Si mundus musica caret, homo animam viventem non habet..."

If a world lacks music, a man has no living soul
-Brother Sebastian

Brother Sebastian viewed the horizon from a dilapidated tower in the old fort.

The crumbling place was not stout or robust enough to be described as a fortress. And Brother Sebastian was not literally a castellan. The Music Bearers had found the disintegrating remains of this abandoned and rat-infested sandcastle five years earlier. They decided it would make a perfect place for a seat of learning. The brotherhood liked how it was-cut off from the mainland by a spit. They also appreciated the clear, unobstructed views from the ramshackle towers. The old fort was a long walk from the nearest settlement. The nearest place was the tiny fishing village of Waverside. From the towers, they could see the coastal village in the distance. The self-sufficient fort had its own fresh water supply, and a vegetable garden with herb plots. So journeys from Waverside to the castle were rare.

Since the fort-school had been settled, dozens of young men had been through the shaky gates. They had received a safe and comfortable education inside the 'golden' walls of the fort. Brother Sebastian was not actually a castellan — a castle captain — although he acted like one. As keeper of the fort, he took care of all the daily maintenance of the broken-down buildings. He assumed responsibility for the governance of the college. And he took on the role as 'father figure' to the boys and senior member of the teaching staff.

But today, Sebastian seemed concerned.

Brother Sebastian peered down into the mouth of a tiny river that trickled towards the village of Waverside. The village sat in a snug dip between two wooded slopes. He felt anxious because the girl had not arrived. A girl from the village travelled to the fort each week. She typically came with fresh loaves and dried fish, though she had not arrived this week. Eight days had passed since they had last seen the girl. It was eight days since the staff and boys had eaten fresh bread.

When the girl came, she would usually leave two baskets of food at the gatehouse. The girl would take away two empty baskets left for her. She never entered the fort: she had never stepped foot inside the place. But was allowed two silver pieces for each visit she made. She typically tucked the silver coins into the bottom of her basket. This was a tremendous amount of money to pay a village girl, more than sufficient payment for her trouble, and the monks knew it was more than sufficient to purchase her silence. The monks were over-generous for good reason — so she'd kept her mouth shut. If she kept their secrets safe, the shillings would keep coming. The girl knew a good deal when she saw it.

Sebastian felt in his bones that something was wrong. Something had changed in the fishing village. He distinguished a spiral of black smoke that rose from the centre of the settlement. It was difficult to determine accurately which building smoked — because it was far away — but it seemed certain they had set one of their major structures alight. Sebastian also noticed it became quiet on the mud road that led out of the village and into open country. It was as if the residents of Waverside had been told they could not leave. Generally, there was a lot of hectic activity around the edges of the village during daylight hours. But in recent days, the road became deadly quiet.

∼

The day's tutoring went on, as usual, at the fort. Sunlight awakened the boys for first prayers. Then, after exercises, they started a busy working day. The sudden decrease in protein supplies meant meals had to be strictly rationed. But, after mealtime, they placed the boys in various rooms for tutorials, to be trained by expert Music Bearers, who acted as teachers.

During the day, each boy spoke privately with Brother Sebastian. He encouraged them to speak, confidentially, about anything that bothered them. Topics included subjects such as how their bodies were changing. Or the vivid dreams they were experiencing. Or any number of minor problems. Brother Sebastian tried his best to answer all their questions honestly. In his experience, the boys' questions were frequently about growing up. The lads in the fort were fast developing into young men.

Elis took advantage of his first one-on-one session with Brother Sebastian to raise a question that had been on his mind since he had first arrived at the fort.

'How are you getting on Elis?' Brother Sebastian asked.

There was an opening in the roof that let in some weak sunrays. Sebastian invited the young novice to come sit in the light so Sebastian could distinctly see him.

'I'm enjoying it very much,' Elis told the senior monk. 'I am trying my best to learn everything that is taught.'

Brother Sebastian nodded emphatically, though he said nothing. He left a long space so that Elis might fill the void with words of his own.

'I have been thinking about girls,' Elis blurted. He emptied the thoughts from his mind as hastily as he could. Not that he had any impure thoughts! Though he admitted to himself that he felt lonely since his arrival at the fort. Other boys had told him they experienced intense dreams about girls. They said they sometimes felt stimulated by such dreams. They said they felt unclean afterwards. These boys said that they needed to discuss these feelings with tutor-counsellor. But the problem Elis experienced was deeper than that. It felt more profound than carnal lust. It felt like hurt burnt inside him. An empty feeling. Food, prayer, exercise, or learning could not remove or sate it.

'Thinking about girls is normal,' Brother Sebastian told him. The monk seemed wise as a sandpiper. He smiled and nodded in a way that urged Elis to continue.

'Well, the thing is — where are the girls?' Elis asked after a long pause.

Elis lacked a mother's love. They *all* did. The brotherhood took away a mother's love, at a most tender age, and replaced it with the love of music. Struggling parents handed their kids over to the monks because they couldn't make ends meet or could not offer their children protection, or future. They handed their infants over before they could talk or crawl. The church powers then entrusted the older women of the Order to take care of the growing youngsters during their infant years. Older women of the Music Bearer community provided the young lads with a much-needed maternal presence in the early years. But when the boys approached adolescence, they were cut-off from the females, mainly because they had to determine to be celibate.

Elis missed the company of women — young and old. He missed the younger girls the most. And, principally, he missed Cinnamon. She had been his best friend and closest confidante. He wanted to admit to Brother Sebastian that he thought about her every day. Elis wanted to express how much he loved her. He wanted to tell the Brother how much he missed her... so much it hurt. But words neglected him.

'The girls you grew up with, Elis, they started upon an alternative path...' Brother Sebastian explained. 'But you will meet them again one day. They will help you carry out your missions. You will have many happy times with them.'

Elis felt his heart jump for joy when he heard these words.

'Now, remember Elis,' Brother Sebastian continued, 'You can only love these girls with your heart. Not with your body. You know that you don't you? You can never love a girl — er — substantially.' Sebastian shook his head to reinforce the notion that sex was denied. 'You will take holy vows of chastity next Michaelmas. You will swear to keep your body and mind pure.' Elis knew this, so he nodded.

'And where is my mother?' the boy asked. He felt uncomfortable talking about her now, just after discussing sex. But he had already decided that he must ask the biggest questions upon his mind.

'We do not know where your mother is, Elis. Though we pray for her every day.' Then Brother Sebastian changed topic. 'Do you remember when you started singing?'

This question surprised Elis. It didn't seem relevant. It came unexpectedly. So he took a moment to answer: 'I do not know when I started to sing. I never thought about it before. I just sort of, you know, I just sort of knew how to do it right away.'

'Your mother reported that you started singing when you were in the cradle,' Brother Sebastian proposed. 'Yes, you started singing before you could talk. You started singing before you could walk. You started singing before you could think.' Sebastian allowed these facts to sink in: 'Which is why your mother left you for the taking. She loved you, she genuinely did, but knew you had been blessed with a rare and powerful gift... the gift of the harmonic root. She had no choice but to leave you for taking.' He stared at Elis. 'If the Black Hounds discovered you — they would have killed you. They would have punished your mother, too. So, right from your earliest days, she ordained that you would have to come away with us, to learn our ways, to be part of our holy mission. This way, she understood as must you, you will use your natural gifts. You will help humanity and glorify God with music.'

'Why do the Black Hounds hate us so?' Elis whispered.

'My boy, they do not hate us. It is not hatred that sits in their hearts — but it is *misunderstanding*. They do not accept our view of things, that's all. When a man does not understand another man's point of view, things become deadly dangerous. The Black Hounds are *afraid of us* because we choose to think differently to them. That's why they try to hurt us. Our task is to make them understand. One day, with God's help, we will get them to understand.'

16

THE CANTICLE OF THE FALL OF THE FORT

On the first full day of Zadock's visit, the Black Hound told the newly promoted Commander of the Guard in the coastal town of Waverside to issue a proclamation.

It was a formal notice directing everyone to heed the following two explicit instructions: Villagers could not leave the confines of the fishing village unless they were told otherwise. And the Black Hound did not permit boats to sail from the harbour. Each villager was advised of this ruling, personally.

A few hours after issuing the decree, a peasant-boy left the village to collect firewood from scrubland outside the community. Zadock saw the boy leave the boundaries of the village. So he sent one of his guards to fetch him back.

At noon, the peasant-boy was executed on a tree.

His body dangled by the roadside. Openly displayed as a warning to others. The Hound put the boy to death as a reminder to all. The villagers must take orders from Zadock seriously.

After this incident, Zadock began a personal inspection of the village. He looked for anyone or anything that seemed to be out of place. When he entered the holy place of the village, a small fisherman's chapel, it dismayed him to find that they used the sanctuary as a warehouse for salt-fish barrels.

Plainly, the old Port-Reeve, presently placed under arrest for murder, had allowed this to happen. So Zadock had the chapel torched. If the sinners of this village could not use a chapel well, then they should lose it, he decided.

Since his arrival in the small fishing community of Waverside, the village-folk's lack of discipline had appalled Zadock.

The Black Hound decided it was a godless place.

Later the same week, a little after sunset, Zadock met with ten men of the village watch. He told them they had to arm themselves. He told them that, after midnight, they would attack the fortress on the hill.

There was much murmuring about this. At least one man mumbled that the fort was empty. Another said ghosts haunted the place. After warning the men to keep superstitious thoughts to themselves, and prepare to arm, Zadock ordered the freshly promoted Commander of the Guard to issue another proclamation — this time declaring a night-time curfew.

Zadock had discovered that the fort on the hill was only reachable across a thin path of sand. The villagers called this link a sand-spit. He also found out that the only time they could traverse this spit was at low tide. So he needed to get his 'volunteer' army up to the fortress without being seen, but at low tide. He decided he would take them single file, just after midnight.

Zadock ordered they allowed no torches or flames on the march. His Palatine Guards took charge, issuing instructions and cross-checking for understanding. An hour after midnight, they haltingly brought the men from the village towards the sand-fort. They trod across the spit of land that emerged only when the tide was low. They achieved all this in complete darkness.

They instructed the men of the watch to remain silent. They were told that they would be sentenced — instant death — if they refused to follow orders when required.

They led progressively the men to the fort. Once at the walls, the men were divided into sections and told to remain still. The Black

Hound instructed them to lie low and keep out of sight. They would remain hidden until Zadock gave a pre-arranged signal. Upon the signal, they would enter the gateway and take the fort.

One of the Palatine Guards was doubtful about his ability to keep the 'attack' secret. But Zadock convinced him he had done enough to secure the yield of the village men. 'And how are we going to enter the fortress once we get there?' asked the curious guard.

'Through the front door, of course,' Zadock replied with a dry smirk.

~

In the pale light of early morning sun, when all watchmen were in position around the walls of the fort — they shivered as they hunched into position — Zadock made himself visible.

He wore his black habit, with the dark hood pulled tight around his head and face, to protect him from needle-sharp salt-breeze. He wore black gloves and the fanged-cross — the sign of the Black Hounds. The emblem glistened in the weak sun. Zadock walked fearlessly to the main gate of the fort where he whacked onto soft, wet wood with his gloved hand. Bang! Bang! He figured most inside the fort would be up-and-about at dawn. And, soon enough, they would respond to his knock.

Brother Sebastian was first to be startled by the sudden knock-knock at the main gate. How could anyone approach the old fort without being seen? They had placed lookouts since first light. Why hadn't anyone seen an approach?

He decided he would have to answer the door soon enough, but first needed to put the pre-prepared evacuation plan into effect. If it were just a harmless bashing at the gate, a passing vagrant pleading for bread, perhaps it would be fine. It would be a valuable drill. He had discussed the evacuation plan with other senior members of staff frequently. Though it was true, they had never found time to rehearse the drill properly. So evacuation was not a foregone conclusion. There was no telling if the plan would go easily. Some boys were already awake. Some teachers still slept. But, using his most efficient and dependable staff, Sebastian got the boys wide-awake softly, swiftly and attentively. He gathered his staff together and told them they would need to evacuate the building. He insisted they had to go right away. The boys were used to sudden secret escapes. So this was a game for them.

So the Music Bearers took the boys down a shadowy corridor. This led to a small sea-gate at the rear of the fort. The sea-gate opened above choppy green waves. This gate was out of sight — a secret opening in a sea wall. The wall protected the old fort from crashing waves and eroding salts. Tethered at the base of the wall were several small coracles. These were round, smooth-edged watercraft, constructed of wood and leather. These primitive boats were difficult to manage and might capsize in waves. But they took one adult and two, perhaps three, children. They were almost unsinkable, but the boats were not ideal for open water. They might freely turnover in choppy waters, though if they capsized, they could still use them as floats to ride the waves.

Outside the fort, Zadock pounded on the main door. His knock become furious. The Music Bearers had little more time to evacuate the fort. They ushered along the boys and hushed when they asked too many questions.

Sebastian could not avoid the moment any longer. He went to the wicket-gate at the main entrance. He peered through the aperture at a dark figure pounding his fist on the door.

A pang of anxiety shot through him like an electric bolt. The visitor was, unquestionably, a member of the Black Hounds. Today was going to be a difficult day.

∼

Brother Sebastian opened the gate and greeted the man. He viewed a stranger dressed in black. Sebastian welcomed the stranger as if he were a long-lost brother, which, in some sense, he was. Brother Sebastian received him with the same gentle smile he might offer a cleric from any branch of the mother church. He unlatched the gate of the fort with all the enthusiasm he could muster: 'My brother. How are you? Please forgive my sluggishness. We get so few visitors at early hour.' Sebastian smiled as he beckoned the stranger forward.

Zadock, the Hound, was also magnanimous: 'Salve! Salve! Oh! Brother, I seek forgiveness. I did not wish to intrude on morning rituals. I apologise. It is an unfortunate transgression, but one that can't be helped —'

'Come in, come in,' said Sebastian. The two men kissed each other on the cheeks. They hugged each other as if best of companions. An observer would never suspect that these two men had never met before or were, in fact, mortal enemies. These acts of artificial friendship were part of the theatre of ritual. Played out, in part, because both men were fully tonsured monks, so proper formalities had to be observed. This was the way of things. But also the theatre was maintained, so both men had time to put their elaborate plans into effect.

'Alas! Alas! I cannot come into your domain right away,' Zadock suggested. 'Protocol does not allow me to enter the fort unless I am invited. That invitation must be from the guardian of the fortress, the castellan. You are he?'

Brother Sebastian considered the thin, dangerous man that stood before him. He felt genuine compassion in his heart. They were both of comparable age. Taken to this place by circumstances, they had no control over. They were both a long way from home. They were both windswept and tired. They were both in need of a decent meal. They were both men of God. They were both members of one Holy and Apostolic Church. Yet, despite these many similarities, they were destructive enemies. Today they would dance with death.

'I understand the protocols,' Brother Sebastian replied. He wished to keep the theatre going as long as possible. 'As a matter of fact, I do not mind presenting myself as warden of the fortress. So, yes, I am he. I am castellan.'

'So be it,' Zadock said. His smile left his lips. He appeared as grim as any man might be. He was about to perform a distasteful task: 'Can I ask you to indulge me, brother? Please forgive this —' Zadock frowned.

Sure, sure. Anything,' said Brother Sebastian.

'Sadly, I did not come alone. I came here with others. I should have made that clear from the outset. I apologise. I came with armed men. I intend to take this fortress.'

'I see.'

'So, as castellan, would you do me a great honour — and complete my formalities — and please invite my men into your domain. It is purely a matter of protocol. Nothing more.'

'I understand,' Sebastian said with a nod.

Brother Sebastian walked through the wicket gate and out from the safety of his castle walls. He stopped near the entranceway and waved. As far as he could tell, there was nobody out there. But he knew the farce ought to be acted out. He continued with the strange script. It had to be adhered to, for the sake of the boys. Every second counted. Any time wasted here — wasted performing perfunctory tasks — was more time for the urgent evacuation of boys and staff. After a short while, Sebastian heard a rustle. Then lumbering. Soon he realised people were hiding outside his fortress. They lurked unseen by walls. He also realised that he was offering a pre-arranged signal. A signal they waited to see. The village watchmen and the Palatine Guards had been told by Zadock that the Castellan of the fort would invite them in himself. He'd promised them they'd go through the front door.

The Palatine Guards were first to cross the threshold of the fort. They followed Brother Sebastian inside. They took their place alongside the Black Hound. The other men from the village filed in behind. Sebastian examined the two Palatine guards. One was a professional soldier. He appeared to be a mercenary. Doubtless a native of the northern tribes. The other wore the sign of the scourge, so was identified as the torturer.

'Now we are all here — and formal protocols are complete — I can introduce myself,' the Black Hound said with a smile. 'I am Zadock. *Del Santo Ordo Fratrum Hubertus*. I am sure you understand why I am here. These are my guards and advisers,' Zadock pointed to the Palatines.

Brother Sebastian stared at the other men behind. They seemed dishevelled and tired. 'And these other men?' he asked.

Zadock made a dismissive gesture: 'These men are from the village. They are only here to help me make a complete and comprehensive search of the fortress. I apologise for their presence.'

'I see — ' said Sebastian.

'I'm sure you understand I have proper authority to search this place,' Zadock continued. 'The Pope affords imperial authority. I will take into custody any person I suspect is guilty of heresy or perversity. To obstruct, impede or inhibit a Hound is a crime...' Zadock pointed to his torturer. 'Tartax, here, will stay with you. And, if we can proceed right away, we will start the search.'

Brother Sebastian smiled and nodded. Though otherwise, he remained silent.

Zadock gave instructions to the Palatine guards and then the watchmen of the village. After that, they all went to search the sand-fort.

'I will supervise the search. I will keep you informed of developments,' Zadock told Sebastian.

∽

After an hour, Zadock returned to Brother Sebastian, who stood with the torturer, Tartax. Both men waited at the main gate. Brother Sebastian recited prayers and turned prayer-beads. Tartax stood rigid. Impassive.

'They are all gone,' said Zadock. He appeared most agitated. An esteemed enemy had outwitted him. He had calculated this raid for days, had travelled miles to get to this remote place, and had experienced many difficulties along the way. Yet now, at the last hurdle, he had lost, probably, his biggest catch ever. He had missed his prey by minutes. Zadock had checked the beds of straw in the dormitories and found they were heated. Zadock had estimated that at least twenty, perhaps thirty, heretics had escaped justice before they had come into the fort. 'It is only you that is left behind. You are to be the sacrificial lamb,' Zadock whispered. He had to admire the Music Bearer for his courage. Zadock looked to the torturer: 'Tartax will have work to do this day. I hoped to avoid such odious stuff...'

Brother Sebastian did not speak.

'So silent now, are you, brother?' asked Zadock. 'Yet so talkative earlier. How your mood has changed!'

Sebastian nodded.

'I expected as much. However, I seriously demand you tell me where your brood is. I command, passionately and soberly, and under threat of physical penalty that you should speak now. Tell me where they went.'

Sebastian smiled a righteous smile. Though he continued to turn his beads.

Zadock considered the possibilities. The others could not be far away. Their beds were still warm. They must be somewhere nearby. They had boiled water on the stove. There was enough food on the table for ten or twenty souls. There was sufficient bedding for thirty. The guards had searched the slops. Foul-water had been found in buckets. This meant several men had stayed in the fort. The cellars and rafters were still being searched. The missing individuals might yet turn up. Or there was some other secret way out of the fort? A passageway that they had not yet discovered? And, sure enough, even as Zadock reflected on these possibilities, the Palatine guard came back and whispered into his ear.

'Ah, developments, developments. I shall return in a good time, gentlemen. Then we'll have work to do. You will need to talk.' Zadock glared at Sebastian. He nodded to the torturer.

~

They took Zadock up a ladder and guided him along a narrow corridor.

The shadowy route led to a sea-gate at the rear end of the fort. The Black Hound stared out of the sea-gate towards the churning waves. Then he scanned the horizon. There was no sign of boats. He checked along the coast — towards the fishing village. They would not be stupid enough to go in that direction, so they must have gone along the coast. They had to be hugging the shoreline. Otherwise, undoubtedly, they would be visible. Zadock took this information in before he walked back to the main gate to question Sebastian.

Prior to this, he instructed the Palatine guard to dismiss all the men of the village. They were free to return to their homes. But he advised them to go back to sleep. Because he might need later them for errands. But now he had an unpleasant task to perform. He waited a while in an alcove. To prepare himself. And say a brief prayer for his victim.

After praying, Zadock returned to Sebastian: 'Will you tell me where your brood has flown? I command you, in the name of the Holy Father, tell me now...'

Brother Sebastian smiled. He continued to recite the five decades of the Rosary.

'Tartax! Take the beads from him.' The torturer snatched the beads from Sebastian's hands. 'This is your last chance...' shouted the Black Hound. 'Tartax, prepare your tools...'

The torturer opened his leather bag. He pulled out a pair of metal tongs.

'Answer me,' demanded Zadock 'Where has your brood? Now is the time to recant your depraved practices...'

But Sebastian made the sign of the cross over the tongs. He blessed the torture's tools.

Zadock may have been a wicked man, but logic motivated him as much as the church law. He knew the Vatican Code — known as the *ad extirpanda* — it gave discretion regarding torture. All he needed was a 'half-truth' from the heretic — and he could use whatever means necessary to gain information from Brother Sebastian. But the Black Hound did not have the luxury of time here. Torture was a slow business. He needed to hasten. So Zadock pondered the implications. He considered what outcome they could achieve in so little available time. After a few moments of reflection, he concluded it would be expedient to leave the sand-fort as promptly as possible. To return to the village as soon as he could. From the fishing village, he might commandeer a vessel. Then he could search along the coastline for the escaped Music Bearers. Thus, torture was impractical, and, in this situation, it was not called for.

Zadock did not have time to organise a proper trial for the heretic. Though he also knew that if anyone found out the Black Hound had weakened, the lapse might strengthen and motivate others So the Hound concluded that if he failed to do something horrible, if he failed to wean others away from the evils of the heresy, if he faltered in any way, things would only get worse. He made a tough decision because something needed to be done right away. Something that would be meaningful and immediately effective.

The Black Hound addressed the torturer: 'Remove his fingers. One-by-one. See that he never plays his demonic harp or flute again...'

Tartax nodded his understanding and prepared the pliers.

'Also, rip out his tongue. So he cannot sing his vile songs.'

'Yes, brother,' said the torturer.

'But otherwise, leave the fool intact. He will be a living testament to our resolve.'.'

17

THE CANTICLE OF THE COG

When Zadock got back from the sand fort, he headed forthwith to the small harbour that was the haven for the village fleet. The Hound passed huts, fishermen's houses, fishnets, lines, crab pots and corkwood floats. He sought the quickest and the most efficient vessel in the harbour. He found a single-masted, square-rigged sailing Cog. The skipper was washing down the deck as Zadock approached.

'Permission to board...' Zadock said. He stepped onto the craft without the permission being granted. The skipper gaped at the Black Hound with a look of concealed disgust. 'How much to hire your vessel? I need it forthwith. To track down fugitives.'

'You cannot afford me, cleric. Now, get off my boat. Or I will slice you open with a billhook.' The shipmaster had no time for pastors or priests. He indicated this with proud body language. He was not at all afraid of the Hound.

Zadock laughed. At least there was one assertive character in this damaged place: 'Now, surely, you do not want to make threats like that to me. I'm a man of the church,' he grinned. 'You don't actually want to cut me with your billhooks, do you?'

'See that I don't,' said the boat skipper. He produced a double-edged hook from beneath his pots. 'Where are your friends now, cleric?' he asked. 'I don't see them anywhere close by — '

'Oh!' said Zadock. He looked around. 'You are pointing out my Palatine guards? They will find me soon enough. I'm sure they are around the village, somewhere.' Zadock gave a vague nod.

'Well, they cannot help you if they're not here, can they?' added the skipper. He continued to eye the monk. Then an idea flickered into his mind that maybe he should fillet the cleric, anyway. What the hell? Feed his scrawny body to the crabs. That would thrill the folk around here, for sure. The Hound suggested he could 'hire' the craft. Money spoke louder than words. 'How much can you afford?' the boat skipper mumbled. Though he held tight onto his hook and waved it recklessly.

'Well...' said Zadock. 'I guess it would be more money than you could earn in a single year. I would pay you generously for your services. I need to fetch my cash, of course. Then I will bring it back here. You will see I have ample funds. I can pay lavishly.'

'In that case, Hound, bring the money back quick. Show me a proper reward. Then I will decide—'

'Of course. And I will need to pay extra... for my two friends. I require passage for three. A days sailing. I need to patrol the coast — keeping close to the shoreline. Are you up for that?' Zadock pointed towards the fort and the coastline beyond.

'It will take time to set sail. Give me half a day to prepare,' the sailor grunted.

'I will double your money if you sail by noon,' replied Zadock.

'I have not even agreed on a price yet — '

'I'll be back by noon with my friends. I'll bring all my money.'

∽

Zadock returned by noon to the single-masted sailing ship. He returned with his two 'friends' — the Palatine guards. He brought with him a simple sackcloth bag. The bag had two straps that went over the shoulders. It was a bag packed with coin. He called on the skipper to gaze inside at all the money found therein. There was, as Zadock promised, a year's earnings inside the sack. 'See, I told you there would be more money than you could imagine...' he said.

The skipper of the craft seemed satisfied, though he eyed the two guards with suspicion. They appeared intimidating and unruly. But the Hound did his best to allay his fears: 'Do not worry about my companions. They will do as I say. Nothing more, nothing less. They will be as meek as lambs, I assure you.'

So Zadock hired the boat. The captain grunted his approval and set sail. And the fishing cog run along the shore. The craft was quick and easy to manage, and it cut through the waters like a hunter's knife. Though Zadock remained convinced that they were too late. He reckoned his quarry had scattered. He'd lost his prey.

∽

The craft cut quickly through the shakes and chills of the coastal waves. And the fisherman knew accurately where the tiny tips of sand could be discovered, or where rocky outcrops were at their most dangerous. When he saw hazards, he made dramatic deviations around them, so the boat never run aground.

Soon, the cog sailed beyond the fort.

Zadock had a good look at the rear seawall. The Hound distinguished the sea-gate immediately from the water and could even determine the rusty mooring rings on the side of the wall. He figured the escaped Music Bearers must have secured their escape-craft to some corroded rings he saw. He cursed himself for not checking the back of the fortress earlier. He should have made a sea-trip there on his first day. If he had seen the wall for himself, he might have prevented their escape. He had made a mistake. And that was inexcusable. He would punish himself later. But for now, he had to stay focused and keep vigilant. Zadock had to keep an eye out for any small craft that had landed on the coast or were still sailing ahead.

'Let me know, as soon as you can, if you see boats tethered on land — or abandoned on the shore,' Zadock shouted to the two Palatine guards. He felt thrilled that neither man was as confident or cocksure as they generally were. They both shook with cold, and their faces appeared greenish and nauseous. These men did not enjoy travelling on water. They had trouble adjusting to the bounce of the waves. Zadock grinned at their discomfort.

After half an hour, the Cog travelled far beyond the fortress. And there was still no sign of any other boat. Either in the water or abandoned on the shore. It seemed as if they had set out too late. Their prey had vanished. Zadock sensed defeat.

But just when Zadock became convinced that the Music Bearers had escaped justice, the skipper of the sailing cog shouted, 'Ahoy!'

The captain pointed at something ahead. It was a tiny speck on the horizon. The monk and the two Palatine guards strained their eyes to see what the speck was. It was a tiny black dot. Or two dots. And the dots were not moving.

As their fishing cog got closer to the dot, Zadock thought the shape or shapes might be seals playing on a spit of land. It almost seemed as if the land had risen, somehow, out of the water. The skipper shouted that the 'dots' or seals, or whatever they were, were near dangerous inter-tidal mud-flats. The cog came up hastily onto those flats. But the skipper didn't want to hit the flats himself, or get his craft stuck, so he veered away, earnestly. Then he slowed his craft right down, so they approached the danger with care.

As they got nearer, they realised the block dots were really tiny round boats — three coracles. Rising mud had caught those tiny boats securely. Near to the coracles stood nine people. People stranded in mud. Three adults and six children stuck fast. As the sailing cog sailed a circle around the hazard, they saw the predicament of the coracles.

These tiny round boats had obviously run aground on a treacherous spit. This was how their boats had got wedged. They, foolishly, had got themselves out of their boats, perhaps to push their craft back into open sea or dig themselves out the gloop with their paddles. But this made their predicament worse. They had got themselves caught in the stickiness. The sludge sucked them down.

'Can you get closer to them, skipper?' Zadock asked.

'It's too dangerous to get nearer. We might get stuck too,' the skipper shouted.

Zadock unfolded a long net. He had discovered it earlier, down by the stern.

'Oi! What are you doing with my net?' quizzed the skipper.

'I want to do a little fishing. If we can get close enough to them — if we can get along the edge of the mud — we might try to cast a net out.'

The skipper saw the sense in that. Although it would take all his skill and sailing experience, he decided it might be worth trying. So he veered off, and circled his boat around, so that the port side of the vessel skimmed along the edge of the mud ridge. Zadock and the two guards tried their best to fling out the long roll of net.

Their first two attempts were no good at all, and they got soaked hauling the net back. Meanwhile, the Music Bearers, who were overwhelmed by mud and sand, seemed too exhausted to wave or cry out. They stood outside their coracles. Some were waist high in mud. Others were glued right up to their knees. They couldn't move. They were in grave danger.

'The tide is coming back. They are fixed tight. It's quicksand out there,' shouted the skipper of the sailing cog. He tried to manipulate his craft back around again, pulling her into the wind, then turning her back into an immense circle, to come alongside the ridge once more. On this second attempt, Zadock caught sight of two more 'black dots' right out at sea — approaching the horizon.

'There are two more coracles out there!' cried Zadock. He looked westwards.

'Stupid, stupid.' shouted the skipper of the cog. 'They do not design those things for open sea. They will turn over with a flick of a wave. What do they think they're doing? They will never cross the channel in such modest vessels.'

The cog came around to make another pass with the net. This time, Zadock and the Palatine guards had more success. They snatched one of coracles with the edge of the netting, so they pulled the small skin boat back towards the vessel. They grabbed the tiny boat and muscled it aboard.

The skipper of the cog watched and wondered what they were doing.

'I'll come around again...' he shouted. He shook his head at these landlubbers. What was the point of hoisting a coracle aboard?

On the next pass, Zadock and his guards looped the net around another coracle. So they dragged this one on board too. The final coracle was in a more awkward position, firmly lodged in the adhesive mud.

'What are you doing?' shouted the captain, his face burned with anger. He'd strained to get his cog around, fighting with the flapping sail all the time, and in all that time, all the landlubbers had achieved was to 'hook' two coracles aboard. They had missed the stranded people altogether. The skipper manoeuvred his craft out into safe water again, but this time dropped anchor. He marched over to Zadock and the guards. He appeared exasperated: 'I know you lot are not used to boating, but please try harder to get the net out to those stranded people. I will come around again. This time, I will get as close as possible. Those poor people are running out of time — the tide runs as quick as a horse in these waters. They have little time left. Those adults are waist deep already. We need to get the net out to them quick. Throw it as far as possible. Get the net to the adults first. Then they might grab hold of the children. We can drag them all out of danger if we act fast and act now.'

'There is no time for that...' Zadock said. The skipper viewed the monk in utter bewilderment. 'We will need to get after those dots on the horizon instead. They are making off...'

The skipper shook his head frantically. 'Yes, they are in danger too — that's true. We can get to look at them in a while. But first we need to rescue these folks stuck in the mud.'

'No...' Zadock said, firmly. 'We will go after the coracles on the horizon now! These people are past saving. There is nothing we can do to free them...'

'What? They are just boys. They will drown...' shouted the skipper. His face flamed with anger.

'Pull up the anchor. Let's go after the others. At least we can help them,' commanded Zadock.

There was logic to this plan. They would try to help, probably, six people — at the cost of nine lives. They might return before dark and make another attempt to get the folk off the mudflats. Or they could get more help from the fishing community in the village. It might be possible to rescue them all. But did they have enough time to do it? The cog skipper doubted it. 'Alright!' he said, finally, and with gruff acceptance. The skipper went to haul up his anchor, then caught the wind again and moved his boat away from the flats and into open sea.

The black dots hitherto seen on the horizon had now passed into the openness of the great expanse. They had vanished. But the skipper made a mental note of their approximate location. They were opposite dark green trees on land. So he checked back at the dark green 'blobs' to adjust his course.

It took him a while to get to about the same point they were last observed. But there was no trace of the remaining two coracles in the open sea.

'They apparently capsized,' commented the skipper, sadness in his eyes.

∽

He did not convince Zadock that they had capsized. The Hound had inspected the captured coracles when they were hauled aboard earlier and, to his untrained eye, they seemed unsinkable. 'If these turned over in choppy water, would they sink? What if they got filled with sea-water?' he shouted.

'I don't know...' the skipper answered. 'Maybe they'd go down. But if they capsized, they might still be afloat. They could be here somewhere, I suppose. Perhaps a person might cling onto the side of one for a short while. But ultimately, any person would slip under the waves. Nobody can hang on for ever...' The skipper pondered the horizon but felt sure there was only a slim chance anyone survived out here in open water.

'Keep sailing,' Zadock told him. 'Head across the channel, to the other coast. That's where they're headed.'

The skipper was not sure: 'We arrived at this point — there is no sign of them. I think we ought to go back to the mudflats and try to rescue the others. It's possible we still have time to save them. But only if we turn back now.'

'Get the money,' Zadock shouted to his guard. He turned to Tartax, his torturer. The man grunted and moved his bulk hesitantly across the slippery deck to find the canvas bag that contained the heavy coins.

Zadock grabbed the moneybag and said, 'Come with me...' The guard nodded.

The skipper of the sailing Cog had meanwhile returned to his sail.

Zadock stopped him by grabbing his arm. The skipper had a perplexed look on his face and waited for Zadock to speak: 'Set sail across the channel. We will follow the fugitives to the other side — ' Zadock made his wishes clear.

'I cannot do that, cleric...' the cog skipper replied, with a dismissive shrug. 'It will be dark soon. We need to turn back to help those poor souls stuck on the flats.'

'If you take us across the channel, I will pay you twice what's promised,' offered Zadock. 'Three times as much! You can have everything in this bag. I will double it when I see my friends on the other side of the water. I will have you paid in gold. They will pay you a King's wage. This I promise because I am a man of God.'

But the skipper shook his head: 'No, I cannot,' he said. 'You might be a man of God; I am a man of the sea. I can't allow the briny to take innocent lives.' He thought about the children in the mud. He thought about his own children. He thought about the children of the village. Money was not important now. He needed to save lives.

'Fair enough,' said Zadock. 'It's regrettable you won't help — '

'Well, that's the way of things — ' sighed the skipper. He shook from the cold and the physical exertion of his expert seafaring.

'Pay the man...' said Zadock. The Torturer nodded.

'No, no, not now. You need not pay me now—' the skipper declared. He wanted to get back to his ropes.

'I insist...' Zadock told him. He passed the heavy bag of coins to the cog skipper. 'Make sure you secure the bag tight around his shoulders, so he doesn't lose it...' The Palatine guard grunted understanding and hurriedly put the straps over the skipper's head, then twisted them as tight as he could manage, around the skipper's waist. The heavy bag was now attached firm.

The skipper of the cog thought something was odd about all this and motioned his shoulders: 'What are you doing? Now, hold on. Get this off me...' But it was too late. With the smallest of pressures, and an elbow to the ribs, Zadock unbalanced the man. The guard helped by turning the skipper's shoulder and pushing. As the skipper turned, he tried to right himself and attempted, hopelessly, to grab on to something. But he could not secure himself in time. He could not regain his balance. His eyes were wide, and with sudden panic, he toppled over the side of his own craft, to plunge into the cold, cruel sea.

Zadock and the guards watched the man flounder in frothy water. The skipper swallowed once or twice and could even stay afloat for a fleeting period, because he was such a healthy man. But the mass of coins in the bag pulled him down. He struggled — and in a supreme effort to save himself, he fought to dislocate his own shoulder so he might release himself from the dead-weight of those murderous coins. But he succumbed. He got dragged down by his reward.

How ironic, thought Zadock. 'Too bad...' he said. 'Now we will have to navigate this boat ourselves —'

'Can we do it?' asked the guard. 'I'm not sure we can —'

'I'm certain we can cross the channel in this old bucket. How difficult can it be?' said Zadock. 'We will presumably run aground eventually. We'll crash into rocks on the other side. It won't be easy. But if we can get to the other side, we can use those...' Zadock pointed to the two coracles they had taken. 'We'll be able to reach the shore in them. That's why I dragged them aboard.'

18

THE CANTICLE OF THE CAPTURE

Atalanta worked as a Music Bearer's consul in a small town. She had arranged two more successful musical interventions after her first intervention with the Verderer's wife.

Even though that first one had not gone well, the Verderer's wife had told everyone how helpful Atalanta had been. So folk around town accepted her. She felt far confident and comfortable in her role. But just a few months into her mission, things went awry.

She slept in quarters with other servants, in a temporary building near stables. A little after midnight, during her deepest sleep, a vigorous shake of her shoulder quickly wakened her. She sat up in an instant. Her heart throbbed and her senses became totally engaged. It was too dark to see accurately who had awakened her, though she felt certain a stranger had entered the room.

'Atalanta, please come with me. My mistress wants to see you at once.' Atalanta heard a strange woman's voice in the darkness. Atalanta's first thought was that the voice belonged to a mother of a child who perhaps needed help through music. She was told to expect that kind of thing. So she was ready to respond swiftly to such a request. She got up from her bedding, bleary-eyed, then wrapped a shawl around her shoulders.

The woman, aged about twenty summers, waited coolly while

Atalanta tried to do something with her hair. Then the woman led Atalanta by the hand. They treaded delicately, so they roused none of the other servants. Once outside, the two women hurried through darkness. They moved past familiar buildings and to the town walls.

Near the gatehouse, the woman led Atalanta through a small arch. She assumed this was the gateway to the main watchtower. After this, the woman took her to what seemed to be an empty barn. Then the woman opened a hatch and directed Atalanta to climb a ladder. The woman followed her up. They emerged into a loft-room. The room had a pleasant aroma of freshly cut herbs with drying spices. The place felt warm and was well lit. Lanterns and candles littered the board floors, a floor prepared with colourful rugs. In the room was an ornate, thin-framed chair. They had placed this in the middle of the rich setting. As Atalanta's eyes became accustomed to all this — by candlelight — she noticed a tall, thin woman, aged about thirty summers, who stood at the far end of the upper room. This lady was dressed extravagantly. She had a small head, with crisp, dark-black hair. She had pushed her hair into a tight bun, and the bun was held in place by an elegant silver clasp. The lady had several rings on her slender fingers. Her lips were mud-brown, and her dark eyes were empty. There was no joy or vitality in that face. If anyone needed a little music therapy, thought Atalanta, this woman undoubtedly did.

The rich lady gestured that Atalanta should settle down on the rug. So she did as asked and lowered nicely in front of the rich lady. The other woman, the other servant, bowed and also knelt. Eventually, the rich lady sat on the 'throne' placed in the centre of the room.

The rich lady spoke: 'I'm sorry that I woke you in the middle of the night to be yanked here.' The lady spoke delicately, but quickly. 'I'm also sorry we had to meet in such a place.' The lady checked around the upper-room — viewing it as if it was an ugly pigsty. Which it wasn't. It was a lot better than anywhere Atlanta had ever seen. 'It's just we can be here without intrusion—' she continued.

As a trained Music Bearer's consul, they had taught Atalanta to talk to, and negotiate with, people from all occupations. That included those of noble birth. So she sat still. She remained attentive. And she nodded her head to show understanding.

'I suppose you do not know who I am,' the rich lady continued, after a moment of contemplation. 'Well, my name is Sophia. I am the Landgravine.' The rich lady let this information sink in before she continued.

For the first time in her life, Atalanta felt amazed, and her bottom jaw dropped. She knew she would meet people of high rank — even Shire Reeves and their deputies. But she never thought she would meet the Landgravine. The first lady of the realm. The wife of the representative of the Holy Emperor, no less.

After the explanation, the lady paused. She sat and looked keenly at Atalanta, as if she tried to take stock of her. 'You people crawl, twist like common lizards…' said the lady. The comment was uncalled for. And the woman spewed it out like an uncontrolled stream of bile.

Atalanta did not know quite how to react to this unexpected outburst. The words caused small tears to develop in the corners of her sleepy eyes. Maybe it was the burning beeswax candles, or maybe it was the potent smell of herbs, but whatever it was, Atalanta felt quite upset by this place and this rich lady. Atalanta felt extremely uncomfortable. She lost her carefully groomed composure for a moment. She knew she'd already lost control of her emotions. And that was precisely what the Landgravine wanted: 'I know everything about your people,' the noble lady added. She narrowed her eyes as she spoke, as if she tried to spy deep into Atalanta's heart. 'I know what you are like. I know how you think. And, of course, I know what you're doing here. There's no need to fool me…'

I am discovered! Atalanta shook with fear. She knew she was in grave danger. A crazy woman was interrogating her. In a secret place. And this crazy woman *knew her secret*.

The Landgravine observed the girl kneeling before her. And with a sudden change of heart, became more conciliatory. 'Now you fear me, that is good. I'm glad you feel nervous before me because I am exceedingly dangerous. I am powerful. I am fabulously rich…' the rich lady looked at her own lap. 'But even though I can be the worst type of enemy to you, I can also be your friend, if you allow me…' The woman offered a sickly smile. 'Any friendship we might develop will be on my terms, though. And under the strictest supervision of my trusted adviser and confidant, Melita — here.' The lady pointed to the other kneeling woman. This was the woman who'd collected Atalanta from her bed. The lady gave the woman a trusting smile. 'So let me start by saying that your time here is now at an end. You will leave this place — and you will re-locate to another place of my choosing.' The noble lady seemed quite certain of this. 'Your departure will be abrupt. There will be no goodbyes. In fact, you will leave tonight.'

Atalanta took in this information. She realised she had to get a message back to someone she trusted. So the Music Bearers could make other arrangements. She would have to be replaced. Her presence in the town was vital. She couldn't leave. Arrangements had to be made. People depended on her. Lives depended on her.

Atalanta at last spoke: 'It will not be possible to leave, I am afraid Madam,' She didn't know, yet, how to address the Landgravine properly. 'I am required to stay here. I have not finished my term of office with my family. I am obligated to them. I should not be able to leave without an explanation or an apology.'

But the rich lady viewed this talk with resignation: 'I expected, of course, that you might object to your abduction, young lady. But I cannot take the risk that they monitor your movements. So you will leave when I say.' She looked across from her throne. 'I want to stress that your departure will be this evening. Whether or not you like it. You will do as you are told. And I really think it would be better if we made our arrangements in the spirit of friendship. It will be much easier to endure for both of us...' She nodded to herself. 'You will travel tonight from this place. Headed for a new home. You will travel incognito. I'm sure you will respect my wishes. I gave Melita permission to bind and gag you, if required. But I think it will not be necessary, because ill behaviour is beneath you, yes?' The Landgravine allowed this information to permeate the room, then continued. 'We will meet again. After a short trial period. I will see if you are suitable for my needs. If you are suitable for me, then we can proceed with the next part of my plan...'

Atalanta nodded. She sat on the mat in silence, though her mind was active. She tried to figure out what the woman said. And what she left unsaid. This was a secret meeting — so she could assume the Landgravine was operating outside her authority. The Landgravine wanted Atalanta to travel incognito, so it might be reasonable to speculate that this was a secret plan hatched by the lady herself. Had the Landgravine made this plan without her husband's knowledge?

That night, Atalanta found herself heaped into the back of a wool-wagon and taken on a long and uncomfortable journey. Abducted by the Landgravine. Now a prisoner.

19

THE CANTICLE OF MELITA

It overjoyed the Landgrave to see Melita.

She stood before him. His comforter, charmer, and temptress. He felt eager to hold her arms. Hungry for her lips. But this was not the time or place. 'This is a massive surprise! I did not expect you. How did you come to be here? Why are you here? How long do you stay?' He was keen as a puppy. The kinglet had not felt so thrilled in weeks.

'The Landgravine allowed me to come down...' There was a long silence. The word 'Landgravine' caused the Lord consternation. She was the main reason for his trip to his half-brother's house, miles away from his stronghold. Miles away from the government, too. But also miles from his wife, which was fortunate.

The kinglet suspected the intentions of the Landgravine. Why would she send her favoured and most trusted maidservant to him?

'Your wife sent me, and to bring Atalanta. She will help you...' whispered Melita.

'Who the hell is Atalanta?' The Landgrave became even more suspicious. Why had his wife sent a female worker? Melita shrugged. It was as if she could read his mind. She pointed to the door.

'She is outside?' he asked. 'Well, show this woman in. Let's have a look...'

They called Atalanta. She entered the handsomely decorated

room and bowed to His Highness, then peered around the room in genuine wonder. It was the most magnificent dwelling she had ever seen. There was fur on the floor, tapestries on the walls, superb furniture everywhere. It smelled great too. It reminded her of fresh flowers on a balmy day.

'So, my wife sent you?' The Landgrave asked. He considered his new maid and decided she was nothing but a child. She looked feeble, too. 'Do you know why she sent you?'

'To help you, Sir. To help with things around the place.' Atalanta answered quietly and bent her knee neatly. Then she grinned as cheerfully as she could.

The Landgrave waved her away. Melita accompanied her out of the door, then told her to wait.

'I don't like it...' His Highness muttered. 'She is unquestionably a spy. My wife has sent a spy to snoop around. Monitor her closely, Melita.' He gazed into the eyes of his love. 'Watch her. But do not let harm come to her... Or my wife will blame me. Keep the spy out of trouble. But crucially, keep her out of my way—' The Landgrave smiled. 'And you? How long will you stay?'

'Me, your Highness?' Melita allowed a cheeky smile to stretch across her face, so her dimples exaggerated. 'I am here for as long as you please!'

The Landgrave beamed. 'In that case, stay close. Because I might need your help with many tasks.' He chuckled.

'I'm happy you said that,' said Melita with a giggle. She nodded her head and made a miniature bow. With that, she excused herself from his presence.

Once the encounter with the Landgrave was over, she met with Atalanta and they made their way, arm-in-arm, to the servant quarters. These quarters were situated on the other side of the stable yard. She greeted the mistress of the house and Melita introduced the mistress to Atalanta. She underlined the fact that both she — and the younger servant girl — were travelling under the safeguard of Her Highness the Landgravine, so, therefore, must receive accommodation that was 'suitable.' The mistress of the house understood the implications of this information, so had the little bottle room cleared out by stable boys. This small room was not connected to the main quarters and had its own entrance. It smelled of dust and mould but, otherwise, it seemed a perfectly adequate place to stay.

Melita turned her nose up at it. Though she knew she would not be spending a lot of time in it, if she could help it. Silk sheets and scented wines awaited her in the Royal bedchamber.

Melita still didn't know if she could trust the girl, Atalanta. She was bothered about her, especially when she let her out of her sight. So decided she needed some kind of insurance. She figured she needed a grip on this girl, or she might run off. The girl was gentle and gullible, and she did what she was told, so some kind of hold over her would not be easy to find. Atalanta had no vices or weaknesses. Well, none that could be employed to any advantage. But Melita felt sure that she would find weakness in the days ahead. And once she found a weakness, she'd use it as leverage.

'Stay here. Don't leave these quarters. I will bring back food, water, and bedding. Try to get rest...' She yapped these orders out as if she was captain-of-the-guard. Then realised she sounded too bossy. So gave a weak smile. Melita rubbed the girl on the shoulder. 'It's nice, isn't it?' Now she spoke affectionately. Rather than barking orders. She functioned as if they were best friends. As if they'd known each other for ages. 'I wonder if there are handsome boys around? I'm going to have a look. Yes, you and I will have fun here. Lots of fun together.'

Atalanta gave the older girl an inquisitive look. A gaze that did not entirely mask the distrust she felt in her heart. She surveyed the room and allowed a sigh of obedience to yawn out. Then she settled into a corner. To wait for her kidnapper to return.

20

THE CANTICLE OF THE LETTER

The weekly messenger delivered urgent despatches to the Landgrave's office.

They also assigned this messenger to bring a sealed letter to Melita. It was from the Landgravine herself.

The messenger delivered the sealed letter, as promised, personally into the hands of Melita. It seemed a pity that Melita could not read. She had never found the time to learn. When she opened the letter, she saw a series of meaningless squiggles. She recognised the seal of the Landgravine at the bottom, though, so knew who had sent it. Melita figured it must be important. She considered the possibility of getting Atalanta to read it to her but remembered Atalanta had been trained by the Music Bearers, so dismissed the idea. Then she thought about asking His Highness the Landgrave to help. He was an educated man. But then, when she wisely thought about it, she realised that both Atalanta and the Landgrave might be alluded to in the letter's contents. So, therefore, neither must be allowed to see the contents.

Who could she trust to read the words of this important letter? This was the first hitch in a plan that, otherwise, seemed thoroughly developed. The snag in the plan revealed the possibility that her mistress, the Landgravine, was losing her grip on reality. It was quite obvious that a house maid like Melita could not read. She pondered on the problem for a day.

Fortunately, for all concerned, the Master of the Hawks had shown an interest in Melita since the day she first arrived at the Margrave's residence. Soon after receiving her sealed letter, Melita contrived a way to 'accidentally' show her milky thigh to this older gentleman as she passed him. Later, Melita deliberately strolled a long route around the estate so she could saunter beyond his cabin. When she saw the Master of the Hawks that time, she produced a generous smile. Also, 'by chance,' she snagged her kirtle on a low branch. This accident meant she showed a little more of her pale milk thigh. The incident led to some obscene suggestions from the older man and flirtatious behaviour from Melita. She loved it! She entirely enjoyed the sexual power she had over other people. She especially loved getting attention from older, influential men. That was her talent and strength. She felt quite proud of herself. Melita had learned that all men, some women too, couldn't resist the lure of her feminine charms.

By dusk she found herself in the Master of the Hawk's straw bed. Her hair became bedraggled, and her clothes were dishevelled. It had been a quick, yet rewarding, fumble. She left the man, although he panted for more. She made an apology, saying she needed to go, to perform other functions. He ached for her wonderful body. He gawked at her with the type of pleading eyes she had seen many times before. He was now decisively under her control. Melita went into the evening air, leaving him begging for her return.

Of course, straight after that, she made her way to the Landgrave's royal bedchamber. Here she was accordingly wined and bedded by the minor kinglet himself.

In the morning, she made her way past the Master of the Hawks. She caught his eye, and he motioned, beckoning her to come into his woodshed. The shed smelled of leather and raw meat. He made his advances in the privacy of that old cabin. Then he invited her back to his bed later that same evening. She did not agree at once, but instead asked him to read a letter that she said she had 'found.' She pulled it from between her impressive breasts, which were hidden under her apron top. The gentleman licked his lips when he saw the buttery curves, though they he only glimpsed them. He even felt the warmth of her cleavage as he took the letter from her hand.

He enjoyed reading the letter to Melita — he didn't actually take it all in. Because, while he read, he thought of the promise ahead. The letter said that Melita was to allow 'the girl' (she assumed, correctly, that this referred to Atalanta) space and freedom. This was so the 'girl' could get in touch with 'her people' (she assumed this meant the Music Bearers, although it was not spelled-out in so many words.) The letter instructed Melita to 'watch over' her charge, yet also allow her 'independence of movement.' This was so that she could collude with her organisation. The writer, Her Highness, the Landgravine, hinted that she would provide further instructions in the days to come.

21

THE CANTICLE OF THE BUCKLES

She was the most beautiful girl he had seen.

The son of the hawk-master had taken a liking to Atalanta, from the first moment he saw her. In fact, it was on the first morning she had had been permitted to go out on her own. He watched her hips as she walked positively across the cobblestone courtyard — and, after that first day, she began to fetch water every day. It took time for him to gain confidence to do anything more than simply watch her go by. But he eventually gained the courage to talk. It started as a simple comment about weather. Then an observation about horses. Afterwards, he found it a little easier to take more time to get to know her.

'Your Lady has allowed you more time to wander, I see—' he dared ask, one morning.

'My Lady?' Atalanta almost spat out the word. It was a secret that she worked for the Landgravine, so how did this strange lad know such a thing? She had been told, strictly, that she should never disclose the identity of her abductor. 'I don't have a Lady,' she said, with a growl.

'But I thought... um, I thought you served the elegant lady with you. I cannot tell if she is a servant or a noble-woman, because she is free to come-and-go as she pleases. She goes into the primary residence late at night. You seem bonded to her, as if you are her servant. Are you not? Please forgive me, I thought she was your Mistress.'

'Oh, yes.' Atalanta understood now. 'She's my — uh?' She was about to say 'guardian,' but that seemed unlikely. Any fool would see through that. Even this chump. The idiot would then ask more probing questions. 'No. She's not my Mistress. She's my friend. She is with me because I'm young. She is my chaperon, do you see? She takes care of me.'

Atalanta decided she could put the issue aside if she attempted to explain what she had been doing at the Royal residence. 'She guides me. She is providing my 'tutoring.' I'm working for His Highness the Landgrave. I help at the main residence. I do occasional work for him—'

'Oh, I see.' The hawk-masters boy didn't seem convinced. He'd noticed that Atalanta had a strained relationship with her so-called 'chaperon', as if she was subservient to her. It didn't seem that the two of them were equals. He also noted that the body language between the two women was not what he expected from 'friends.' There was no warmth shown between them. But he thought better of prying. So instead, he changed the subject. 'Do you like horses? I see you go over to them each day, to make a fuss.'

'Yes.' Atalanta said. 'I love horses. Because they are friendly. But mainly I like them because they are wise. They are never spying on me. They never ask stupid questions ...'

Suitably rebuked, the boy went quiet. His cheeks became pink.

He is adorable, thought Atalanta.

∼

Every day they sent Atalanta to the primary residence where she was handed a small chore to perform. Maybe they found her some light polishing to do. Or perhaps she might be requested to arrange flowers in a vase. Or help to prepare fresh food in the kitchens. But the tasks were never difficult. It was as if they were going through the motions — 'finding something for her to do.'

On her mind was the constant thought that she should contact the Music Bearers. Contact had to be established, as soon as possible. They needed to be told that she had been snatched. They needed to know where she was so they could come and rescue her.

She was sure that there must be a consul allocated to the nearby town. It was about twenty-five furlongs away. It seemed to be a moderately bustling place. Traders from the town frequently made their way to the royal residence. She hatched a plan to make some kind of excuse to go to the town. Then she might scout around to try to locate the town's secret consul. She needed to get word back to them that they had abducted her.

~

The next day, an opportunity presented itself.

His Highness the Landgrave had ordered four buckles from the whitesmith in the town. He was unhappy with the design. He explained he wanted something bigger, with three hooks, not two. Also, he wanted someone 'reasonably competent' to go see the whitesmith and explain his specific requirements in more detail.

In fact, His Highness had asked Melita to do this minor task. But she had suggested they send Atalanta. For the Landgrave, it didn't matter who did the task, it was simply a trifling matter. So he nodded his agreement, mainly because it meant he could spend time alone with Melita.

Atalanta was pushing a mop around a hallway when Melita found her. Melita explained about the buckles and told Atalanta that the coach would take her into town. They would ask the driver to wait for her, and to bring her back once she had completed the simple task. She gave her one buckle so she could describe the 'problems' with it. She was told to inform the craftsman that His Highness would keep all the other buckles until they had adequately made new ones. They had already paid money for this work to be done, so were holding onto the other buckles back, as a deposit.

Atalanta enjoyed her ride into town. She felt like a grand lady, travelling in such a fine carriage. When she peeked out of the carriage, at fields and meadows, she started to think about how she could get used to this kind of living. When the coach arrived at the market-town, it halted. The driver parked by a still-pond.

Atalanta went to find the whitesmith's workshop. It helped that she did not know the layout of the town. This provided her with the excuse she needed, to talk to numerous market traders, and most of the town's other inhabitants. Although she was trying to locate the whitesmith's shop, which she discovered immediately, she also continued to make other general enquiries.

She had already concocted a story that she might tell people. Because, clandestinely, she was trying to establish where the Music Bearer's consul could be discovered. And, of course, that fact would be a secret. This information she needed would not be disclosed by anyone. Especially not to a stranger in town.

So Atalanta told folk she had experienced sleeping difficulties . She told everyone she met she was new in town and asked them if they knew someone who might know a remedy for insomnia. She told them she had terrible bad dreams at night. Some folks directed her to the apothecary's garden. Others simply shrugged their shoulders and said they didn't know anyone who could help. Some directed her out of town, saying she should try the nunnery in the adjoining village.

But one person, an older woman, who washed wicker baskets by the pond, pointed out the casking yard. The woman told Atalanta to talk to the brewer's wife. She suggested she should tell the wife about her problem.

So Atalanta went to the brewer's yard, and she found the brewer's wife. The wife wiped her hands on an apron as she entered the daylight. Atalanta apologised for the disturbance. She was evidently interrupting the woman's work. Atalanta said one of the townsfolk had directed her here. She explained she was experiencing sleeping troubles because of bad dreams.

'Then it is my handmaid you need to talk to...' offered the older woman. 'I'll get her for you. Wait in there.'

She led Atalanta into a flint-built storeroom. The brewer's wife called out.

A girl arrived. She wore a neat pinafore. Simple shoulder-clasps held the pinafore to a plain under-dress. Once the older woman left them to go back to her toil, Atalanta went through the secret greeting code with this girl. She waited for the correct responses and attentively noted the rhythms and silences between words:

'Be filled with the Spirit.' Atalanta said, in a low tone.

'We exalt him...' the girl replied.

'Our mutual friend, Paul sent me—'

'Silas, was he there?' The girl asked.

'He was. He was...' Atalanta replied.

There, the code was accomplished. Atalanta smiled and threw her arms around the younger girl's neck, as if she kissed a long lost sister, which, perhaps, she did. Both girls smiled joyfully, then hugged each other gleefully. But the younger girl seemed puzzled. Why had this new consul been sent to town? Did they think she was not competent? Was she still not trusted to deal with things? This other girl's presence was a bit of a mystery. The Bearers never sent two consuls to the same town.

~

Once back at the primary residence, Atalanta sought Melita to explain the news about the Landgrave's buckles. She explained it had been a successful visit to town. Obviously, she did not tell Melita that she had secretly contacted the Music Bearer's consul while there. She also decided, at this early stage, that it would be prudent not to tell the consul, or anyone from the Music Bearers, about her abduction. She had made contact — that was an important start. But Atalanta was still trying to figure out how best she could rationally explain such a complicated situation. She didn't want the Bearer's assuming she had been in any way complicit.

She reasoned Melita would hand her over to the authorities, without a moment's hesitation, if called for. Especially if she suspected Atalanta had betrayed the trust of the Landgravine. Who would believe her story of abduction, anyway? It seemed a tall tale even to her. So she waited to think things over well. She knew she must consider each nuance, and think out a proper strategy, before she told the Music Bearers about her plight.

22

THE CANTICLE OF JAMIN

The days slipped-away for Atalanta.

She spent morning hours in the principal residence; they were easy. Then spent afternoons with the falcon-master's son. She learned that the falcon-master's son was known to everyone as Jamin. He was two summers older. And even though he was nervous, he seemed very interested in Atalanta. She felt pleased he controlled himself during their several meetings.

But, one afternoon, when he demonstrated a method for cleaning feathers from a coop, the couple found themselves within the confined spaces of the bird-shed. He pressed his body close to hers. He could not help it. He put his arm around Atalanta's waist. He did not try to kiss her. Or caress or rub her anywhere. He simply wanted to embrace her, so he could feel her sweet breath against the hairs on his neck.

She didn't know how to respond to this cuddle. She knew, deep in her heart, it was not to be. But she rationalised that there was nothing wrong with a hug. A squeeze was a natural thing, wasn't it? And the guy wanted to protect her, so it made sense, didn't it? Also, she wanted to feel protected. His embrace meant nothing more than that. A protective hug.

Jamin tried nothing else with Atalanta, though he was smitten. It was true. He sensed some reluctance from her. It was as if she held back. Clearly she wasn't ready yet. Jamin prided himself on his restraint. He was beginning to grow fond of her and didn't want to jeopardise things by pushing her. Though he wanted nothing more than to kiss her mouth. To keep her the entire night through. But instead, he wished her goodnight. So he returned, with a smile, to his own quarters. So she could return to hers. Alone.

Days went past like this: Light work in the morning. Lovely meetings with Jamin in the afternoon.

One evening, The Landgravine's favourite, Melita, returned to the servant's quarters late. It was the first night the fornicatress had even been back to the servant's quarters in a week. 'I got another letter from Her Highness,' she told Atalanta.

Atalanta didn't know, till then, that Melita had received an earlier letter. In fact, she didn't know Melita could read. She listened attentively to her news.

'Her Highness intends to come here—' continued Melita. 'She is going to travel clandestinely into town. She will remain disguised, of course. She will stay at a secret location. She wants you to know these plans because she has asked to see you.' Atalanta seemed amazed. 'Yes you. She says she will reveal everything to you when she sees you. That's when she will ask you to perform your duty.'

23

THE CANTICLE OF THE FALSE PRIORESS

Her Highness the Landgravine travelled to the city of Castle Acre in the guise of a Prioress. This was befitting of her 'real-world' rank and status. She planned to stay in the old castle that sat on the hill. It overlooked the city walls. It was private enough to be secure, yet palatial enough for her requirements.

Her assistants included two guards, a driver, a messenger, and her most dependable maids. They were all sworn to absolute secrecy about the trip. They were told they were not to disclose her true identity to any person, on pain of death.

Of course, her favourite and most trusted maidservant, Melita, was not with her on the journey to Castle Acre — because she was already there. Snooping around and spying. As she always did. They had sent Melita to Castle Acre in advance to make all the provisions for a trap. A trap that was about to be set.

The vengeance-filled wife was going to surprise her husband. She was planning a surprise that he would not like. A surprise that would cost him his title. And his life.

They had given Melita the responsibility of looking after and observing the behaviour of the little Music Bearer's consul called Atalanta. This girl had been snatched from her 'home' city and taken far away. Here, to Castle Acre. The Landgravine looked forward to seeing her most trusted servant again. She also looked forward to telling the Music Bearer's girl about the next steps of her plan.

Her Highness arrived at the castle at dusk, arriving at the gates from the hills. This approach was uniquely arranged, so others would not observe the Landgravine's arrival. She didn't want her coaches to be noticed by anyone who used the main road that led to the nearby town. Once the Landgravine had settled into her quarters, she waited impatiently for her girls to attend her. She expected the arrival of her trusted servant Melita and the kidnapped Music-Bearer's girl, Atalanta.

The two girls arrived at the castle gates, dressed in miserable, smelly shawls. Garbed this way, they appeared to be peasants. This was important, because if any enquiring folk had seen them on the road, they could not guess their true identities.

The guardians of the castle did not let them in at first — so convincing were their disguises. But Melita explained they were there to see the Prioress. This was a passcode and the chief gate-keeper recalled an earlier briefing. So he cautiously allowed them through the gates. He emphasised they must go straight to the west tower and told them to report personally to the staff of the 'Prioress' there. He evidently still believed they were peasants pleading for alms.

So, a few hours after sunset, the two 'peasant' women made their way to the tall tower in the west, to be shown to the main lodge by one of the trusted maids. They entered a large room that had been hurriedly provided. The castellan of the building had richly prepared it. He aimed to provide the 'Prioress' with small comfort, although he was not told her true rank or title.

The two 'peasant' women were summoned into the largest room and told to kneel on a rug in front of an ornate carved chair. Soon, the 'Prioress' entered from the main hall. She approached them and Atalanta noted she was dressed in a wimple and charcoal habit. She wore a light-grey topcoat, hung across aristocratic shoulders. She gestured for Melita to rise. Then she gave her a big hug. She seemed happy to see the girl. Melita was her most trusted confidant. Then the Lady made a cursory nod towards Atalanta before she sat upon her throne.

Her Highness was the first to speak: 'You have contacted the Music Bearers?' She spoke candidly to Atalanta, though her head tilted towards her beloved Melita.

This direct question upset Atalanta. How did the Landgravine guess she had been into town to contact secretly the consul? Atalanta had truly told nobody what she had done. Therefore, she did not know how to respond to the question. If she said that she had contacted the Music Bearer's consul, then she would be damned. Condemned for the act. But if she lied about it and said she had not... that lie would also be telling. Before she could fill the silence with a satisfactory answer, Melita saved her.

'I think I can help my little friend here. She has some kind of short-term memory-loss...' Melita smiled with confidence. A flicker of amusement flashed across her face, 'The simple answer is, yes. She has.'

This revelation amazed Atalanta. She was about to protest her innocence but could not find the appropriate words to explain herself. Now, her stomach turned. She rubbed her palms together. She felt anxious. But Melita continued. 'I arranged for her to travel to town on the pretext of organising replacement buckles. And that was when she stealthily looked for her Music Bearers. The driver of the coach watched her meet and talk to several citizens. The driver reported back that she slipped out of sight just after she spoke to one of the town's folk. She headed for the brewery. The driver did not see her for a while after that.'

'And you guess that was when she connected with the Music Bearer's agent?' The Landgravine asked.

'Yes, I do.' Melita replied, with a nod.

The women regarded Atalanta with critical gazes. They looked her up-and-down. It seemed as if they waited for an explanation. Atalanta felt a twinge of fear, deep in her heart. She wished she could sink deep into the beautiful carpet under her knees. She wished that God had blessed her with the power of invisibility.

Atalanta could not bear the silence any longer. Those condemnatory stares were drilling into her soul. She felt small tears forming in her eyes. She dared not look up. Nor look into the eyes of her accusers.

'Yes...' Atalanta murmured, finally. 'I saw the Music Bearer's consul when I went into town for buckles. But I promise I did not tell anyone about my situation here. I swear!' Tears streamed down her cheeks. 'I have told no one that you forced me to come here, lady. I have not, absolutely not, given away your true identity. Please believe me.'

The Landgravine did not seem startled by this outpouring. She didn't even seem moderately upset. When Atalanta glanced into the eyes of the false Prioress, it encouraged her to see the Lady smiled.

'Well, well. That was expected...' said the Landgravine. She spoke in reassuring tones. This gave Atalanta a renewed sense of hope. She felt her strength and courage flood back.

'You will need to be brave girl...' Her Highness continued, 'Because you have yet to fulfil entirely your role. The next phase of my plan will require far more obedience from you. I'm going to give you explicit instructions. Follow those instructions absolutely, with diligence and loyalty, and you shall be free.' The Landgravine paused, then went on. 'If you do as you are told, I pledge, we will leave you alone. I will even arrange things for you, so you can start a new life here at castle Acre Far... away from fear. Far from the influences that control you. Do you want that?'

'Yes I do...' Atalanta replied. She nodded gratefully. She breathed deeply. Trying to preserve her strength.

The Landgravine turned her attention to her trusted servant Melita: 'You have been observing the girl, I hope—'

'I have,' Melita said. She cast Atalanta a knowing look. As if she could see precisely into her heart. She peered at the younger girl's dewy eyes. Then continued to smile her perceptive smile.

'And what did you find out?' The Landgravine asked.

Atalanta didn't know where this conversation was going. Once, when she was young, she saw a stringed puppet at the county fair. The puppet-doll was forced to do all kinds of crazy things; made to dance, to climb and even to fly. All the kids laughed. All the while, the puppeteer was almost invisible. That was because the crowd focused on the little puppet. He jumped up and down. He responded to hidden strings that were pulled this-way-and-that. The puppeteer manipulated things behind the scenery. But the puppet did all the work. Atalanta felt like that poor puppet. Others pulled her strings. Others made her do things she didn't want to do. She was controlled by everyone. Though, she had no free-will of her own.

'I observed that the girl begins a close friendship with a boy,' Melita told the Landgravine. 'The boy is the son of the Falcon Master. He is a nice-looking lad. They have been seeing a lot of each other. I think they have grown fond of each other.'

Atalanta felt her cheeks blush. How could Melita know about Jamin? Was there nothing that she could keep secret from these two witches?

'Well, well...' said the Landgravine. She smoothed out her skirt. Perhaps pondered on the information. 'Right, young lady. Listen up. If you want it to be so, I can arrange for you to stay here at Castle Acre with this boy. I have the power to make dreams come true. Did you know that? How does that sound? Once you have performed your duty to me, and my plan is complete — I will help you stay here, with your new boy-love. I promise we will leave you alone once your duty is performed. Then you may start a new life. Away from all the influences and obligations that have burdened you for so long...'

Atalanta considered all this. The suggestion tempted her. In fact, she had been thinking about starting a new life with Jamin, anyway. She had wondered if it could work for them. She asked herself if she cared enough about him to give up everything. To give up on the long years she had spent studying to be a Music Bearer's consul. She knew the answer was yes. But Atalanta had never heard of anyone leaving the secret order of the Music Bearers. Perhaps nobody ever left. Well, nobody left alive and breathing, anyway.

The Landgravine abruptly interrupted her thoughts: 'I expect you will want to know what I need you to do... And that's why I came all this way to see you, in person. Because I did not want you to be confused. I am giving my instructions personally. That way, there is no risk of any misunderstanding...' The false Prioress gazed at Atalanta. 'What I'm about to tell you is extremely confidential. Your life will be at risk if you dare utter a single word about this plan. Do I make myself clear?'

'Yes, Your Highness.'

'Right. I need you to make another connection with the Music Bearer's agent in the town.'

Atalanta nodded. Melita examined her expressions and checked her body language. Making sure she understood the instructions and didn't give away odd signs of flakiness.

'When you do that, I want you to organise, forthwith, a Music Bearer to attend this town. I want the call to go out for a Bearer, straight away. It is imperative that we have one here, now, you see. To complete our plan.'

Atalanta studied the Landgravine. 'But.... Your Highness...' she stammered. 'It takes a while for a Music Bearer to come around. They arrive on rotation. We do not expect the next Bearer here till the full moon...'

'I understand...' The Noble woman said. 'But I need one right away. You will exaggerate the problem. They will listen to you. Because you will make it sound dramatic. You will report that someone — an incredibly special person—will die! Yes, that is right. Unless we summon immediately a Music Bearer, a high-ranking person will die. It is imperative that a Bearer attends this town at once—'

Atalanta sat still. She took in this fresh information. She reflected on it. Perhaps it would be possible to do this. She didn't know for sure. 'And who might I say should die — if a Music Bearer does not take part? Who would this special person be?'

Both women, the Landgravine and Melita, smiled. This was the moment they would have to disclose their most secret of all secrets. The most important part of the plan. The Landgravine spoke: 'My husband, of course. His Highness the Landgrave.' She paused for dramatic effect. 'He has been feeling weak of late...' she continued. 'The poor man he has been overworked. He has not been sleeping. He has been suffering from depressions and fears. He needs immediate help. The type of spiritual help that can only be administered by a Music Bearer. Otherwise, he may expire. He will die soon, unless you help him, Atalanta — this is your moment. You must save him. Music must save him.'

Atalanta's eyes widened. Her mouth opened to show a shimmer of glossy tongue. She was shocked to hear this. She was being asked to call a Music Bearer for his Royal Highness? 'But — if it ever became disclosed that His Highness required a Bearer of Music to cure his ailments, if that ever came out, wouldn't it be the end of him? He would have to give up his position, wouldn't he? Or worse. They'd lop off his head for such a thing, wouldn't they?'

'Yes, Miss. They presumably would—' the false Prioress offered a grin. 'So now you understand the complexity, the gravity, and the severity of the situation. You also understand why I demand absolute secrecy. I trust you will do your duty. I'm handing a significant task to you. The life of our beloved Landgrave will be in your hands. I pray you will succeed...'

Atalanta gasped.

'Before you go, girl — I have something to give to you,' said the Landgravine, abruptly.

Melita was unhappy to hear this. Why was the abducted girl about to be given a gift?

The Landgravine felt around, then revealed an object that was shaped like a horseshoe dish, wrapped in fine silks, and fastened with ribbons. The thing seemed expensive, thought Melita.

Her Highness fixed Atalanta a steady gaze while she steadily unwrapped the beautiful package. Atalanta felt the strain. She tensed her neck as she tried to catch the first glimpse of whatever was inside the fine wrappings.

Finally, the coloured ribbons slipped away, they made a wonderful sliding sound as they hit the floor. Then the false Prioress pulled away the final layers of silk, to expose the hidden object beneath folds and covers.

Melita stared at it. She was puzzled. This was not a valuable object. Why had it been packed so wonderfully? It appeared to be some kind of contraption, an old kitchen tool perhaps. She had seen nothing like it before. Was it a vegetable cutter? Why was it wrapped so expensively? What would Atalanta do with a kitchen vegetable-cutter?

'So Atalanta, do you know what this thing is?' asked the Landgravine.

'I do, Your Highness.'

Melita gazed at her in doubt. Really? Do you know this kitchen tool?

But the object was not a kitchen-tool. Atalanta recognised it as a phorminx. The phorminx was the oldest of all stringed instruments. A type of rudimentary harp once played by David as he sang his psalms.

Both girls observed the object in wonder. But for varied reasons. For Melita, she stared at the thing with a sense of envy. She asked herself why the new girl had been offered such a precious gift. She wanted to know what her reward would be. Meanwhile, Atalanta looked at the thing with curiosity. The Lady had taken a colossal risk to bring the object here. If they caught her with a musical instrument, she would surely be imprisoned. She would face the toughest of questions. She would doubtless be put on trial for heresy. Then would be condemned to death. Even the Music Bearers do not carry musical contraptions around with them, for fear of discovery. It was too dangerous. They taught Music Bearers to make instruments from natural objects that are found along the way. And even when they created such instruments, they had to be entirely de-constructed after use. Rendered back into individual, non-suspicious components. Then the pieces were turned back into the soil. Nobody ever possessed a musical instrument. This item was extremely rare. And it was a reckless folly to carry it around like this.

The false Prioress extended her elegant hand—offering the precious gift to Atalanta. But the girl resisted. She didn't want to grab hold of a musical instrument. Understandably.

'Oh, come now, girl. I brought you a precious gift. I had it with me all this way. Now you reject it?'

'I am grateful, Highness. It is just...' Atalanta struggled to explain. 'This thing, ma'am. It is not a safe thing to possess. It is dangerous to even have it in this room. Holding a tool like that is a serious crime. Punishable by—'

Atalanta did not like to finish the sentence. But the penalty for possession of a musical instrument was death.

'Well, I need you to take it, young lady.' The Landgravine said, with authority. 'You will take it now...' She seemed very insistent. 'My husband, His Highness the Landgrave, will need his mind soothed by the singing of songs. Soft sounds will accompany those songs. They will play the sounds on this — um — is it some type of lyre? He is of royal blood, you see, so he must have the absolute best. Don't you understand that? He must have the best music that is available. So take it — keep it hidden until it the time is right. Then pass it onto the Music Bearer. So he can play soothing sounds upon it. Then my husband will be repaired. And all will be well in the realm...'

Atalanta remained unsettled. She resisted taking the stringed instrument for a few moments more.

'Take it. Hurry. Before someone steps in ....'

The Lady leaned to pass the phorminx. 'You may have it destroyed after use if that is what worries you. These silks and bows are too elegant for you, so I will give those trifling gifts to Melita...'

At last, Melita's eyes grew wide, and she beamed a smile of thanks.

'I also brought a rough sack, so that you can hide the instrument. Begin by hiding it in this bag. Keep it dry. Then the thing must be moved to the Music Bearer when you see him. You will instruct him to play it to my Lord, the Landgrave—' With that, the Landgravine, who posed as a false Prioress, passed the phorminx to Atalanta. She gave the silks and ribbons to Melita, who studied them with pleasure. Quickly afterwards, the noble lady felt around behind the seat, and produced a rough sack. She pressed the sack into Atalanta's hands. 'Here, stick the beastly thing into this. Keep it covered. Show no one. Except the Music Bearer. Now, both of you, go."

24

THE CANTICLE OF THE PHORMINX

When the two girls got back to the servant's quarters, after their secret rendezvous with the Landgravine, Melita made excuses about the need to 'slip away' to do chores in the pantry before morning. In fact, she wished to visit His Highness the Landgrave in his bed. Melita wanted to taste sweet dinner wines and slurp down oysters. She wanted to relax on a woollen mattress and feel silk between her toes. Most of all, she wanted to feel kingly hands upon her body. She hurried off immediately, even fleetingly kissing Atalanta on the cheek, like a sister.

Atalanta decided that the first thing she needed to do was get rid of the infernal phorminx. What was the Lady thinking? She should never have brought this to her. Atalanta thought she must be unbalanced. Atalanta thought hard about a place to hide such a terrible thing. Where would be safest? Surely not here in her bed-sack. Nor anywhere in these quarters. Some nosy maid would certainly locate it. Where else then?

As she crossed the courtyard, a thought struck her. She did a U-turn and headed back towards the edge of the property. This is where several outbuildings were located. She found what she was looked for. She cracked open a fragile door. She heard a flap and a rustle as she entered. Nothing more than she bargained for. Then she felt around in the dark until she located a pile of dry wood with her hands. She had seen the logs collected the day before. She heaved up some of the lower timber. They were heavier than expected, but she moved them once she exerted herself. After that, she stuffed the sackcloth bag containing the phorminx under the lowest logs. Then she let the looser logs settle down upon on the thing.

Satisfied she had left the secret object in a safe place, Atalanta made her way back to the servant's quarters, brushing her hands as she walked. She promised herself that she would tell Jamin — the son of the Hawk Master about it all. The complete story. From beginning to end. She would confess completely everything. He deserved that. If she had been honest with him from the outset, then maybe she wouldn't be in this ungodly mess.

The next morning, Atalanta searched around for the boy, Jamin. But she could not find him anywhere. She supposed he must be at the principal residence. She completed her morning odd jobs. Then she went to the falconry to find him. He was not there. She asked about. No one had seen Jamin all morning. Maybe he had taken some birds out? That was doubtless the best explanation for his disappearance. Her morning, spent doing pointless chores at the primary residence, dragged. Atalanta felt apprehensive that she had not seen Jamin yet. She pledged to herself that she would tell him everything. But Atalanta felt a knot of anxiety grow in her stomach. She knew something was awry.

Soon before she was due to leave the residence, to return to her own quarters, Melita stopped her. This was commonly the time of day that Atalanta looked forward to meeting Jamin. In the afternoon, they would share innocent moments together.

'Well, at last I have found you …' said Melita, as if Atalanta had been hiding all day. She had not. 'We will need to travel down to the town this afternoon. So you can tell the Music Bearer's agent about what expected, yes? Remember what she instructed? We need to organise a Music Bearer to come immediately here, to this place. I will come with you. To supervise. And see this 'agent' for myself. To ensure all arrangements are moving forward smoothly—'

'You will go with me?' Atalanta asked, nervously. She felt a twinge of anxiety shoot through her belly. She would have to think swiftly.

'Yes, yes. Why? What is it?'

'The consul... The secret Music Bearer's agent. She will not talk to me if you are there. They have instructed her that she may only talk about such things when we are alone—'

'Well, introduce me as your trusted companion. Tell her how you and I get on. Tell her we have been friends for many seasons—'

'That will not help. That will sound even more suspicious. She will suspect a trap. She will not speak to me about such things. They instructed us to change the subject if someone else is present. There is a code. We have a code that must be rigorously observed. She will only speak of such things to a Music Bearer or a consul. But not when another person is present. Because those persons might overhear our codes...'

'Well, can you not teach me those codes now? We could learn them together, as we travel to town, in the coach.'

'Melita, with the greatest respect, it takes many months to learn and practice just one code. They have a special tone and complicated rhythms. It takes hours just to learn the patterns and pulses of sound.'

'I think I understand...' Melita said, beaten. 'Well, I will go with you to the meeting point. Then leave you to do your magic codes. And you will have to tell the agent to get the Music Bearer to come here right away. Tell the agent that we need help, fast...'

Atalanta nodded.

'And bring the thing with you. You will need to give her the thing. So it can be given to the Music Bearer.'

Atalanta seemed puzzled: 'What thing?'

'You know, the kitchen cutter noise-making thing. Bring that as well, so we can pass it along to the next person.' Melita referred to the phorminx. The stringed instrument entrusted to Atalanta by the Landgravine. The instrument that Atalanta had already hidden in the falconry cabin. Curses, she thought. Now I will have to find it again, from where she hid it.

'I need to recover it from, er, my quarters.' Atalanta said.

'Well, do it quick. I'll see you in one hour's time. At the main drive. We shall travel in style.' Melita's eyes twinkled. 'I asked the Landgrave if we could use his best coach. He agreed!'

Wonderful! thought Atalanta. So much for a sneaky trip into town.

Atalanta rushed to the cabin of the Falcon Master to retrieve the hidden phorminx. There was still no sign of Jamin. She crept into the cabin and headed straight for the pile of wood. That's where she had hidden the instrument late last night — under one of the lowest, largest branches. She had to lever one of the jutting logs off, to lift the stack back. At first, she could not believe it.

The phorminx was not there.

A spasm of anxiety shot through her bones. Perhaps she had buried it deeper in the woodpile than she remembered? She'd hidden it in the dark, after all, so perhaps that was possible. She remembered she couldn't see too well when she had tucked it away. She knocked off all the upper layers of timber, then took off the heavy pieces too, one by one. Until she got to the lower, lighter, ones. Eventually, she revealed the remaining few logs. These were the logs at the base of the pile. But undoubtedly the phorminx had been removed. Who had taken it? Now she was running out of time, because Melita expected her at the carriageway in a few minutes.

Atalanta had to run to the grain store to collect another sack, so she could hide the 'musical instrument' inside it. She collected the sack, returned to the Falconer's cabin, found the flattest, most warped piece of timber available, then stuffed it into the 'new' sack. After that, she hurried to the principal residence. To meet Melita.

The coach journey to town was not pleasant. Atalanta's mind was full of fears and concerns. But Melita beamed with joy. They had organised an ornate carriage for their brief journey. It had upholstered cushions and carpets, and the smell of expensive oils. There was a lamp that could be lit, once dark. Atalanta placed her 'precious' sack on her lap. It seemed smaller and lumpier than before, thought Melita.

They arrived at the town, and the carriage was placed obtrusively right outside the main lodging house. Everyone looked at it. Some locals even peered inside to see who the regal visitors might be. Two servant girls alighted, and folk seemed disappointed they were not visitors of note. The coach didn't contain any Earls or even their Countesses.

Atalanta rushed off to see the Music Bearer's consul at the brewery. Melita followed behind, keeping her distance. At the brew-house, Atalanta contacted the brewer's wife, as she had done before. And, like last time, the wife called for the younger girl to attend.

The girl arrived, and Atalanta noted she wore the same apron as before. She was younger than Atalanta remembered. How old were they these days? She looked a little older than fifteen summers. Still, whatever her age was, the girl was the local consul for the Music Bearers and had to be admired for that.

Atalanta went through the correct code of greeting again. As was required, she waited for the responses. And made sure that the rhythms and tones were impeccably correct.

'Be filled with the Spirit,' Atalanta said.

'We exalt him…' said the girl.

'Our mutual friend Paul has sent me …'

'Silas, was he there?' asked the girl.

'He was. He was.'

The girls were happy to see each other again. The young girl glanced quizzically at the sackcloth bag that Atalanta clutched.

'What is that object?' asked the consul.

'Oh — this? It's only a lump of wood. May I leave it here?' She opened the bag to reveal a mouldy looking log.

'Why are you hiding a piece of wood in a sack?'

'It is a long story,' said Atalanta. 'I won't bore you with it.'

'It is good to see you again,' the girl announced. 'I have many questions. I have been thinking about your last visit. I have not been here long, you see. I'm new. So, I wanted to ask you… is my performance lacking? Is that what they think? Are you here to replace me?'

'No, nothing like that. I'm here because…' Atalanta needed to think this through. She did not want to get this poor, innocent into any trouble. She did not want anyone to get into trouble. But she was being manipulated by a powerful lady who predicted her every move.

So she needed to use all her cunning if she wanted to work out a way to escape from her puppet-strings. She would tell the girl what she needed. And that was all. She would perform her function — as she had been told. Then would wriggle herself free from the tangle. And run away.

'I need you to get a message out. It is essential that you summon a Music Bearer here. At once—'

She expected the new consul, this young girl, would now ask questions. So Atalanta had planned, in her mind, some excuses to tell. She expected the girl would doubtless deliver an explanation about how it would be absolutely impossible to get a Music Bearer to attend before the next full moon. Atalanta prepared to argue the point, to stand her ground, if necessary.

But the girl did none of these things. She did not respond in any of the ways she had predicted. Instead, the young girl smiled, and said: 'Yes, this is good. He is supposed to be here in a few days' time, anyway. Maybe before twilight tomorrow...'

Atalanta was astonished to hear this extraordinary news. Of course, it would please her mistress. Things were surely going to be a lot easier to arrange than she'd expected. But, even so, she felt curious about his early arrival.

'Was he not due until full moon?'

'Oh, yes. That was the old Music Bearer. That was Brother Chad. But they promised us a new one. A younger, different friar. Fresh from training! I think that Brother Chad has been handed over to some other region. Because the Hounds recognised his face. So we will get someone brand new. Just think... a Bearer filled with ambition and courage. He will arrive soon. I can't wait to see him...'

Atalanta considered this information before continuing: 'Well, that's good. I suppose. But there is vital information that I need to give you. This new brother has an important 'patient' to see right away. I can make all the arrangements for you — so you do not have to get involved. Tell him he will need to attend the principal residence — up on the brow.'

'That's where His Highness the Landgrave is staying, isn't it? You came in that wonderful coach? Everyone is yakking about it. It's the talk of the town.' The young consul had started to put two-and-two together.

'Yes...' Atalanta said, moderately irritated. But she continued. 'You will get word to me when the Music Bearer arrives? So I can make last-minute vital arrangements to get him up to the grand house on the hill?'

'You are staying at the royal residence?' the girl asked, her eyes filled with wonder.

'Yes, I am...' Atalanta replied. 'I remain in servitude, of course,' she added.

∼

Atalanta returned to the primary residence by coach. She told Melita the barest of details about her meeting. But explained how she had contacted the consul and the consul had gone along with the plan.

It was late. But Atalanta needed to see Jamin and explain all that had happened. She felt the need to tell him everything. It seems that nobody had seen the boy all day. So once Melita had scurried off to the Landgrave's bedchamber, Atalanta went to the cabin to wait for him. She cracked open the door, then walked into the dark. She would wait his return. She curled onto the floor, laid upon her cloak. She reclined in silence. In sober contemplation. As her eyes closed, she slipped into a gentle slumber.

A squeaking noise from the cabin door awakened her. It being opened, quietly. In trod a figure. She could not make the person out, but Atalanta tensed all her senses. She forced her herself to hear, struggling to recognise any familiar pattern of sound. Listening to how the figure breathed. She even tried to detect an aroma above the smell of bird lime and rotting beams.

So she would not alarm the figure. She spoke deliberately and delicately. 'I waited for you. I have been waiting...'

She heard no response. Only heavy breathing.

'Where are you, Atalanta?' came a voice. It was him. The boy, Jamin. Thank God.

'I am here —' Though she remained laid upon her cloak at the far end of the cabin. He came forwards. Only then did she stand. Their breathing was heavy. He took her in his arms.

For the first time, he squeezed her tight. Then he placed a kiss on her lips. The first kiss. And it was gentle. Then a soft touching. The touching became long and enthusiastic. Atalanta thought her legs would melt. She pulled him onto the warm cloak, where they clung together, strong, and close. She felt that they would never escape each other's arms again. They clung together for what seemed like hours.

'I worried about you. Where have you been?'

'His Highness wanted some excellent sport. He is lively these days. Full of energy at the moment. He wanted to take three birds out. It has been a long day. I am only just back from hunting—'

They hugged hard. She needed to tell him everything. It needed to all spill out. But first she had to question him.

'Where is the thing, Jamin?' she asked.

There was no answer.

'The thing from the woodpile. Where is it?'

'I guessed it was yours, Atalanta...' the boy said. 'I got it into a safer place. I had to move it quick, or one of the lads would have certainly found it. They come here to collect dry wood for the fire. They would have discovered it. So I took it and hid it in a better place.'

'How did you know the thing was mine?' she asked.

'I am an observer. A bird watcher, don't forget. That is what we bird-fanciers do. We observe young hens and study their behaviour. I've done it all my life. My father taught me and my grandfather before that. We observe a lot by watching. That's what they taught me.' Jamin hugged her stronger as he continued. 'I know you have been keeping things from me. I know you live two lives. You pose as one thing, a servant girl, yet you are something else. Something higher than that. You twist and turn like a falcon in flight...' He kissed her forehead. 'That is not a terrible thing. It is your natural state. You weave, like a bird might do, on the wing. When I saw you go into my cabin last night, I knew you went in with an object...' She listened keenly. 'I saw you leave later, brushing your hands on your skirts.

When you left, you did not have the object with you. So I figured, correctly, you left it in my cabin. I did not mean to be observing you. Please believe me. I did not set out to study you. I am curious, that's all. I notice things…'

Jamin couldn't see it now, but tears were welling in Atalanta's eyes.

'I have to tell you what happened to me…' she whispered. 'I need to tell you who I truly am. The reasons I am here. The reasons I left that awful thing in your cabin. I have to be honest with you, Jamin.' Her heart felt as if it would erupt if she did not release the pressure. So she told the boy the entire story. She mumbled it from beginning to end. She left nothing out. About how she was a trained to be a Music Bearer's consul. About her first meeting with the Landgravine. About how she had been kidnapped. Even about the plot to trap his Highness. And about how she was offered the phorminx, to trap the kinglet.

Jamin listened to all these things.

Together they hatched a plan.

25

THE CANTICLE OF THE CROSSING

"Sine cantu in spiritu quomodo potest esse beatitudo?"

Without song in the spirit, how can there be happiness?
-Brother Kem

It was a miracle that Elis had survived.

The small coracle had made its way across the channel. He and his guardian were both alive. Delivered by the hand of God.

One day, they would voice this tale in a great and historic canticle. Though it is a tragedy that we should be remembered in our prayers since nine Music Bearers died that day, drowned upon mudflats.

The other coracle, the one that did not get stuck in the perilous mud, was surrendered to the sea. So three more Music Bearers had perished.

Elis had only vague memories of the day. He recalled the boys had risen from their slumbers early. Tutors took them to a secret passage, and the boys thought it was a game. They liked games, so they were in good spirits.

The boys loved to play games that took them out of their classroom for a period. Their Masters led them to a high door in a steep wall. Then they were told to slide down a rope. At the bottom they were told to sit in a small boat. Two boys burned their hands awfully, on their way down this rope, but the master's did not scold the boys for going too fast. Thinking back, that was curious. One boy fell in the water near the boats, and everyone laughed at his soaking. Elis realised there were problems with this game, right from the start!

Once they had slid down the rope, the boys became separated into small groups. Two in each boat, with a master. Except that there was an odd number, so Elis had to be on his own, with one tutor, in his boat. He tried to exchange seats with other boys, but no one would trade with him for this game. Typical, he thought. Nobody wanted to be stuck with a Master for a companion.

The tiny boats — the masters called them coracles — were difficult to operate. They equipped each Master with a short paddle. And with that paddle, he was presumed to steer and drive the boat. Most of the teachers had never done this before, so had trouble making their boats move. They couldn't get the sculling action going. They were expected to describe figures of eight with their paddles, but just splashed and flapped the water with the silly paddles. They needed to get the tiny craft away from the fort walls promptly, so all joined to push and paddle with their hands till they got away.

After a while, as the morning steadily grew brighter, the small flotilla of coracles rowed, paddled, and dabbled themselves up the line of the coast. Finally, the tiny boats manoeuvred out from eyeshot of the old fort. Now, the masters relaxed a little. They tried harder to get the hang of the difficult sculling motion.

The rag-tag flotilla broke up. Some boats were well left behind. Some were going around in circles. To an onlooker it might have looked like silly: like a sea-dance of whirligig beetles. Circling frantically round-and-round like this, all the boys laughed because was so much fun.

The small line of boats made their way, as best they could, beside the coast. The soil was sandy all along the way along. With large dunes protecting the dank swamps that might be discovered inland. All the teachers looked for trees, so that they could safely bring their boats in to land. They could hide their boats in woodland if they found any. After that, they could make off on foot.

But ahead was just furlong-upon-furlong of sand banks, soggy dunes, and squelchy mud. Some sands were watery and had many waders upon them. These birds strode through the muds on stilt-like legs, pecking at the residue with long beaks, searching for worms and molluscs. It didn't seem as if any of the beaches were dependable. So the little squadron of coracles continued their way along the coast.

By now, Elis and his tutor were quite a long way ahead of the others. Not only were they carrying less weight than the other boats, but his tutor — named Kem — performed the sculling action perfectly. He could move their craft rapidly and effectively. Kem steered their boat carefully, too. A little way back from Kem and Elis was another coracle. This boat also had a moderately competent rower on board. They left the rest of the boats behind.

Ahead, Kem saw danger. He recognised mud-mounds that peeked from beneath rapidly moving waves. The coracle had a flat bottom, and he reckoned he and Elis weighed little, so he judged they might skim across the mud. But, as they approached the mudflats, when Kem got a closer view, he saw how he must work around the mud-banks because they were quite extensive. Certainly, they were too marshy to cross. The trouble with this plan would be that they would have to go further into treacherous deep water — out into open sea.

These small boats could not take gigantic waves. Coracles were estuary and river craft. Kem viewed out across the horizon. At this stage, things were still moderately calm on the open sea, but he knew that when bigger waves tipped and rocked the small boat, things would get distinctly unpleasant. It would be dangerous to go into open water. But did they have another option? The mudflats could not be passed. Kem earnestly looked for a stream that flowed between the slimy bulges of mud but could not see any other way to cross them. It was a tough choice. Should he slide over the sludge —

and risk being caught or trapped? Or should he head out to sea — detouring around the mud, but risk being over-turned by the first enormous wave that came along? Kem could not stand in the coracle, so could not see the size of the mudflats. That made up his mind. After much doubt, he decided to risk it. He would take the craft out to sea.

The coracle that followed behind Elis and Kem saw them change direction. Entirely consistently, this craft followed them into open water too. But the other coracles, those that were left behind, those that did not see the mudflats, so did not witness the last-minute deviation of these two tiny boats.

When the other group of boats arrived at the treacherous mudflats, the masters decided, out of necessity, to ride over them. The lead coracle got quite a long way across the beds. Yet the little craft became stranded on a sticky bit of the mud.

The other two coracles skimmed past this first one, and their masters used paddles to stop their small boats, spinning them around, so they could go back to help the first one that got lodged. But it was useless. That coracle was glued fast in the sticky sludge.

All the Music Bearers were previously exhausted, anyway. And the mud looked inviting. So it was not long before one monk decided to push his coracle onto the bank, adjacent to the first stricken craft. Then he chose to vacate his little vessel to help-out his colleague. He motioned that his boys should get out of the boat too, so they could help.

When the monks first got out of their coracles, their feet sank immediately into the fine-grained mud, burying deep. At first, the kids thought this was great fun. They pulled out a foot, and the sucking sound from the mud resembled rude belches and farts. Then other feet got stuck too. So those feet had to be sucked out, also making vulgar noises. Each foot swallowed up air before they could release it.

By now, the Master who had first got stuck in the mud was not so merry. He could not move his feet at all. He was sunk up to his shins. Unable to move, he motioned for the others to help him. All of them readily jumped from their small boats to help their friend. None of them understood — at that moment — the immense danger that they were in.

In no time at all, the teachers, each of them, were stuck in the mud. Not only that, but they found that if they moved at all, they sank deeper. Even waving their arms around meant they got sucked further into the slime. Some kids could move, because they were lighter, but even these kids moved haltingly.

So these kids were told to get paddles from the craft, so teachers could get leverage. To get themselves out. But even this was useless. One boy never got back to his boat. He sunk in a place that was even more liquid. He stepped into a spot where the mud was just like gel. He went right down—up to his waist.

They diverted the other lads to help him instead of helping the Masters. An adult yelled that the kids should not get close him. This adult also instructed the boys to take their cassocks off and fling them out to the stranded boy. So they could drag him back. It made sense. Just one boy did though, because the other boys simply did not understand.

It wasn't long before all the Music Bearers, boys, and men, were utterly stuck in the slurry. As they wriggled and squirmed, it made things worse. Even twisting or bending an arm meant they would sink a little deeper.

Then they saw a fishing vessel approaching. They whistled — to gain attention but could not wave. Because each time they tried to lift their arms, it sucked deeper them into the mire.

Elis and Kem were a long way out into the open sea by then. They could only guess what had happened on the mudflats. They saw a sailboat speeding along the shoreline. *The enemy,* guessed Kem. So, even if they wanted to, they knew they could not go back to the coast. They'd have to stay in dangerous open water until the sailing boat had gone.

Kem laid down his paddle and rested for a while, to take stock of the situation and preserve his energy. He watched as the sailboat turned in large circles. Kem realised the sailboat tried to avoid the mud flats, just like he had done. But could not understand why the fishing craft was going back towards the mudflats again-and-again.

Then he assumed the craft was just a little fishing. Maybe it was not sent after them, after all. Perhaps, the vessel was putting out nets. That was the perfect explanation. That was probably why the craft zig-zagged in a dramatic fashion around the mud, he guessed.

Kem was pleased to *think this* until the sailing ship accomplished a dramatic *change* of direction and began to head straight for them.

Well, he thought, they could *not* be throwing nets at that speed. He was right, of course. It was the enemy. And the enemy was on the chase.

Kem grabbed their paddle, then began furiously sculling the little coracle into the vastness of the channel.

He sculled with all the energy he could muster.

As if his life depended on it. Because it did.

26

THE CANTICLE OF THE TIRED LADY

The great and exalted travelling consul known as Temenos became old.

She was getting slower and forgetful. Her bones were painful. Her fingers did not work as fast as they once did. In fact, she had given up on the phorminx — the oldest of all stringed instruments. The Music Bearers favoured it because it was the easiest instrument to craft They could easily create a yoke for the strings — a ram's horn or timber fork worked well. Then a strong crossbar might be soundly lashed into place, tied stiffly into the arms of the yoke, with a thong. This kept the entire structure in place, tied securely to an additional cross bar at the base. The Music Bearers called this bar 'the bridge.' Then strings of gut would be added. They would tie these between yoke and bridge. Slacker playing strings, those with the deepest notes, were born far from the player's body.

The Music Bearer did not have to be nimble to play a recently made phorminx. Such an instrument might be simply strummed, rarely plucked. But even this became too much for Temenos. Her gnarled fingers could no longer get juice out of the strings.

Her crucial role, like that of all travelling consuls, was to get messages to and from towns and cities across the realm. Infrequently seen by Music Bearers themselves, travelling consuls like Temenos would criss-cross the land, delivering news and instructions to the girl-consuls who were integrated inside walled-settlements. So, she figured, it wasn't important any longer for her to play an instrument.

Temenos frequently met with her girls — she knew each by name. Temenos carried letters and memoranda. She advised and moved the girls out of harm when she predicted it. She provided dates, times, and secret codes for them. All these facts demanded secure storage.

Temenos, like other travelling-consuls, deposited such facts in her mind. But now her memory was not so good. She was becoming old. She knew she needed to take a rest. To see what God had planned for her.

Temenos travelled the earth in the guise of a wealthy widow. Known by all she met as the 'Lord-Lady' — she was a popular figure. This clever guise gave her power, influence, and charm. Her flattery would seduce men. Traders would protect her. Even churchmen bowed in her presence, because she was one of the most generous benefactors in the kingdom.

She travelled alone, without protection. Using great wealth, a cunning mind, and her network of allies to get into and out of tricky situations and difficult places. She travelled everywhere. Unharmed. Never hindered.

She had always favoured the regular canons known as the Nitrian Brothers, whose parsonage they set in a wooded area surrounded by a dry, sandy heath. This Canonical Order had been sympathetic to The Music Bearers. They were extremely helpful. Very trustworthy. They were steadfast.

The Nitrians differed from other cloistered monks. They worked within the larger community. So these priest-missionaries came into contact with Music Bearers from time-to-time. The Nitrian Brothers ran the community hospital for the area. Therefore, they were often the first to know about folk who might need therapy through music. When they discovered someone who could not be served by 'normal medicine,' they contacted Temenos. Temenos arranged a visit from a Music Bearer. It was a good relationship they had developed. And it had lasted a score or more years.

Temenos was glad to stay in the Nitrian canonry for a few days. If those days turned into weeks, months even, who was she to argue? It was God's will.

The Nitrians offered her sanctuary and a cell to sleep in. They provided her with honest food and crystal-clear waters. She determined to rest. She also decided to ask the Leader of the Nitrian Congregation about her failing memory and painful bones. To seek his guidance. Who knows? He might even provide a miracle salve or a marvellous drink that would soothe her bones and brighten a dimming mind. Then all her pains and anxieties would be retired. But, although she trusted God, she did not think that it was likely.

Instead, she believed that God had prepared an alternative path for her to follow.

But now, it seemed, the Almighty wanted her to rest.

27

THE CANTICLE OF KEM

Elis and Kem were in a terrible state when they eventually landed their coracle on the far beach.

They had travelled all the way across the Channel. Doubtless this was the first and last time any person had crossed such a huge stretch of water in so flimsy a vessel.

Elis had passed out two times during the voyage, through fatigue and thirst. Kem was not much healthier. Yet, he had to carry the boy ashore. He lugged him across a shingle beach, then through prickly gorse hedges that thrived in the harsh, salty wind.

Kem peeked behind a dune, where he saw three lakes, square in appearance. So he ran towards them, almost tripping over in his eagerness. He placed the boy on a grass bank, then slid down the slope and into the water.

But the water was salty.

'Damnation...' he said aloud, looking up to heaven.

So Kem went back to the boy and plucked him up. He ran as fast as he could along the edge of the lake. He carried the boy towards a line of bushes. He knew Elis would not last much longer without fresh water.

Kem sprinted into a line of berry bushes. Each branch was spiked with thorns and the spines tore cruelly into his skin. Birds flew off in alarm as he crashed through dark green leaves. Kem looked for something in particular. Something he knew he needed. In the end, he found it.

He located a bowl in the knotted trunk of a berry tree, a natural cup hollowed by nature between stem and bough. It held about a goblet of rainwater. Not the best water to drink. But better than the brackish stuff in the lakes. But how could he get it into the boy? He tore at one pocket of his habit and pulled the sack cloth away. He stuck it into his mouth and chewed. But seawater had encrusted the cloth with salt. Not good at all. He could not use it as a flannel for the boy to suck on. So Kem went to the far end of the bushes, where he found reeds that grew in a muddy ditch. He broke two reeds from a stem. They were green and flexible. No use to him. The third reed was better and could be used as a straw. He broke the reed and returned to the boy.

He pulled Elis close to the natural bowl of water and levelled him alongside of it. This used up the rest of his strength as he lifted and stuck the reed into the corner of the boy's mouth.

'Suck, suck...' he whispered.

The boy drifted in-and-out of sleep. His eyes flickered. His skin felt icy to touch. It did not look good.

'Suck, suck...' Kem pleaded again.

The boy did not respond.

'Please, please, help me God...' Kem prayed aloud. 'Help me now —' And the boy responded.

Elis opened his eyes a little and even gave a weak smile. He sucked at the straw and Kem heard him gulp down a tiny trickle of water. It was enough to save him.

The next challenge was to get the boy somewhere warm and sheltered. Kem felt tempted to wait in the bushes. He actually considered snoozing under the berries. But he knew sleep here would be fatal. For both of them. The cruel winds blew kisses of death all day and all night. There was little shelter under the prickly thorns. And when the sun went down, they would both freeze. Added to this, the land was subject to sudden flooding and rushing tides. The place was a threat to life and limb.

No, Kem realised they needed access to fresh water. A stream was best. Plus proper food to eat and a sturdy canopy for shelter. Most, they needed civilization.

So, with great difficulty, Kem raised the boy again, to carry him on his shoulders. Across a flat, grassy pasture towards far-off woods and then, he hoped, to valleys where he might find some help.

By dusk, they had found their first woodland. But this was only a fringe of deciduous trees. It seemed unlikely that any rivers or streams ribboned through these parts. The land was too flat. Kem placed Elis down onto a leaf-pile cushion at the borderline of what appeared to be an ancient forest. The woodland had a musty, oaky smell. Birds made their last calls of the day. Soon creatures of the night — bats, owls, rats, and badgers —would come out to seek food.

Kem dropped his own body into the leaf mound next to the boy, dizzy with fatigue.

In a few moments they were both asleep.

28

THE CANTICLE OF THE POACHER

The old Poacher hurriedly checked his snares.

He found, through years of experience, that the traps always worked best on the edge of the woodland. His feet were clad in furs, laced with leather trim, and he wore makeshift gaiters wrapped solidly around his shins, up to knee-height. He wore a smock made of flax; it swelled with yet more fur. A brownish pelt hat topped off his head. His milky eyes seemed too large for the proportions of his yellow, wedge-shaped face. His cheeks seemed permanently sucked in, so hardly exposed two blackened teeth.

At first, he thought he spied a dead fox.

More worryingly, it could even be a dead deer. A deer carcase would mean involvement with the authorities. It would mean lots of questions. He first saw the body yonder, under an old oak. A brownish lump. He glimpsed it out of the corner of his milky eye. He always glimpsed things, never saw them. That was the way with hunters. Predators did not like to stare precisely at their target because your quarry can sense when you are watching it. So you put on an act — you pretend you cannot see it. That way, your prey won't sense your approach.

But the brownish lump was not a dead fox under the oak tree.

Nor was it a deer, thank heavens. It was a dead man and his dead child.

Not being one to make rash movements, the poacher had grasped that the secret of plundering was to see, but never to be seen — so the old poacher approached the brown bundle cautiously. He watched, he waited, and he listened. Maybe there was money to be had here: rings of gold, clasps of silver, knives a-gleaming, or beautiful jewels. But he reprimanded himself in silence. There would be none of that because rich folks don't die in the woods. They don't even go into the woodland unless they are a-hunting. No, this pair was a tramp and his boy-apprentice. And, because that was the case, then they would smell strong they'd possess nothing. Not so much as a snot and bogey. However, he looked anyway. To prod at the bodies with a stick. And search for any medallions or crosses that might be attached to their scraggly vagrant necks.

The old poacher eventually got to the brown bodies. He approached from the west, with the wind behind. So he didn't give away his own stink. Also, so he didn't make noise, cracking twigs on the way. The technique meant he could come onto them from behind an enormous tree trunk that sprouted between. From such an angle, he might spy their bodies in secret.

They were monks. One was mature, with broader shoulders. The other was much younger — a teenager. The poacher saw breathing. Though their breaths were shallow and irregular. Neither lumps were stiff, which, he decided, was a great pity: 'Sod it...' he whispered. 'There goes my medallions and crosses.'

But an interesting thought also crossed the poacher's mind. These two might be fugitives. Wanted by the law. If they were outlaws, then there might be a bounty... the authorities would reward him for their capture and return. There may still be money to be made from these bones. So, with a grin, he revealed himself, and worked out his strategy from there. So the poacher stepped out from behind the tree to make himself known. The older monk roused. He was in a bad way. His mouth was as dry as a nun's linen loincloth. His every bone ached, and each tendon was cracked and tormented. This older monk tried to stretch, but even that felt bad. He looked at the poacher, though he could not speak. His lips seemed glued. He could scarcely see because salty gloop had fastened his eyelids. When he finally tore his eyelids open, a yellow liquid escaped, and the yellowness made things look opaque in the early morning half-light.

The boy did not wake at all. He seemed grievously ill.

'Well, well...' the old poacher muttered. 'What do we have here? Two monks. In the woods. Stayed here the night, did we? Nowhere to go, have we?'

'Water? You have water?' the older monk rasped.

The old poacher passed over his water jug to the monk. The top had been plugged with a filthy rag. Kem didn't have the strength to pull the plug.

'Here, let me.' The poacher pulled the rag for him.

The water tasted good. Kem, sensibly, limited himself to a few drops. He let other drops dwell on his chapped lips for a few moments to soak them. Then nodded his thanks to the poacher.

'If you want food and shelter, come back to my cabin. I do not want to eat out here. Not now, there are too many people about.' With that, the poacher studied the foreground, as if it were very much likely he would see a group of people approaching at any moment. 'And the boy? Can he walk? What's got into him?'

Kem looked at Elis. The boy lay motionless on the leaf-bed. He needed proper medical help. Let's get him to the cabin, he thought. Food and water might revive him.

'You will need to bring him, brother. Not me. My back, you see. I cannot lift a thing,' commented the poacher.

So Kem lifted Elis and carried him along. He followed the old poacher. The trip was arduous. Not only because the poacher lived a long way into the forest, but also because he moved so painstakingly slow. For every drop of leaf, or chirp of bird, they had to pause, while the poacher listened for enemies. Then, off they would trudge again. But only a few steps. Before coming to a sudden halt again because the poacher 'thought' he heard the snap of a twig. He stopped many times.

He also paused frequently to check his pitfall traps. He found a squirrel in one, so broke the animal's neck. Now they had something to eat! Eventually, after a protracted trek, they arrived at the poacher's hidden cabin.

His lodge was not big enough for all three to enter, so one had to stand outside at all times. Kem put Elis into the poacher's bed-sack. Whilst the poacher diligently prepared the squirrel for the fire. Then he invited Kem to come outside also, to let the boy rest, and take a drink of water from his rainwater barrel. Kem drank greedily from the tub with a wooden spoon.

When the poacher came to spit and roast squirrel, he was ready to talk.

'So, are you two Music Bearers?' The direct question was stark. It was also difficult to ignore. But Kem tried to ignore it, anyway. He looked into the thicket.

'So, are you?' The poacher asked again.

'What makes you say that?' Kem said.

'The facts, *the facts...*' the poacher persisted. 'I ask myself questions. I give myself answers. I wonder why monks have no place to go. I ask myself why monks sleep in a forest. Why do monks become sickly? I say: church law wants these monks. Monks flee from justice. These monks are escaping. These monks want to go home. Then I ask myself: why does the law want these monks? I answer myself: because these are Music Monks—'

'I see...' whispered Kem.

'Also, I ask myself: Why has this monk got a child-monk with him? I answer myself: Because the child monk is a novice Music Monk. The authorities asked us to keep an eye out for such monks! Also for anyone travelling at night with a child. They asked us to provide sightings. The authorities offer an award.'

'Yes, I know that.'

'So are you then?'

Kem glanced at the poacher. The line of questioning displeased him, but he needed the cooked meat more than anything else in the world. He couldn't turn down the chance to eat. He also needed liquid from that water-butt. More particularly, though — he needed to get Elis to a safe place because it became obvious that the boy needed proper care. Elis was in a bad way. All this had to be paid for, yet Kem had nothing to barter with. They must compensate the poacher. So Kem admitted what he was a Bearer.

'Yes, yes, I am a Music Bearer. If you prepare the meat for me and promise to help me, I will sing for you. Do you want that?'

The old poacher smiled so widely that his face turned from trilateral to square. Tears formed in his old eyes. 'It would be wonderful, brother, if you would sing for me. Yes, I will help you. Please sing for me for me. I will help you both. I have not heard a song since I was five summers old...'

'Do you have a cradle song?' Kem asked.

'That, I do, brother. My mother saw fit to get me one. But it has been many years since I last heard it. I no longer have it in my head. Any song will do for me now. Any song.' The poacher was overjoyed.

After the cooked meat, brother Kem searched around the forest for a certain type of seed, or a pinecone, anything that could produce a ratcheting sound. He needed that type of sound for his song. He found what he searched for and returned to the old poacher.

The poacher now seated on his favourite log and licked his dirty fingers. Kem showed the poacher how to scratch out a raucous beat on the cone, using the back of a knife. 'You said you had not heard a song since you were five summers old. What were the circumstances of your last remembered song?' Kem asked.

'It was a deathbed song. For my mother.' The poacher replied. He had a sad look in his milky eyes.

'Then we should sing a song for your mother. She waits in heaven for you and is attended by angels. She waits for you to join her in everlasting song. She prays for your salvation.' The poacher nodded and Kem thought he saw a teardrop well in the corner of his eye. 'Shall we do a song for her?'

'Yes, I would like that,' the poacher said.

'What do you remember about your mother?'

'Her name was Anna. Her hair was the colour of dirty straw. Her face was like leather. Her eyes were dark green. I loved her all the same. Though she thrashed me hard with a sweeper. She didn't have to go so soon...'

'Good. Focus on your mother's face. We will sing this song together.'

Brother Kem placed his hand onto the old poacher's wrist to slow down the pace of the rhythm stick. Then he stared intensely into the poacher's eyes.

He sang the song. Pure and clear.

29

THE CANTICLE OF ANNA

'Oh Anna. Remember us. As we remember you.
With flaxen hair. Golden skin. Eyes so green and true.
We ask, Oh Anna, that you pray for us.
You have gone before us,
To prepare a place for us —
In the Summer Palace,
Of food and wine
Filled with music of peacetime.
So light a candle for us now,
High in heaven's brow.
So we know which way to travel—
So the light can lead us.
With bread of life, well fed.
Perfect and true.
Like you.'

∼

When they had sung the whole song twice through, Kern asked the old poacher to take part in repeating the chorus:
 'As if we were,

Perfect and true.

Like you...'

They sang the song three times. The old poacher cried. The Music Bearer put his arms around the man and rocked him tenderly. Then they said prayers of devotion together.

After nourishment, Kem decided to leave the poacher's lair. Elis was still not responding perfectly, but at least he seemed stronger, and it looked as if he could go on. Kem asked the poacher to provide him with directions to go somewhere, anywhere, where he could gain help for the young lad. The old man advised him they should keep walking straight, with the wind at their backs, until they reached an old straight road. From there, they should head north. The poacher offered to take the monks to the road, but Kem refused the offer, because he didn't want to creep along at the poacher's slow speed. Kem needed to get moving promptly. He still had to carry Elis, who remained floppy with fatigue. Even now, Elis did not react to stimuli, but at least he was not comatose.

So Kem and Elis made their way through the tangle of forest, burring, snagging, and snaring themselves on thorn, root and bramble. Finally, after a complicated journey, the Music Bearers stumbled out of the ancient timberland and onto a drover's road. Kem tied Elis to his back of with a prayer rope, so he would not fall-off during transport. They headed north.

After a while, Kem saw the edge of a small parish. They climbed a muddy slope to go around the boundaries of this village. They didn't want to be noticed. Looking down from a hill, Kem saw how far they had walked. From this vantage point, he also had some idea of the long trek ahead. The road shot straight into the horizon — and there it disappeared.

At first, Kem decided it would be safer to walk alongside the road, not upon it. But this became progressively hard. It seemed impossible to make progress through the brambles, thorn bushes and nettles. There was another problem too: they were still 'dressed as monks.' If strangers saw them on the road, they would surely report the sighting. Kem made a tough decision. The boy's long-term health was at risk, so Kem walked along the drover's road, in plain sight. He figured that at least he might get some furlongs walked out if he stuck to the road.

Near dusk, Kem supposed they closed-in on another parish. This one seemed bigger than the last. Lanterns gleamed in the distance, and he could hear farmhouse animals fussing. Kem negotiated deliberately around the edge of this village. He almost stirred a bunch of wild geese that were contentedly munching fresh grass in a water meadow on the Eastern side. After trudging a wet valley, he crossed a slow running stream. The tired monk edged his way across country until the village was behind.

Across the horizon, not too distant, was a group of trees. This ancient woodland was a screen for several chapter buildings, hidden by deciduous shrubs and hedgerows. It was the home-building of the Canons Regular, also known as the Nitrian Brothers.

Kem and Elis arrived at the Nitrian canonry as night drew in. The noise made by Kem limping along the driveway to the main house attracted attention from the Canons. One of the Nitrian brothers rushed out to help. Then, others were hailed to help. Someone ushered inside the Music Bearers and Kem watched as Elis was transferred to a special place — a closed chamber — where he might be offered proper medical care.

They took Kem to a simple cell where he was supplied with honey-bread. Then he was presented with warm herbal tea, made from barley and ground apple. Kem soon fell into a profound slumber on a mattress made of fresh bedstraw.

∽

An elegant older lady came to see both of the Music Bearers while they slept.

She had been staying with the Nitrian Brothers, briefly.

. The elegant lady watched Kem's deep breaths. She inspected his hands. He did not even stir as she tenderly lifted his arm to inspect the fingers. The lacerations on the tips were clear enough. They were the give-away sign. This young man had newly plucked, tuned or played a stringed instrument. Probably a phorminx.

The graceful lady then went to see the younger monk.

He was just a teenager. He seemed exhausted, malnourished, and seriously dehydrated. He was the most precious thing she had seen for a long time. He was, undoubtedly, a novice Music Bearer.

This boy is the future of music, she thought. If music is to endure in a murky world, then this one *has to survive.* To ensure the survival of music, sacrifices had to be made.

She could not know, at that stage, what sacrifices they had already made to protect this boy. But she knew in her heart what sacrifices had to be made in the future. He was the future of music. She was the history of music.

After visiting the two slumbering Music Bearers, the refined lady went to see the Leader of the Nitrian Congregation. She explained she would leave the Canonry immediately.

'I'm sorry to hear that, Lord-Lady Temenos. You have not yet thoroughly recovered from your maladies. I have yet to heal your hands. I wanted to create some medicines you might need...'

'Yes, Father, but I'm sorry I have to go. The arrival of those poor, unfortunate brothers at your door has caused me to reconsider my position —'

Once she had seen the monks, and had recognised them as fellow Music Bearers, she knew she had to buy them time. A diversion was called for. She realised she was the only person alive who could create a diversion that was large enough to put a Hound off the scent. These brothers had evidently been 'on the run' for a while. Most likely, the hunt-team approached them rapidly — were perhaps nearby. Ready to make a kill. They would be in the neighbourhood right now. Tracking the blood.

If she could distract or divert the scrutiny of those hunters, for long enough, she might provide the Music Bearers with enough time to recover strength and move to a safer place.

'I need to take some things with me. I need my horse saddled for travel. And I need to remove your altar screen and take a mallet...'

The Leader of the Congregation listened to the request and nodded shrewdly. 'Take what you need Lord-Lady. God speed. May you be blessed.'

After this, Temenos took one last glimpse of the sleeping Music Bearers. She vowed she would do everything in her power to help save them.

Then Lord-Lady Temenos left the Nitrian Canonry for the last time.

She rode into the night.

Upon an alternative path laid by God.

∽

The old poacher did not go straight to the authorities to collect his reward.

He left it a day-or-so before he travelled to the Burgess of the nearest settlement. To report the 'sighting' of the Music Bearers.

It is true that he wished to secure himself a reward—but far more important than that was the conservation of his own hide. If anyone, somehow, ever discovered he had sheltered two outlaws, he could certainly expect interrogation, torture, and punishment. But if he could contrive a compelling story about his encounter with the holy men, he might stay alive. Even if it meant he betrayed the trust of those good Music Bearers, who had shown him nothing but peace and benevolence.

So early in the morning, he made way to the office of the Burgess. He waited until noon, before the clerk saw fit to see him.

'Hurry, I haven't got all day for a stupid hypocrite like you —' the clerk said barked.

'I wanted to report a sighting of two fugitive brothers. I want to claim my reward...' the old poacher explained. 'I saw an adult and a child. They headed towards the canonry of the Nitrian Brothers—'

'How do you know where they headed?' asked the clerk. It was a good question.

'They travelled the old Roman road. The boy was being carried by an older friar, who seemed lame. I figured they headed for the Nitrian hospital—'

'But how did you know these two were fugitives? They may have been Benedictines for all you know. Were they dressed as monks?'

'Yes, they were,' the poacher replied.

'In that case, the men you saw were not Music Bearers. You waste my time. Everyone knows the heretics take the guise of other workingmen. They disguise themselves as toolmakers, scriveners, and artisans. They would never travel together. They only walk alone. And they never 'dress' as monks. This is a crazy story. I should caution you against wasting my precious time. What day did you see these brothers passing?'

'T'was the day before yesterday, Sir.'

'And time?'

'A little after dawn.'

'You rogue! What were you doing on the road at dawn? I have a good mind to report you to the Verderer's men. You realise, I hope, that poaching is a crime punishable by death?'

'Yes sir. I was not a-poaching, honest. I was trying to find dry kindle-wood, that I was.'

'Get out. If I find you were poaching, I'll have your skin off your back. Do you understand?'

'I do.'

But the old poacher felt absolved. He'd washed his hands of any responsibility for the Music Bearers. The matter had been honestly reported. It was not his fault that the jumped-up clerk did not believe him. If the brothers had escaped, well, there was no harm in that. Because it was the will of God. However, the poacher had preserved his own skin.

The clerk of the Burgess made a note of the old rogue's report, anyway. That was his job, he did it earnestly.

A few days after he filed his report, a fox-faced, black-hooded monk entered the office of the Burgess's clerk. He asked to see reports of any recent sightings of suspected Music Bearers. The clerk of the Burgess showed him the last report, the report from the old poacher. The black-hooded monk seemed happy with this sighting. It was about two monks traversing the old Roman road. He was principally interested in the fact that they travelled to the Nitrian Canonry. The black-hooded monk rolled a silver coin in the air, and let it drop onto the ledger: 'Make sure that the informant gets this reward...' his fanged-cross glinted in the morning light.

'Yes, brother,' the clerk replied.

But, once the Black Hound had left the office, the clerk pocketed the money.

'The hell I will give this coin away to a ruffian...' he said loudly. 'I filed the report and questioned the man. So the reward is legitimately mine to keep.'

He felt a stab of fairness run right through him. 'I did well today,' he whispered.

30

THE CANTICLE OF THE FIRST MISSION

Elis satisfactorily recovered from the effects of his sea-journey.

The Nitrian brothers cared for him and nursed him back to full health. Once fit for travel, the Nitrians organised safe transport for both him and Kem, out of the area. Their chosen method of transportation was a wagon containing barrels of salted fish. Unfortunately for Elis, he had to travel in one of the empty foul-smelling barrels — it had been punched with holes and filled with straw. But the smell of fish helped to put off guards who might stop them on their travels.

Kem rode up front with the carter. They made their way to the next safe community, where Elis was to continue his training and his development as a Music Bearer. The journey was uncomfortable, and it lasted almost two days. Elis was glad when he eventually arrived, late afternoon, at a humble courtyard in a cloistered community.

The building was on the edge of a small village. The original clerics of this priestly house were long gone, and so the Music Bearers had been using the dilapidated mission-building as a base for their training for over a year. They taught six young people at the centre. With just two tutors. They were glad to see Elis, and they were even more pleased to see Kem — he added to the staff.

Typically, a novice would expect to be trained for at least six more at a centre like this. But things were getting desperate. The Black Hounds were having considerable successes all over the realm. They were tracking down and capturing all the Music Bearers. It was never safe to stay in one place for too long. It was also clear that the local communities required more help from the Bearers. So novices had to be trained fast. Faster than was judicious.

The most important lessons that Elis had yet to learn was how to help those in need. These lessons included instructions on how to provide basic music therapies. Elis already possessed a good understanding about how to create soothing sounds. He already knew how to utilise the shapes found in rhythms and songs. But now he would learn how some of these shapes would create a sense of peace, to soothe listeners. He would also learn that other shapes would urge listeners to become more active, perhaps agitating them into action.

Elis learnt how music was communication. Music could talk immediately to a person's heart — even though that person might not understand any actual words or any conventional language.

Elis had to learn how to assess what type of treatments were called for. Then how to provide the best treatments that were available. It would take a good deal of experience before he would be adept at the craft of Music Bearing. But they expected Elis to practice repeatedly the techniques and explained he had to be ready to apply them in half-a-year.

Elis also had to learn one more thing: a 'trade' or a skill — something that he could conduct with some aptitude — that was over-and-above his skills as a Music Bearer. That was because this trade or skill would be his assumed role when he was travelling. They would expect him to travel separately and pose, with credibility, as an itinerant craftsman. He would have to assume a false identity. Clearly, Elis could not travel as a monk or friar because this would raise many questions and prompt suspicions. Neither could he reveal his true identity or true calling — unless the secret town consul had prepared such a thing.

The idea of the town-consuls fascinated Elis. His tutors explained that almost every town had a consul. These consuls lived amongst the people. They were the female members of their secret society. They were girls similar to his beloved Cinnamon — always 'foundlings' — the community had brought them up to provide a lifetime of service.

They would expect Elis to contact one of these female consuls through a series of protocols. The protocols were secret signs, codes, and passwords, and they had to be committed to memory in the manner all other information was kept — through song.

Even the geography of a region had to be memorised through song. Music Bearers carried no maps. So details of placenames, rivers, hilltops, moors, ridges and ley-lines were all stored through something they called plainchant. Plainchant was a wonderful way to learn facts and was an easy way to retain and recall information.

Little by little, Elis formed 'pictures' in his mind about the geography of an entire region. He could go through various rhymes and chants in his head, and these would help him pin-point certain way-markers or places of interest on the 'map' in his mind. The length of pauses calculated the distances between sites. Slower rhythms suggested hard going. Proportions, say, for example, stronger sounds or more emphatic tones, highlighted the sizes of forests or lakes.

Elis was eager to start a mission on his own. He was excited to meet a consul — a girl. He hoped and prayed he would meet Cinnamon again. And she would remember him.

~

On his first true mission as a Music Bearer, his mentor, Kem, would accompany Elis.

The mission was to be a challenging test.

This first mission would form part of a final assessment. The target settlement was a community a few miles from a large market town known as Castle Acre.

Before Elis left for this, his first mission, Kem wanted to impart one last lesson.

Kem held a stick and pointed the end towards an insignificant creature on the ground.

'Notice how the ant works...' Kem told Elis. 'He is a free spirit — beholden to no other. Yet he is part of a living hive. He shares the same body but works alone. For the worker, like this one, danger is everywhere. Everything in nature despises him. Yet he is part of one body. He never forgets that the love of God shines upon him.'

Elis looked on, fascinated by this tiny creature. The ant seemed to understand that he was being observed — so he ran around in circles to show how happy he was. After a little while, the ant scampered to a tiny pebble. There he came face to face with another ant.

'Watch how your ant interacts with the other one...' said Kem.

Both ants touched tentacles. It seemed as if both jumped back in shock. It was a small jump. But the jump seemed important. Because Kem harrumphed and said, 'There! Behold.'

After that interaction, the ant Elis watched ran faster. This time, the ant ran in an altogether different direction, leaving the other ant to run back the safety of the nest.

'They will use their special, secret signals to inform others of danger. They will warn each other of significant changes. They will share information about where the best syrup can be discovered,' Kem said. 'Of course, we look for souls to feed, not sweet-stuffs for our Hive Queen...but otherwise we are similar creatures.'

The ant scuttled across crumbled steps towards an old, cobbled courtyard. Elis observed the ant all the way, as the tiny creature gambolled down. The little creature made way to a weed thistle. And then ran towards a small pool of water.

The ant stopped at the edge of the pool, to peer at the surface as if it looked down at its own reflection.

At that moment, a black shape swooped.

A dark shadow fell on the ant. A crow landed near the water.

A cruel beak nipped out and snatched up the little ant.

'Danger is everywhere...' Kem said wistfully.

∽

After this last lesson, Elis travelled under his assumed name. He purported to be a scrivener. Part of his recent training was to develop enough skills to convince others he was what he said he was: a travelling craftsman. To these ends, he'd studied the craft of scrivening up to apprenticeship level. He carried the guild-papers too and wore a guild pin that authorised him to work in the assumed role. A scrivener did not carry any tools or paraphernalia — this is how they liked it. The Music Bearers preferred to travel light.

On his journey to his first mission, Elis stopped one night at a friendly hostel. He paid for his keep with a couple of small coins. He had never made payment by coin before. He felt entertained by the concept. It seemed unfair to him that he could swap brown circles for something as precious as food. But Kem, his mentor, told him that a scrivener paid by coin. And that's why Elis must learn this strange custom.

As Elis approached the next village, the place where he would perform his first mission, Elis practiced how to 'become' his alter ego.

Kem explained how he had to 'undo' his original personality — even try to take on new traits — so anyone who met him would remember these observables. They would broadcast this misinformation to all those who sought knowledge about him. It was the type of trickery that would be essential if Elis wanted to disguise his proper mission — and to avoid any detection.

Counter-surveillance was an integral part of his new life as a Music Bearer. Elis was required to be vigilant of his surroundings at all times, aware of anyone who might watch him, no matter how innocent they might seem.

Kem also asked him to make several detours along the way. Sometimes this meant doing U-turns along a path, so he might end up approaching people he had passed earlier in the day. At other times, he would start on a track that would take him in entirely the wrong direction – before taking a detour, rather late in the day. The fresh path would lead back to where he first started. All these precautions were doubtless necessary because, as Kem frequently told him, spies and enemies lurked everywhere. Behind every tuft, barrel, and hassock.

Eventually, Elis was drawn to a lovely settlement that was hidden behind a dark curtain of green trees. The place had a few well-thatched buildings and pens of livestock on the outer limits. Chickens ran openly in the forest nearby.

Kem told Elis that he should approach the village consul. He pointed out the runes, carved into stone, near the well-spring. He invited the young friar to decipher these runes. They then both went to find the consul.

Kem watched from a distance as Elis completed the coded protocols that needed to be recited, correctly and meticulously, with the consul. This was before she would talk to him.

The coded greeting satisfied the female consul, so she welcomed Elis to the village. She ignored Kem, who stood some way off, but she seemed aware that he regarded his charge.

The town-consul explained two children suffered from what she described as a kind of 'sleeping sickness.' Elis was worried that the cause of the symptoms could be some infectious disease. So it may not be something that he could handle.

'Have you reported this disease to a healer?' Elis asked.

'Yes,' the consul said. 'The sisters came to inspect the children. They agreed that an infection did not cause the disease. They examined the adults of the village, too. They could not find signs upon the children's skin.'

Elis knew what this meant. They had taught him that marks, red shapes, or spots on the skin, might alert healers to a malady or a disease. 'The sisters could not find any blemishes on the bodies. So they believe a state of mind caused the symptoms—' the consul confirmed.

'Do these people have cradle songs?' Elis asked. The cradlesong was the 'seed' for all music therapies. The cradlesong was the most important mechanism utilised by the Music Bearers.

'Yes, they have cradle-songs. They understand the old ways. They are in tune with such things'

They invited new mothers to allow the Music Bearers to provide new-borns with a cradlesong, so this answer caused Elis to smile. Cradle songs would be chanted smoothly to the baby, whilst rocking.

These cradlesongs would 'stay' with the child for life. They, the Bearers, could use the song to 'unlock' the mind or mood of a person. A brain engages with music if it 'understands' it and has experience with it.

The town consul took Elis, the freshly trained Music Bearer, to meet the concerned mothers. They took him to a warm stable where a small child slept. The child's mother joined him there. Elis asked broad questions. Then he quizzed the mother about the child's health history. Elis asked if they had tried any conventional remedies. The mother said they had tried everything but that they could not awaken the child.

'And do you have a cradle-song for your babe?' Elis asked.

The mother said yes, she had.

'It is safe for you to sing that song to now, show me how you do it...'

The mother took the child into her arms and rocked him tenderly. She hummed. Elis thought the rocking motion was a little too fast. Perhaps the hum was not chanted at a high enough register. So Elis showed the mother how to rock the baby at the correct rate. He recognised the cradlesong she had used so he asked if he could take the child from her. She agreed, so Elis cradled the boy and copied the cradlesong, singing it in lower tones than the mother — starting deeper, then increasingly reaching a higher pitch towards the end. This was the first time he had indeed performed a song with an actual living baby. In training, they had always used dolls stuffed with straw. The baby felt warm in his arms. Elis became nervous as he rocked the child. He repeated the cradlesong several times.

'Repetition is important,' Elis told the mother. She smiled and nodded.

She knew that familiar music increased the likelihood of a response. A brain processes songs differently to spoken language. So songs worked well when normal spoken words did not.

Spontaneous improvement was not unheard of, though not expected. Elis had to manage delicately the expectations of the mother. The child did not respond. There was no immediate success. But repeating the cradlesong regularly might help.

The second child that Elis saw that day had been in a coma for ten days, with no signs of improvement. He had taken a tumble from a barn roof. So his circumstances were different.

Elis tried a cradlesong on this child too. But was also keen to try some mechanical vibrations. He searched for a wide reed that he might use to create a low-pitched sound. Once he found the reed, he produced a pipe.

Elis played the pipe gradually, with long deep puffs. Whilst he did this, he asked the mother to sing the babe's cradlesong. He knew he needed to create low vibrations, like a drone, if this was to work at all. He knew the sound should sit 'beneath' the higher-register of the triggering cradlesong performed by the mother.

The mother found that the music relaxed her. She felt, honestly, that healing happened. She acknowledged she had experienced a spiritually uplifting event.

By the time Elis had left the village, he felt happy he had passed on good advice. He felt sure that he had at least started some useful remedies. Though he felt less happy that he hadn't seen immediate results.

But he had tried his best.

∼

Once they left the settlement, Kem gave Elis the feedback he needed. Kem said he was pleased with the progress his young student made. He told him he was especially impressed with how Elis dealt with the 'disappointment' of not providing solutions or miracle cures — because not all therapies were instantly effective. Elis had come to terms with failure as well as success.

He was now ready for independent missions. It surprised Elis to learn this news: he had expected the training to go on far longer, but Kem was adamant he should begin on actual missions. At once.

So the two Music Bearers held each other for a while. They gazed into each other's eyes. They had been through so much together. But now it was time for Elis to travel alone. Kem directed him onto a road that headed towards Castle Acre, then kissed him tenderly on the cheek.

'God be with you every step of the way,' Kem said, then he waved him off.

Elis started the next stage of his journey with bubbles of excitement in his belly.

31

THE CANTICLE OF THE SCRIVENER

The new Music Bearer named Elis arrived at Castle Acre on the following day.

He did not need a mentor any longer. He now acted independently, as an entirely trained Bearer.

Elis had disguised himself as a scrivener. He carried papers, but they had been falsified. These papers allowed him to perform as a scrivener. He also wore their guild-pin, a pin that had been plundered. This marked him as a craftsman of his profession.

His first task was to locate the secret town-consul for the community at Castle Acre. As they had trained him to do, he found the well-spring in the middle of the market square. Every town had a well. It was typically placed centrally. They had taught Elis that a Bearer would find clues at a well-spring. Such clues would lead him to the right place.

Sure enough, at the well, he found strange markings engraved on the outer ring of stones. Deciphering these elaborate engravings was difficult, but after a while, he worked out the code. It informed him that had to make his way to the brew-house.

He entered the stone courtyard, where he was approached by the brewer's wife.

She sized him up. Although dressed as a scrivener, the boy was too pasty and thin to be a tradesman. He wore wearing a brooch, but he had positioned it in quite the wrong place. It seemed this lad was malnourished and had wandered to the town alone. Yet a true craftsman would have been well-fed and would have travelled in the company of others. The brewer's wife had seen young lads like this many times before. She could see straight through his disguise. She knew precisely what he was. He was a Music Bearer. God! They got younger every day!

'I suppose you want to see my girl?' she asked.

Elis smiled at the woman. He recalled the special coded greeting he needed to share with the consul when she arrived. He went over it calmly in his mind. This was to be only the second time he'd used it. The coded greeting had to be performed flawlessly or the consul would not deal with him. The rhythms were especially hard to get right.

After he practiced the coded greeting in his mind, a girl appeared from the brew-house. She was clad in a plain smock with a clean apron that covered a long skirt. She appeared young, about the same age as Elis.

Elis realised he did not need to use his special coded greeting on her. Because he knew precisely who this girl was. His heart sang with joy. He felt a special type of happiness that threatened to overwhelm him.

This girl was his Cinnamon.

They embraced. They held each other hard. Neither could speak. They cuddled. Tears escaped from the girl's closed eyes. Elis felt his throat squeeze shut. His eyes blazed, too. He thought he might cry.

After a while, hugging in the brew-yard, the girl sobbed. 'I hate this place —' she told softly said.

Elis silenced her by stroking her hair. He attempted to soothe her sobs. He never thought he would see her again. Ever. Yet now she was in his arms. They should never have been separated in the original place.

'I hate this place,' she said again.

Elis peered deep into her eyes, and she shared his gaze. She already felt safe because she was with someone who loved and respected her. She wanted to be away from this place. Away from all of it — forever.

'They sent another consul—' she explained. 'A girl who is much more experienced than I am. I think she has been sent to spy on me. They sent her to watch over me because I'm useless. I am sure of it. This other consul is high-and-mighty, and she lives in the Royal residence...' Cinnamon continued her sobs. 'She reports back to them — telling them how useless I am. Elis, I can't do this anymore—'

He calmed her with a soft kiss on the brow. Then he rocked her.

Elis had already decided what to do. Tonight they would run away together. Flee from this madness..

32

THE CANTICLE OF THE BELLS

It became too late to travel, so once Zadock had obtained valuable information, from the Burgess's Registrar, about the fleeing Music Bearers and their whereabouts, the Black Hound dismissed his Palatine guards — he pointed to a comfortable inn on the fringe of the village, there they might settle down for the night. The Hound then found himself a cool place under the skies to retire, as was his routine. He unfailingly found most comfort when he exposed himself to the harsh elements. The sleeping place he located was partially out of the wind and the threat of light rain. He crouched under thatched eaves that belonged to a parish long-house. Zadock felt more fatigued than normal — he felt especially weakened since their perilous channel crossing. So he pushed his habit close around his neck, then pulled his long hood around his ears. After prayers, he closed his eyes.

∾

The first light of the morning had not even broken through dark clouds, when Zadock became startled by a strange sound. His eyes fluttered open. He tried to understand what he heard. Then it happened again. A distant gong. Some hellish chime.

It was a weird noise and sounded depraved, corrupting to his ears. The Hound actually thought he had dreamed it. But then he heard the chime again, so knew it wasn't a nightmare. He tried to put a word to the insidious intonation, then realised, with a shock that run through his veins, precisely what the sound was. It was the toll of a bell. And a bell was a musical instrument. A bell was banned. Utterly illegal.

The bell clashed in the night. It rang a mysterious message. They could only use the message in the most extreme circumstances. It was a message of calling. The bell called out in the night for Zadock. It waited for the Black Hound to respond.

He stood and stretched his muscles. There it was again. Chung!

The sound echoed around the village walls. It alarmed geese in the field. The clatter of birds rose in the sky, honking in fearful agitation. The next beast to become unnerved by the strange signal was the Hound's torturer, Tartax. He stumbled through the front door of the inn and made his way promptly to the Black Hound.

'How many? How many times did it ring?' Zadock questioned, snappily.

But the torturer did not seem to know. He vigorously scratched his head, trying to eliminate invisible bugs in his hair in an attempt to get his brain functioning. The strange unearthly noise confused him. Chung!

'There it goes again. Get to the home of the Burgess and find out where the sound comes from...'

Tartax grunted agreement and made his way to the best house in the village; the house where the Burgess lived. Meanwhile, Zadock went into the inn to wake the other Palatine guard and prepare him for an immediate trip. Because, unquestionably, they would travel soon to the source of that infernal noise. Chung!

∽

Tartax returned from his sprint to the Burgess's house. He brought along with him a bleary-eyed companion.

'This is the Burgess...' announced the torturer, out of breath.

The Black Hound gazed at the stupid-looking Burgess, with his stout-faced and gangly features. He cast him the most contemptuous stare he could manage. 'How many times did it ring?' Zadock questioned. 'How many?'

This direct line of questioning agitated the thickly fleshed burgher. He gawped at this strange vagabond who barked questions — a thin man dressed as a monk — and wondered whether he should bother answering. But the fanged-cross hanging around the monk's neck caused him to bite his tongue and think twice about how he should proceed.

'Nine, brother. Nine chimes—'

'From where?' the Hound shouted.

'Presumably from the only place that has a turret. The tower at Hoxne Priory. It is about fifty furlongs from here. The sounds must originate from on high, so I guess it's from out there. Everywhere else is flat.'

Zadock took in this information, then waved forwards his guards.

'There is no time to lose,' he directed this comment to the Burgess. 'You must bring us horses. We will need your best man to guide us. We will ride to Hoxne as soon as we can. We need to start right away. Bring horses now.'

The Burgess was about to complain about being given orders from a mere monk. And so early in the morning. He considered taking issue with this dishevelled cleric in black — perhaps to question his authority. He found the monk's manner insulting. They should not order a man of his position about. But Tartax, the torturer, glared with a sinister expression. He licked along the top row of yellow teeth, to imply that the Burgess might be devoured, once killed — if he thought of hesitating or arguing. So the fat Burgess bowed in obedience, then departed into the morning air to find horses. And to scream and shout at his own followers — who wouldn't question his authority.

~

Just before the sun had risen across far-most flatlands in the east, Zadock and his two men, with the Burgess's appointed guide, headed towards Hoxne.

The monks who so begrudgingly greeted them when they eventually arrived at Hoxne did not greet them with the equal speed or indulgence that matched the rapidity and urgency of their race to the Priory , where the only tower in the area was located. Two grumpy coenobites came to welcome the horsemen, almost reluctant in their sluggishness. They took possession of the horses and took the animals away, then two others beckoned the strangers to come inside.

Zadock reasoned that their *Horarium*, a strict timetable of prayers and devotions, must have been confounded by the fuss and commotion caused by the tolling bell. So, although he silently cursed their disrespect, he excused the coenobites for their lethargy and crabbiness.

The Black Hound and his men were grudgingly invited into the main Priory building. Zadock dismissed the guide from the village, turning a coin for him to catch, and thanking him for his service. The man seemed satisfied with the role he had played in these events. He rode promptly back to his bed. And doubtless spent the penny he'd earned on ale.

Before entering the main building of the Priory, Zadock checked across the roof structure at Hoxne. A tower of flint and mud loomed over other squat buildings. The tower had two oval, dark openings. The tower looked just like the body of a monstrous tawny owl. The owl-shaped turret loomed high, silhouetted against a dark red sky. So that's where the sound came from, thought Zadock. Though now, thank the Lord, it had ceased its horrible clanging.

Once inside the main priory building, the Black Hound approached a large door that was situated halfway along a primary transept. The coenobites conducted him and his guards beyond cloistered zones towards a large semi-circular apse. Here, the Black Hound motioned to his guards. It was time for them to leave him. Zadock asked a coenobite to take his men to the refectory. His Palatine guards did not have to observe any strictness of order — they were free to eat, sleep and rest, as they pleased. Zadock assumed they would be most comfortable in the frater house. The main meal of the day was far away, even for monks, but bread, soup and even cold beer might be found for a weary traveller who entered these holy walls. That was the monastic way. Obedience and charity.

After his trusted guards had departed, going to grab their food and drink, Zadock prepared with prayer. Then he entered the modestly decorated apse. The Black Hound made his way along the walkway, past empty rows of pews, to arrive at the most impressive seat of all. Like the others, it was a simple wooden chair, but this one was placed high on a platform at the centre of an oval chamber. Upon this dais chair sat the Prior of Hoxne. The Prior was a man with a whitish beard, and Zadock guessed he might be aged about forty summers. He had slender fingers and a pinkish hue to his lower arms. Zadock speculated that it had been many years since this lump-of-a-man had done a day's arduous work. The Prior seemed manifestly cold. Indeed, it's true that a nasty draught had fermented around the high-domed area, so the high-cleric had pulled a large black cloak around his neck, to cover his bony shoulders. He wore a black hat, a nightcap, and had a blanket of sackcloth across his knees.

'We must persevere despite these many obstacles...' the Prior said, as Zadock approached.

As was customary, the Black Hound bended his knee, then kissed the extended finger-ring of his monastic superior. 'We must fight for our true King,' the Prior continued, ignoring the kiss as if it came from a nobody.

'Indeed, indeed—' Zadock agreed. But what was this all about?

'There is a cosmic battle going on, you know, between good and evil. The horned one is all around us...' the Prior continued to mumble. 'That is why we choose to live honestly and apologetically. So we can consider cosmic events, in prayer. But today, we have been overwhelmed by demonic forces. It is a test of faith—'

Zadock had enough of this rubbish. 'Forgive me, Excellency, but you called me here. What is this about? Why did you make the call of the nine bells? Why did you summon me?'

'I my son? Do you think I called you?' The Prior seemed visibly shocked by this outrageous accusation. He brought his delicate fingertips to his fleshy cheeks, then squeezed them together, forcefully. It was a gesture of dismay and horror. 'Not me. No! Not me, my son. I am not the guilty one. The sinner created that terrible sound. The evil sound was created by the one you seek—'

More conundrums, thought Zadock. Is nothing easy anymore?

'Where is this guilty one that you speak of?' Zadock asked, hoping to get a straight answer.

'Arrested, bound. Kept prisoner in our dungeon. Confined. For trial. Taken and held.'

'Good, take me to him then — so I may see the culprit for myself—'

'Him?' said the Prior with all the astonishment he could muster. 'Him? Him?' The Prior waved his hands about dramatically. 'No, my son. It is not a him. It is a her. We have a female penitent in our dungeon. And she awaits your interrogation...'

33

THE CANTICLE OF THE HOXNE PRISONER

They showed Zadock the way to their prison at Hoxne Priory. This was where any sin-filled monks might be detained overnight, so they would reflect on delinquent ways.

Almost immediately, Zadock realised the cell was not big enough for his 'specialist' techniques of interrogation. He heard the Prior trailing behind. The older man already puffed. He was out of condition.

'Help us persevere. Help us persevere,' the Prior mumbled, as he shuffled along. He played absently with his prayer-beads.

Eventually, Zadock arrived at the dungeon. He peered inside, not knowing what to expect. At the far end of a simple square room, with no natural light, was a bed fashioned from wooden planks. No bed of straw for this prisoner, thought Zadock. The only dim light came from torches situated in the hallway. The make-shift cell had no bars, but a series of wicker spindles. The spindles had a doorway knotted into them. It would be easy to push out the whole contraption out, thought Zadock. So much for a dungeon!

In one corner of this holding-room knelt a nun.

The nun wore a grey habit covered with a frayed black scapular. She had placed a white scarf around her neck. The veil fully exposed her face and a prominent aristocratic-looking forehead. She tied loosely a brown rope around her waist and had her arms crossed in meditation, with a look of serenity upon her face.

Although he was uncertain of it, Zadock guessed the kneeling woman was about fifty summers old. She was not overweight but did not seem slender either. He imagined she had doubtless enjoyed a good, rich life. Zadock noted the nun had an air of calm steadiness about her. This seldom appeared in others, although he recognised the qualities in himself.

This should be interesting, he thought. To interrogate a nun that was self-composed. Let's see if we can destroy her calm and that balance! She will not allow her secrets to flow freely. No, not this one. The music-finder would have to be smart and deviant if he were to exploit his skills on this evildoer. Zadock allowed a ripple of excitement to flow through his muscles at the prospect. Then, promptly, he chided himself for feeling gratification. He promised that he would punish himself later for this depraved thinking.

'You are my inquisitor?' the female asked.

Zadock did not expect the nun to speak first. In fact, he had not expected her to speak at all. In his experience, they never spoke. They prayed in silence because they knew what was to come. So her words came as a shock.

'Not I, my lady,' Zadock replied. 'I am simply an implement. A holy vessel. Like yourself.'

She sniffed. 'When will I be quizzed? I have much to tell you...'

'I see,' said Zadock. He felt confounded by her openness. Her willingness to engage was remarkable and also puzzling.

He turned to the Prior. 'What happened? Tell me how you found her...'

The forwardness of this question and the Hound's boorish manner irritated the Prior. The disharmony and chaos caused by the whole incident disturbed him and he didn't like to be addressed in a familiar way by an underling. 'Like you, and most of the Hoxne Hundred, that terrible sound awakened me. It sounded like the gate of heaven clanging shut.' He shuddered when he recalled the evilness of the sound. 'Their sound hath been heard in his coming...' he quoted. 'So I sent my coenobites to the high tower. There they found this female, though she was not dressed in the way you see her now. You should note that. When we found her, she wore cloth of rich and ornate quality. The plain habit you see her now dressed in, she recently turned to. She discarded her fineries once she entered this holy place.'

'Yes, *yes*...' Zadock said. He was not interested in what she was wearing upon her skin— for heaven's sake! *Just get on with it, you old goat,* he thought. He hissed under his breath.

'She was positioned by the apertures in our tower. We found her in possession of a flat metal screen. Like a shield. Or large platter. But whatever it is, it was a most unpleasant thing. She had with her a hammer. Of some quality. With that hammer, she was found hitting shots onto the shiny metal plate. The terrible noise she created with the plate and hammer... well, they were evil. And those sounds made you appear.'

'I need to see this noise making device,' Zadock told him.

'Yes, of course. The evil thing is left in place,' replied the Prior 'We would not touch it, for fear of contamination. And damnation.'

'I'm glad your people did not touch it. You will need to leave it in place until it I can handle it properly.'

Zadock then turned his attention to the nun in the cell. 'If you're so happy to talk, answer me this.... How did you know how many times the bell should toll?'

The nun looked at the Black Hound with a serene gaze. 'Nine Bells. Nine bells. Untouched by man. That is the signal to call you a Hound from slumber, is not it?'

Yes, it was. It was a signal as old as time, though nobody had used it in centuries. How did she this odd nun have such intimate knowledge of the ways of the Hound?

'We'll talk about such things later, sister,' Zadock suggested.

~

He headed back to the main body of the priory house with the Prior.

'Of course, there will need to be full investigation. Complete and fair. I have sent word to the Bishop,' muttered the old Prior.

'You did what?' Zadock hollered. He could not control his growing impatience with this foolish old man.

The Prior looked alarmed. Then took control of himself. He managed a few deep breaths before he gained his confidence to continue: 'Well, I needed to report this, my son. So I sent a rider to the Bishop's Palace right away. With word of what happened. And my messenger informed his Lordship that we captured a Music Bearer. And invited him to organize a formal process—'

Damn it! thought Zadock. He did not want to be stuck in this hole, waiting around for a show trial to commence. While other prey was — this very hour — sneaked away. He had to capture the other rats too. The ones he had been hunting for days. Or they'd scurry out of sight before he could capture them all. 'Well, I cannot wait for anything like that, Your Excellency. I have other urgent matters to deal with...'

'Oh! I fear it is quite impossible...' The Prior said, with a haughty chuckle. 'You cannot leave now brother.' The Prior managed to recover his full stature. 'I also sent word to the Lord Bishop telling him we have an expert. An expert on such things. And the expert will oversee the investigation until it is possible to organize a plenary session of inquiry. That expert, as I am sure you recognise, my son, is you. You are welcome to stay — as our guest of honour— until we complete the entire process.'

'God help us,' Zadock muttered under his breath.

∼

The following day, as part of his investigations, Zadock went to the strange owl-like tower in the Priory grounds.

From that tall place, the curious sounds had issued on the night that the nun had been captured. Inside the tower, in the uppermost room, he found a metal plate hanging from a beam. A length of rope fixed the plate to a roof joint. The thing hung near one of the eye-shaped openings that looked out from the highest point.

Zadock imagined that the 'thing' the lady had hit during the night was a makeshift semantron — a rudimentary bell like those used in monasteries, in ancient times, before music had been outlawed by the church. In ancient days, it was used to call monks to prayer. Although this semantron was composed of metal rather than made of customary wood. Zadock imagined that the metallic nature of the 'thing' meant it sounded stronger and louder. The nun had made the sound more effective by hanging it from a rope before she struck the plate with a hammer.

Even though he had been a Black Hound all his life, Zadock had seldom seen a musical instrument for real, so this apparatus intrigued him. He had found discarded broken pipes with holes in them and had once seen a little line of catgut strung to a root. But the semantron was the first complete instrument he had seen. So he inspected the components carefully and deliberately. Near the altar plate was the mallet. They had left this resting on the floor. Zadock imagined Temenos had hit the plate with this. The resultant noise must have sounded shocking — the ring from the plate resounding all over the neighbouring countryside.

Zadock cautiously took up the hammer — to weigh the thing in his hands and assess the effect it had when it hit the bell-like semantron.

The shiny metal dish hung there magnificently. It shimmered a little in light breeze. It gleamed in the soft light of the morning. Abruptly, Zadock became tempted to beat the dish with the wooden hammer, himself, just so he could discover musical noise would sound like. Then he scolded himself. Such was the witchcraft of the Music Makers. That such vile impulses could pervert a holy cleric such as him. It was unthinkable.

After leaning out of the window-openings of the tower, to discern what the range and scope of the horizon was like from this prominent place, Zadock scrupulously packaged the 'proof' he had found in the tower. He placed the semantron into a clean bag, then put the rope into a silk purse and the hammer in a leather satchel. He took the exhibits back to the main body of the house where he had one of his guards place the articles in a locked storeroom, a place where they kept community funds. Then he prepared to savagely chastise himself for the feelings of excitement and gratification he'd experienced during the day.

34

THE CANTICLE OF THE INQUISITION

It took over four weeks before the full panoply of a regional Episcopal Inquisition could be adequately organized. Precious time that Zadock the Hound might have spent on the chase. The entourage, due any day now, would include record keepers, oath preservers, guards on horseback, soldiers, prison officers, and teams of lawyers. Of course, all these powerful figures would have their own employees, cooks, handymen, servants, and hangers-on.

The inquisitors had already been chosen directly by the Bishop. They would preside over the session. These were to be assisted by six magisters — senior government officials of the local area. Not only was the soul of a heretic in danger, but also their false teaching endangered the souls of many. So a full and fair trial had to be arranged.

This was frustrating, Zadock thought. Why did 'justice' take so long to organize? If the Pope gave him a competent torturer and the paper authorities he needed, he could 'root out' heresy in just a few days. At a fraction of the cost of putting this 'show trial' on.

There was no doubt about it, justice took time. Plus money and effort. In fact, justice was an industry. An industry created out of fear.

Sometimes Zadock wondered who was most afraid of whom. Most people assumed that the more frightened of the two sides must the heretics. After all, they were the ones who were being persecuted and exterminated. But when he saw just how much effort and expense went into the annihilation of these few men and women, just a handful of souls, it made him understand how frightened The Church must surely be scared of these few folk. He concluded that it was the authorities who were more frightened than the music bearers.

Zadock spent the intervening days before the trial talking to the accused. She had introduced herself as Temenos, and she had freely provided her aliases. She listed her friends. They were all illustrious church men, dignitaries, and merchants. She had provided useful accounts of her travels over the past year. Zadock found all this information to be valuable. Temenos was erudite, charming, and considerate. She was cultured. She was well behaved. In fact, Zadock kept having to recite the line over-and-over to himself: We must purge evil. To stop himself falling for her.

She was a seductive woman. Of course, he reminded himself, she was a sorceress. And that was why she controlled so much power.

After five days of interrogation, during which time he did not have to resort to any torture at all — he was able to assemble a list of five charges against her:

—Creating a subtle confusion of minds
　—Creating an advantage for Satan
　—Violating God's command
　—Cross-dressing

The inquisition took a long time to prepare.

But eventually the day came when officialdom was ready to start the trial of 'Lord-Lady' Temenos.

The talk about town was that this was not just the trial of an important person. It was also a trial for 'music' itself. The whole concept was to be examined and evaluated by this inquest. The case 'Against Music' was to be put neatly by the Cardinal's own chief advocate— the distinguished Dominican Friar named Bernard Morlàs. He had been all around Europe speaking at trials like this one. He was an exceptionally gifted orator and famed for his intolerant attitude when it came to Music Bearers.

Morlàs introduced his main ideas during the first morning of the sessions. He stood and spun around in his red-lined habit. Then he faced the public for the first time. He glared at the gathered masses before speaking directly to the panel of the Inquisition. This was how he reinforced each salient point.

He started with a clear argument. 'By enjoying the gratifying effects of music we are testing the will of God. We are deciding what is good, what is acceptable, what is perfect. This is the first human sin. It is not for us to decide such things. Let us remember that when a man pleases himself, through song, he is also excluding himself from God.'

'We have heard reports that music enslaves a man. He becomes enchanted by the beguiling nature of its tones and vibrations. An enslaved man becomes addicted by the pace. He becomes intoxicated by the pulsations. In the end, the enslaved man succumbs to the compulsion of those demonic forces.'

'Music promotes the growth of hypocrisy. These secret Music Bearers...' At this point Morlàs stared directly into the eyes of Temenos, 'They lie, cheat, hide and hide. They are frauds and deceivers. This, you all know...' He paused, letting the fact sink into the minds of the crowd.

'Music can destroy the reasoning skills of a weak man. If a man is to work and to pray, then he should not allow himself to be incapacitated by music. Yet music slinks into his mind and will take over his muscles if he allows it.'

'Music is sensual in nature, and it seduces the minds of the weak. We've heard stories of women who heard the lewd language of song. And these weak women reported that they experienced the vibrations writhing into their hearts. Like wicked serpents. They also reported that the movements took over their bodily functions ...' Several members of the public grimaced and grinned at this rude suggestion.

'Yes, they were unable to control their own emotions. And unable to control their own bodies...' Morlàs screwed up his face as he said the word 'bodies.' As if he spat out something that was bad.

'In this way, music is a poison. It corrupts the holy vessel. The mind and the body is a temple. It must not be damaged or corrupted by music.' Morlàs looked around before making his next point, 'Music is frivolous. It will turn a man away from the path of true justice. Music takes a lifetime to learn ... Reports have suggested that it takes months and even years of effort. Days spent learning, reciting, and practicing sounds. Time that should have been spent in prayerful contemplation. Or in silence. Or in proper work.'

'The frivolity of music is a transient joy. It is a short-lived sweetness. Music has no longevity. It diverts a man from his true path ...'

'Music is a false doctrine — it is a betrayal of the church. The rhythmic talking or the singing of words and sounds is a sacred practice and should only be practiced by certain religious orders — religious orders that are properly recognized by the Pope. The Vatican should be the only ones to use music. In their private chapels. This is the law.'

'Music enslaves a person's mind— so that he cannot follow a true vocation. We heard the story of a man who believed he was forced to follow the sin of music. He said he could 'hear' the word of God through songs and rhythms. That is a sin.'

'This was unfortunate, because the man in the story soon became deaf to the real call of God. The man was possessed by promise. That promise was instant gratification — pleasure through the music. But the search for enjoyment consumed him, thoroughly. In the end his soul could not be saved...'

'Music is linked to merry-making, sensuality and depravity. We have all heard stories from the past—' At this stage Morlàs Bernard scrutinised the room. He made sure that he glared directly into the eyes of each person. Many looked away, unable to bear his gaze.

'In ancient times, people danced, and they sang merrily. In those days there was a lot of debauchery and licentious behaviour. Their music-meetings were feasts of indulgence. We all know that. We all know that the music-meetings became orgies. These debauched revels always started with the poisoning of the ears...'

'Singing alters the sacred text of a verse or a psalm so that true knowledge is hidden. We have heard stories that the Music Bearers will emphasize certain words or lines of a sacred text —so that they can reveal what they consider to be the underlying 'hidden' messages. They do this by emphasizing chosen words, using pitch and volume. This is a corruption of the true word. The word of God is written. And it is preached by the ordained priesthood. It is a word spoken. Not to be modified or played around with — for fun or for profit. Prayers that are mutilated in this way, when they are translated to the weaker mind, will encourage erroneous beliefs to be formed...'

'Music contains many false statements. We have heard claims that miracles are performed through music. This is a pernicious lie.' Bernard Morlàs slammed his foot down firmly on the floor, to emphasize this point. 'The followers of music seek worldly benefits. When they should really be looking forwards to the kingdom of heaven. The kingdom can only be revealed through the teachings of the properly recognized church. These Music Bearers belong to a sect. They will lead weak men to damnation...'

'Music is esoteric. The practitioners and their adherents claim specialist knowledge. Through arcane practices. This is evil. Music is similar to witchcraft!' At this accusation, several members of the public gasped out loud. One woman even cried. This was the most devastating formal accusation of all. It would surely secure the sentence of death to all believers and followers— if proven true.

'And finally, let us not forget that the Bearers of Music derive a profit from their scurrilous business. They try to tell us that what they do is for our own good. They try to persuade us that their practices are about rejoicing to the Lord. But their work is not so pure and noble as they claim. Look at this woman. You all recognise her. You know how she dresses. Beautifully. You know who wealthy she is...' The crowd began to stare at Temenos.

'She is rich beyond your dreams ... where did this wealth come from? I say that it comes from practicing music. Because music is practiced for profit. It is a worldly corruption — in a very real sense...'

The prosecutor took a long pause, before he made his final statement.

'So, lest Satan should gain an advantage over us— let the Beast and this woman — at this point Bernard Morlàs pointed his finger directly at Temenos — let them know that we are not ignorant of his evil ways...' Morlàs spun around. Then he dramatically opened his arms, as if he wanted to reach out and embrace everyone in the room, to save them from sin.

With this final flourish, the inquisitor managed to briefly connect the defendant with the Devil himself.

∼

After a day of delays discussing 'legal issues' the process was about to get going again, with the allegations being put to Temenos.

This would be the most important task to be performed by the Hound. Zadock had prepared well for this undertaking.

The rest of the time, during the trial, things were out of his hands. He had to sit and watch. Sit and wait. He was not used to being kept waiting. The natural state of a bloodhound was to be actively hunting. Actively sniffing out prey. Ready to pursue.

Hounds do not like being confined to kennels. They certainly do not like to wait.

Zadock was less impressed when he was told by one of the inquisitor's scribes that the panel will probably break soon, for the weekend. He was told that it would re-convene the following Monday. It appeared that the court only sat for two days. What a waste of a seven-night, thought Zadock.

The weekend dragged by. The Priory was so full of folk that many of the followers and their minions had to camp out in the parkland that surrounded the main buildings.

Zadock had his own cell, and he would not share it with a living soul. He sat silently on the cold-slab floor. He meditated and he brooded. For two days.

On Monday, he was ready to set out the charges against the accused.

35

THE CANTICLE OF THE DEFENDANT

*"Est libertas in musica...
et musica in libertate..."*

There is freedom in music...
and music in freedom...

-Lord/Lady Temenos

Temenos sat in silence.

When Zadock stood, the inquisitors asked Temenos to stand as well, so a cleric could formally put allegations to her.

Temenos smiled, then nodded. She stood with her usual grace.

Her gaze fixed steadfastly on the Hound named Zadock. He wore his usual black habit, with the fanged-cross conspicuously displayed. Everyone in the courtroom knew absolutely what Zadock stood for.

They knew he was an efficient and dangerous extricating tool. Like a remarkably sharp bladed lancet. He was engaged, by the Pope, to do the nasty cutting-jobs that others didn't have the callous nature to complete. The Hound's job was excision; his job was to expurgate the rotten flesh found in society. Often, his 'surgery' went amiss. When things went seriously wrong, the incorrect person died. So, for all those reasons, and chiefly because they believed all the stories they had all heard about this terrifying man, Zadock was the most dreaded, and most loathed, individual in the room.

Five charges were made against Temenos.

The court would invite her to respond to each charge. This was the limit of any defence she might offer. She could also make a closing statement. But could not develop other defences. Certainly, no one would be stupid enough to come forward and speak on her behalf.

Once the courtroom had settled, once all coughs and murmurs had ceased, Zadock started. 'The first charge against you, Sister, is that you are guilty of creating a dislocation of subtle minds...' He paused before continuing. 'As has already been stated, music destroys the reasoning skills of man. If man is to work and pray, then his time must not be distracted by music. But you, quite deliberately, went to a tall place. The tower here in this quiet house. This holy priory. And you hit a bell, the bell of St. Catherine. And you hit it loud and frequently during the night —' Zadock checked around the room, to gain maximum dramatic effect on his listeners, just like the chief advocate Morlàs Bernard had done in previous sessions.

'This bell made a troubling noise. It had the effect of disturbing clerics in their sleep. And it wakened an entire community. So, through these deliberate actions — a day's work was wasted. Many of those people sat here today will attest to this. Also, as you know well, Sister, it is explicitly forbidden that any person should construct or possess a musical instrument... What have you to say to this first allegation?'

The courtroom went quiet. Some of the older people pointed their ears toward Temenos so they might hear her response. The inquisitors sat forward, too. They didn't want to miss an answer.

Defendants seldom put up much of a fight. They went cheerfully to the pyre. Sinners like Temenos genuinely believed they were martyrs.

But Lord-Temenos Lady spoke. Confounding expectations of all. 'You say my actions disturbed a community. For that, I apologise ...'

'Is that a confession? Do you plead guilty to the first charge?' Zadock barked.

Though Temenos had *not* finished. She smiled politely toward her inquisitors before she continued. 'I ask you to consider this... Is not thunder and mighty wind created by God? Is sleep not disturbed by things of nature? You hear a sudden crash in the night... Will you not wake? Though it might be an owl in the barn or a fox loose in the pen. Do you put an owl or fox on trial for disturbance? The answer is no. Because such things are part of a natural world.'

'This is ridiculous nonsense. You're talking rubbish,' Zadock grumbled.

The lady continued, 'My point is that the sounds you heard... they were natural sounds. Sounds as ordinary as thunder and wind. Comparable to a cockcrowing in the morning. Or rain pattering on a ledge. These things are not music — and neither was the sound your heard.'

'Are you *sincerely* suggesting you did not go to the tower to play the bell of St. Catherine? There are witnesses who found you doing it. Please remember they will be summoned to this courtroom to provide testimony. They will say they saw you in the tower that night, with a bell—'

'I am guilty of being in the tower...' Temenos said. 'Nothing more...' She stood tall and proud. Determined and resolute.

The inquisitors and magisters viewed her with hidden admiration.

'They found you in the tower with an evil instrument. How do you disavow responsibility for making that demonic noise in the night?' Zadock said.

Temenos looked at him. She honestly felt sorry for Zadock. He was just a boy. A lonely and *motherless* boy, like all the others. Found in a gutter. Raised by monks. Trained for fighting and hunting. They raised others to run and hide. They were no better or worse than this poor boy. All God's children.

'My brother,' she said 'You said that they forbid a person to build a musical instrument. But I tell you this, I did not build any instrument. If you check the metal plate — the one that played that night — you will see it is not any kind of semantron or bell, as you allege. Rather, it is a part of an altarpiece. An altar-plate from a holy place. Ask your witnesses to confirm this. I'm sure they will confirm what I have said to be true. Ask the inquisitors to inspect the metal plate. They will recognise it as a thing that has taken from a high altar...' Temenos paused. She allowed the information to sink in. 'It is said that you forbid a person to possess a musical instrument. But I tell you that the metal plate was not in my possession. The plate was carried by flex and suspended from a ceiling beam. The thing was not in my possession when the witnesses found me—'

'This is intolerable...' spat Zadock.

His face was turned a deep red. How dare she manipulate his words like this?

She went on, 'And you say I hit the bell of St. Catherine. But this is also a false accusation. I was in the tower with a metal plate — that much is true. I admit it. But the mallet struck the metal. Not I — so your true culprit is the mallet... why don't you bring the mallet here for trial?'

'These are all semantics. Puns and word-games. They mean nothing. Yes, it's smart of you to laugh at this holy court. So smart! But we know you hide nothing. You are guilty, are you not?'

The inquisitors and the panel gazed hard at Temenos. They tried to unravel the words she used. Yes, she had been clever. She had adroitly manipulated the Hound's words. But he was right too. She played on meanings and definitions. The wording might be debatable, but the act was proven. She rang the bell in the tower. That was a crime. Pure and simple.

'I offered my defence, as is my right...' Temenos said. 'I was accurate with my words. It is not my fault that you have been sloppy with yours...' She knew this statement would anger Zadock. 'But my point is this: I am a creature of God. Music is a natural thing. The Psalms tell us we should 'Praise him with the sound of cymbals shouting.' I was helping to praise the creator on the morning they found me. Nothing more, nothing less—'

There was much shuffling and whispering around the courtroom. She had made a fair point. They all knew it. Most were aware of the Psalm she referred to.

Zadock looked a lot *less* happy, though. How dare she say his presentation had been sloppy? He attempted to be precise in everything he did. Her suggestion was a scandalous stain on his character. He put the slur out of his mind, lest it might affect the rest of his performance. But, so far, he felt pleased with her defence, because her answers suited him well — he was ready to make his second charge:

'We also accuse you of creating an advantage for Satan...' he shouted, 'Rebellion is a sin, like witchcraft. Stubbornness, of the kind you possess, is iniquity. You have shown to us today that you have a strong streak of rebellion. Your stubbornness does you no favours. It is your refusal to accept the obvious that means you are guilty of the second charge. The charge of rebellion—'

'Rebellion? Who did I resist? Who did I defy?' Temenos asked.

'You defied the church. You resisted our ways. You attempted to subvert the law of the realm. You persistently suggested, for example, that you are innocent of ringing a bell. So, for this reason, you are guilty of rebellion—'

'So, I am guilty because I offered a defence, am I? So, if I admitted guilt to the first charge, I would be found not guilty of the second charge? What kind of trick is that? It is a game. And I cannot win it! Yet you dare accuse me of semantics? I do not want to answer this charge. I refuse to plead guilty or not guilty. Because the charge against me is unfair. It's a trap. And you, Zadock, you are a dishonourable trapper—'

Once again, Temenos used words that she knew would damage the Black Hound. He hated being accused of entrapment. Hunters never use traps. They went after their prey courageously and with a brave heart. Only a coward would use a trap to defeat his quarry.

There was an air of stillness across the court room as the panel of inquisition contemplated the defendants' last response. There seemed to be confusion, and whispers indicated there was a difference of opinion amongst them.

Finally, to clarify the point of law, the senior advocate, Bernard Morlàs, stood. He addressed the panel, so Zadock was told to sit down.

'If the defendant responds neither guilty nor not guilty to the charge, the court may respond on her behalf. That is for the court to decide.' Morlàs bowed to the panel, then sat.

The inquisitors whispered to each other. They now agreed. One of them spoke. 'So be it...' the spokesperson said. 'You have neither admitted nor denied the second charge. The court has decided that, in the absence of any certain reliance on a well-made defence, it weakens your position. Therefore, we will enter a plea of guilty to this charge.'

There was uproar in the courtroom as many people spoke aloud about their confusions. They were told to keep quiet, while Zadock put the next charge to the accused.

'We accuse you of violating the command of God. You have ignored the teachings of the church. You have worked with sympathy for the Music Bearers. For years, you have been their secret agent. Do you deny this? By doing such things, you have ignored the instructions of Rome. How do you plead?'

Temenos replied with a grin of confidence, saying, 'The Psalms teach us, 'Give thanks to the Lord with the lyre; Sing praises to Him with a harp of ten strings.' Thus we are told to 'Praise Him with trumpet sound; Praise Him with harp and lyre...' I did these things. Yes, I sang my praises to the Lord!'

'So you plead guilty to violating God's command?' Zadock shouted.

'God's command is recorded in the Psalms. I recited them to you. Who are you to ignore the word of God?'

Once again, murmurs and whispers sounded around the court room. Once again, Temenos personally attacked Zadock. This time she accused him of ignoring the word of God, which was, of itself, a serious charge.

The Inquisitorial spokesman once again was asked to deliver a ruling. They instructed the room to keep silent.

'The defendant has not entered a *proper* plea. So, once more, we will enter a plea for her. To the charge of violating the command of God, we enter the plea of not guilty.'

There was more confusion at this. People talked noisily and shook their heads in disagreement. Temenos smiled at the pandemonium she had caused.

Zadock frowned. He knew he was increasingly losing his grip on proceedings. This woman was slipping through his fingers. Like butter. She wriggled free, even as he tried to squeeze her bones in a tightening grip. He had *one last* accusation to make, and this, he was sure, would put an end to her chances.

Zadock stood to put the last charge to Temenos.

'Last, Sister, we accuse of cross-dressing. Everyone knows you dress as a mercer. You travel in armour and leggings. You ride horses. Astride the beast, like a man. In fact, people here call you by an affectionate name — don't they?' Zadock examined the room. He looked into the eyes of the local people. 'They refer to you as Lord-Lady... This is a grave sin. Because the bible says: 'the woman shall not wear that which pertaineth unto a man, neither shall a man put on a woman's garment: For all that do are an abomination to the Lord.' How do you plead? Guilty or not guilty?'

Temenos smiled. 'Brother Zadock. I would only be guilty of what you accuse me of if I were a woman...' She waited to see the response in the eyes of the crowd before she continued. 'You address me as Sister. Yet it is precisely because I am not a Sister that I take to wearing the robes of a male. Neither am I a man who dresses as a woman. I am neither. Yet I am *both*...'

'What?' Zadock slammed his foot hard on the floor, with all his strength. He had finally had enough of this wretched woman. His anger spilled out for all to witness. His face became even redder, his eyes bulged. He shook with rage. He spat, before he continued.

'Do you dare to tell this holy tribunal that you are neither male nor female?'

Temenos became self-composed, 'I'm telling the court that I'm neither man nor woman. Because I am both. God chose me to be this way. I am neither one nor the other. I am both...'

The courtroom erupted into a state of frenzy.

People shouted and cussed. Others laughed or babbled. It took all the efforts of the Palatine guards — who shouted for peace —before the clamour ceased.

Then the normal activities of the court resumed. This was surely turning into a very memorable inquisition. People would talk about it for a long time.

Eventually, the lead Inquisitor was able to speak. 'If the accused is telling the truth, then this is not over. The accused will have to be examined. We should do this immediately. We have physicians here today. They will examine the prisoner to find if she has both male and female genitals. This will be done as soon as it can be arranged. We will return tomorrow, so that we can complete the examination of evidence. Then the results of a physical examination will be revealed to the panel by noon.'

The inquisitors and magisters rose. Everyone left their seats. Still in shock.

Guards came to take away the accused Lord-Lady Temenos.

She went readily with them.

36

THE CANTICLE OF THE DEFEATED HOUND

Outside the court, Zadock collapsed into a wooden pew. He felt utterly defeated. This woman, this thing — she/it — had made him look like a fool.

Now, she/it was going to get away with everything. She had created so much confusion in the court's simple minds; she had interrupted proceedings with such success, that he expected she'd be released, to go unpunished. And Zadock could not allow that. He could not allow this evil creature to escape. Especially since she/it had made him look such a fool. He had to do something. And he should do something today.

Zadock felt entirely defeated when he'd left the courtroom at the Priory. 'I was mocked, I was goaded, and I was derided by her...' he mumbled under his breath, as he trampled the slabs, on the way back to his cell. But then he abruptly diverted because he had an impulsive idea. He headed to the laundry area. Dozens of people had stayed at the Priory for the inquisition. Far more than usual. There was not even enough space to accommodate them all. So they camped henchmen and unnamed intermediaries in the park-grounds around the main buildings. Many of these faceless people passed by the Hound named Zadock without even noticing him. He plotted a new strategy in his twisted mind. He found that the laundry area was vacant. Two gigantic tanks containing chilly water were on one side. Another barrel smoked, and it smelled bad. They had left blocks and boards unattended for cleaning.

Then he found what he searched for. A damp sack. It will be perfect, Zadock decided. He also picked up various sundries, habits, shawls, scarves, tatty cloths and dirty hoods and cowls. Nothing special, a few shabby clothes. Just what he needed. These would suit his purpose admirably. The Hound stuffed them into the sack he'd found. Then he looked around, to be sure he hadn't been spied upon, then he left. He returned immediately to his cell to meditate and ruminate.

Zadock sat for hours. In darkness and solitude.

As was his proclivity — he sat on the cold stone floor. He had never used a bed-board in his life.

He closed his eyes tight. He waited for the appropriate time.

As darkness drew near, Zadock left his cell to make his way past agents, messengers, and runners. These folks scampered hither and thither. Like rats in a maze, he thought. Parasites!

Zadock quietly paced to the cell that was the temporary home of the captured Music Bearer's travelling consul, known by all as Lord-Lady Temenos.

Guards were positioned outside her cell. They recognised Zadock at once. They were going to let him slip past, but saw he carried a large bag.

'No food or drink for the prisoner. Do not offer her anything,' commented a guard.

'This is just damp clothes for washing. I will leave the sack here if you want.' Zadock opened the bag. It reeked of damp and mould. A guard had a cursory look, then waved Zadock away, before fluttering his hand emphatically across his nose, to brandish away the awful whiff.

The Black Hound moved towards the cell of the Lord-Lady. He saw she was on her knees, praying quietly.

'I'm sorry to bother you at this late hour, Sister,' Zadock whispered.

Temenos smiled in recognition, as if he was a kind friend. 'I expected you to come, Brother.' She had an inscrutable expression on her face.

'I wondered if we might talk...' offered Zadock. 'Nothing more than to clarify points—' The Hound seemed in a conciliatory mood. He made sure the tone of his voice had a calming effect on her.

'That is your duty and function, Brother...' suggested Lord-Lady Temenos. 'I am your prisoner, to treat as you wish.' She regulated her tone, as he had done.

'Perhaps it would be helpful if we continued our brief discussion in a superior place...' Zadock offered. He viewed the cell and sniffed the air as if he detected an unpleasant aroma. 'Somewhere, perhaps, where you will find comfort...'

Temenos seemed puzzled by the suggestion and frowned.

Zadock pointed to the guards at the entrance, 'I think we might be over-heard here, Sister, this place is small. Let us go somewhere quieter, perhaps?' He left her to ponder on the suggestion, then returned to the guard who had earlier asked him about his bag of clothes.

'I'm sorry to bother you again,' said Zadock. 'I'm going to take the prisoner for a short walk. To the high altar. She wishes to pray and make last confessions. Do you want to bind her accordingly? To be sure she may not escape. Would you see her hands are bound behind her back? We do not want this little bird to fly just yet...' Zadock laughed at these words. So the guard joined in with a cheerful smile of agreement.

The guard glanced towards the holding-cell. He knew Zadock was in charge of the prisoner. And, of course, he realised Zadock was a trusted holy man. However, he still felt a shadow of mistrust in his old bones. So he made a comment. 'Much as I depend on your intentions, I do not think it's a clever idea, Brother. The prisoner should not leave the cell. They have given us instructions she remains here. We have been told that she is to be confined here until she returns to the panel of inquisition in the morning—'

'Yes, I understand...' Zadock said. 'But who gave such instructions?'

The guards looked at each other. Neither could remember who

gave the directions. In fact, when they thought back on it, they remembered the directive was given by Zadock himself. There was silence from the guards.

So Zadock continued, 'And where is the harm? The prisoner wants to make confessions before daylight. She faces new challenges in the morning. It will be a busy day for her. This will be a minor act of mercy on your part, yet God will richly reward you for this inconsequential consideration, in heaven...' He grinned as he added: 'And in any case, she will be tightly bound, because you will see to that. She will be back in her cell within an hour-or-two. That will provide you with the opportunity to get a cup of mead. Also, perhaps, a little meat to keep away the cold. Before you start your long night of vigilance—'

The guards nodded agreement. One pulled down the fragile cage. The other got Temenos to stand, so he could tie her arms behind her with a strip of leather.

The guards even thanked Zadock as he led the prisoner away.

'You'll be back in an hour?' asked one.

'Doubtless sooner,' Zadock replied.

'As long as it gives us ample time to get food and drink,' mumbled the guard. He licked his lips.

Zadock grabbed a burning torch from the wall as he left, then ushered the prisoner out of the cage. He instructed her to walk in front. His hands were full, with the flame in one hand and the sack of clothes in the other.

'Let's have no trouble from you, sister,' he exclaimed, with compelling authority. Loud enough for the guards to hear his command.

'I have my hands full — so I trust you to behave.'

'You will have no trouble from me, Zadock...' Temenos said. 'I will be as meek as a lamb.'.'

37

THE CANTICLE OF THE DIPPING CROW

Once they had left the Priory 'dungeons,' Zadock guided his prisoner towards one of the main chapels.

They walked calmly and pointedly.

Some people ambled past them. But nobody paid much attention to the Hound, Zadock, and his prisoner. Everyone was fully absorbed with mundane tasks. Running around for ungrateful employers.

When they got closer to the chapels, Zadock pushed Temenos forwards with his knee. She looked around, and he nodded that she should head towards the main entrance. He manipulated her with his elbow, so she walked out of the main Priory building.

'What is this, Zadock? Where are you taking me? Out into night air? I assumed we were going to the chapel?'

'I thought you'd rather go somewhere else. Somewhere you feel safe. Somewhere high and holy.'

The Black Hound glanced at the watchtower. The turret reminded him of a giant owl. With vacant 'eyes' that were the slots in a sheer flint-wall. The gigantic bird stared out — looking over surrounding horizons. The tower was oppressive, yet magnificent. High and holy.

Temenos observed the dark structure. 'I understand,' she responded. 'You will take me to the tower...'

Then she walked, now quite willingly, towards the entrance.

Once at the base of the tower, Zadock pushed open the heavy door. Then he motioned for her to climb the ladder-stile that led over a threshold and through towards the doorway of the main building.

But she gazed at him with a smile of sympathy and curiosity: 'Brother, this is hopeless. I cannot move over obstacles with these restraints. Please untie my bonds, so I may use my hands to steady myself.'

Zadock took out the knife that he always carried from the scabbard on his back. He twisted her firmly, so she faced away from him. He could hear her breathing intensely and could see her chest rising and dropping. This sent a shiver of excitement through his bones. He cut the ties speedily, so the leather thongs fell onto the dusty floor. She focussed on the bindings curiously. Didn't they need to be used again?

Zadock motioned her towards the stile. Inside the tower, she knew there was a long ladder. Zadock told her to climb the ladder to get to the top of the tower.

He lifted the flaming torch — to provide her light for the ascent. 'Do not slip, Sister...' he said. 'I'll keep the light bright so you can see your way. Once you're up to the top, I will join you.'

When he was sure that the Lord-Lady was at the top of the tower, Zadock pulled the heavy door closed. The bolt was on the outside. But the door closed strongly enough from the inside.

He then opened the washing bag he'd brought with him. He pulled out the bundle of clothes. Then he gathered them into a pile by the doorway. He pushed all the damp clothes into a heap by the entrance. He put the flame to the corners of the damp bag.

He watched, satisfied, as the frayed edges of sackcloth glowed. After a few seconds, there was a flash of flame. Soon the whole sack caught fire.

When Zadock was moderately confident that the bag was well alight, he dropped the burning flame and also the sack onto the pile of clothes. Now he had little time. He would have to climb the ladder in darkness. He needed to reach the top of the tower and join the Lord-Lady in a merry dance.

After a struggle to climb to the top of the tall ladder, he felt weaker than usual. Zadock got to the uppermost rail. He sat and paused, to take a few deep breaths. He felt drained. But the Hound gathered his strength to look around. He saw two slits — the eyes of the owl — they only offered a faint glimmer of light. It was by one of these window-apertures that they had found Temenos on the night she had been captured. It was a high place. She had struck the bell atop the highest place in the district. So the sounds would ring out across all the County. She had created a diversion that night. He understood it now. She had played him all along — all this while she had played for time, diverting him, to allow others their escape.

She was a smart one, this 'Lord-Lady.' He had hated no one so much in all his life. But now she would pay for her sins!

She greeted him in the darkness. 'I smell smoke, Zadock,' she whispered.

It was the first time she had shown any sign of anxiety. The shiver in her speech made him feel joyful. Though she could not see the cruel smile that stretched across his face. Nor could she see the sharp blade he held like a dagger behind his back.

Zadock wiped a cobweb from his forehead, then went after her.

He grabbed her by the shoulders and pushed her violently towards one of the slotted windows. It was a dreadfully long way down from the top of the tower. And the windows were now the *only way out*. The wet laundry burned below, the smoke and fire blocked any exit. And soon that smoke would rise through the tower, cutting them off and suffocating them both. Soon, they would have to make a choice: choke to death or plunge into night air. Until that moment, they stayed by the fresh air of the open aperture.

'What do you want?' Lord-Lady Temenos asked.

Zadock could smell the dread on her brow. He felt the damp sweat under her armpits. He breathed in the aroma of fear, he sniffed it long and hard. He took in the heady bouquet because it pleased him. He liked to witness pain.

'You and I are going to fly, Sister...' he said. He whispered the words close to her ear. 'Just like Daedalus, imprisoned in the lofty tower. Like Daedalus, our only escape is through an open window.

We must fly from here — if we want to escape the smoke! We will fly together! Isn't that appropriate?'

'You're crazy—' she said.

'Did you think you could escape justice?' he continued. He ground his teeth. 'Did you think your insults could be ignored? There will be justice tonight, though. *Ha ha!* We will give them a show...yes?' He nodded towards the encampment below. Down in the make-shift campsite, on the grounds of the Priory, people attended their business. 'Everyone came to see a show didn't they? So we will give them what they came here for! Tonight, we will go down in history, you and I —'

'And if I do not choose to jump?' Temenos asked.

Zadock lifted his knife to the soft skin below her right ear.

'You have a choice, of course. You may die a thousand cuts. Or you may be overwhelmed by choking smoke. You may jump with me, willingly, into night air. Or unwillingly. That is for you to decide. But I assure you, to go willingly, will be the fastest. And at least you will have the privilege of travelling with me through night air, hand-in-hand. For one last trip... into oblivion.'

Temenos sang.

At first, it seemed to Zadock that the woman sobbed. Because he had seldom heard singing. But soon the sob became a chant. And the chant became a hymn. And the hymn turned into an anthem. And then he realised it was a song.

Zadock could not tolerate the noise. 'Stop it! Stop it! You will draw attention. Stop the diabolical chant...'

Zadock wanted to stuff his fingers into his ears to halt the evil sounds that came from her wicked mouth — but he held the knife with one hand and the prisoner's elbow with the other. So he pushed his knee hard into her backbone, then edged her ever closer to the window slot.

Soon she would lose balance.

But Temenos did not stop her intonation. She filled her lungs with smoky air, to sing even louder. Her eyes were full of tears and her heart thumped hard, but still she sang loud and clear. She sang the strongest and the oldest song she knew. She sang it flawlessly and she sang it bright— and she sang emphatically into the night air: 'He who dwells in eternity...'

Zadock was about to twist the knife into her milky-white throat before he chucked her body out of the window-slot.

But something made him stop. He thought he heard a noise.

Zadock could not figure-out who had entered the upper room of the tower, but someone had. But even through the smoke and tears — in the dim light that glimmered through the window-slits — he saw a shape. It was unmistakable. It was the shape of a young man.

The figure came promptly, and with noble purpose.

Some sound or movement briefly interrupted Zadock from his thought processes. In that split second, it gave the intruder the time necessary to cut across the room and take the knife from his hand. The stranger snatched the knife by the handle. He tugged it hard — and the blade went sliding to the floor. Then the dark figure grabbed Zadock by the neck, and the stranger's nails dug deep into Zadock's tendons to pull him bodily from the window.

The figure was stronger than Zadock. Fitter and more agile. More useful with younger hands. Within seconds he had pulled Zadock away from the opening, and into the centre of the room. Zadock saw that blood dripped from his own neck, his shoulder was doubtless dislocated. He could not see perfectly because of the rising smoke. The smouldering fumes choked him. His head was swimming.

'Come here to me — my lady,' shouted the unknown figure.

Zadock could almost see the dark shape beckoning Temenos.

She rushed into the stranger's arms, and then the dark stranger hugged her with great compassion.

She had been through a terrible ordeal. 'We have to go. Now!' shouted the mysterious figure. He led her towards the ladder.

Though Temenos found it difficult to descend the ladder, because the smoke burnt her eyes, she persevered. She choked and racked with pain. She felt bad. And was bruised all over. The dark figure waited until she was down the ladder. He followed. The pile of clothes still burned at the bottom of the tower. The fire puffed great clouds of evil-smelling poison into the atmosphere. But the pile was pushed to one side of the entrance. And the door was ajar.

The stranger pulled at the door —with all his strength— so Temenos could squeeze through a gap. Once outside she collapsed onto wet ground. There, she coughed up some smoky vomit as she panted.

'No time for that, lady. We need to keep moving. Come —'

The figure hauled her to her feet. Then he half-dragged her, running in small steps away from the tower, and out of the Priory grounds.

Temenos thought her heart would stop at any second. She felt physically sick and believed something was going to explode inside her. Her bosom heaved uncontrollably. Her legs were likely to give way at any moment. But the stranger stayed with her, coaxing her along, helping by dragging her arms.

Ultimately, they reached the main entranceway that led out of the Priory grounds. They made a sudden right turn and scrambled through thick hedges, trees, and shrubs.

Temenos saw that thorns tore her skin, and she felt her face bloodied by hanging branches. Her hair became matted and wet. Her legs felt as if they were on fire. She had never been in so much pain in her life. At last they reached a clearing. Here, Temenos spotted three horses. She also saw the outlines of two knights. They stood nearby. The stranger, her rescuer, barked orders. It became obvious he was the man in charge.

'Mount up! Mount up...' he shouted. 'We have to get out of here. Fast! She is too weak to ride. I will take her. Fix a lead rope to the other beast. We need to be off. Head east. We cannot use the road — keep moving until we get a few hours from here...'

Temenos was too weak to ask who all these men were but was grateful for the rescue. though, at this stage, she wasn't sure if she had been saved or snatched. But at least she was still alive..

∼

Folk camping in temporary tents around the grounds of the Priory were, by now, standing and gawking. They looked at the high watchtower because it seemed on fire. They saw endless plumes of dark smoke billowing through the eye-like window spaces at the very top of the structure.

Someone called to fetch buckets of water. But most viewed the fun. They appreciated the spectacle for what it was: a diversion. They took the view that it was none of their business, but something to look at. An escape from the humdrum.

Some of these folk might have seen a black raven-like figure appearing from one of the window cuts in the tower. They might even have seen this black figure dip and dive into bitter blackness. A few folk declared they saw a giant crow-like creature flying from the tower. They reported that it flapped its ghastly wings several times, to gain altitude. So it might fly away and towards the stars.

Others were fairly sure what happened. They reported that they saw a figure *plummet*. The said a dark body crashed onto the stony ground below. And that's where it remained, inert and lifeless.

38

THE CANTICLE OF THE PAN AND POT

Several hours passed since Temenos had been rescued from the smoking tower at Hoxne Priory. So now, the man in charge of their escape, considered it safe enough for them to slow the pace. Shortly after this decision, they found a place to camp.

The two other riders dismounted first and erected a temporary shelter. The young man in charge got bags of bedding from the packets tied to the extra horse. He handed Temenos a flask of water.

'Here, drink—' she was told.

These were the first words he had spoken in hours.

Once a shelter had been built, the young man in charge put laundry inside it — then he called the Lord-Lady over to the entrance. He pointed inside the shelter and instructed her to get some sleep. Then he ushered his men inside the shelter too. There was not enough room for four inside the accommodation.

'Where will you go?' Temenos asked.

'I'll sleep in the rain,' the man in charge replied.

This baffled her. 'Come with me inside with me — I do not mind. There's no need for false modesty or shyness. We should not leave you in the cold and wet...'

But the man looked into the shelter, shuddered, then shook his head. He had made his mind up. 'I prefer the harshest environment,' he explained.

∼

Next morning, when light filtered through the canopy of damp trees, and birds started their plaintive morning calls, the noises of dawn wakened the guards. They started fixing things up and checking over horses. Temenos woke too. She immediately realised how badly she ached all over. Her shoulders and backbone were most painful. When she tried to stand, her legs almost buckled beneath her. Her neck was sore, her legs bruised, and her arms were scarred. Even her head felt battered.

She glanced around the makeshift camp, trying to see if she might find the person responsible for her rescue the previous evening, the mysterious young man in charge. Then she saw a stack, bundled close to a tree. It was a mound of discarded clothes that had perhaps been left in a disorderly heap for someone to collect. As she examined the clothes, something about the heap bothered her. There was something unpleasant about the way it was wrapped. Something was wrong. She could not put her finger on it right away — but then felt uneasy about things. All things. All the things that had happened to her in recent hours. She felt more uneasy than ever before.

The pile of clothes stirred. Then she saw two arms poking from the pile. The body of a man climbed out of the sack. It looked like a spider leaving behind a pea-shuck. All arms and legs, and a discarded carapace.

Then she understood why she felt so disheartened by this sight. Because, as the man rose to his feet, she realised what he was. Not who he was, but what he was. The young stranger was another Black Hound.

This one was much younger than Zadock. Slightly leaner, too, if such a thing was possible. This Hound possessed beady eyes that were sunk deeper into his skull. And like Zadock, a face that rarely smiled. This Black Hound dressed in the identical black habit Zadock wore. Why hadn't she noticed these things before? Then she saw a glint. The emblem of the fanged-cross. It hung proudly around this man's neck. That proved it. This man was her sworn enemy.

After that, Temenos scanned the other two men. She had assumed both were knights, the night before. Now she realised the men were members of the Palatine guard. Their job was to protect the young Hound. One guard wore the insignia of the torturer. The emblem of the scourge. His task was to gain confessions. It now dawned on her that she was their little fish. She had been rescued from the pan. But now, it seems, she found herself in the pot.

∼

Before starting on the next stage of their mysterious journey, Temenos thought she'd earned the right to ask some questions. 'Who are you?' There was no reply.

'Where are we going?' she demanded.

'We have little time to answer idle questions — all you need to know is that we head for the next city —'

'Am I your prisoner?'

'You are my hostage. You will do as you are told, ' was the young Hound's curt reply.

'Why did you rescue me?'

'Because I need you alive.'

'Tell me your name?'

'Questions, questions...'

After this was a period of silence, before the 'new' Black Hound spoke again.

'Can you ride?' he asked.

'I can,' Temenos told him. Though it's true she ached all over. She decided she would rather sit with this young man, so she might ask him more questions, than to ride alone. 'I would rather not ride alone, sir. I am weak with pain,' she explained.

'Very well. We will take the other mount.' The Hound shouted over to his men. 'Let the beast I used last night in the escape have a rest.' They prepared the animals accordingly.

'Telson...' the young Hound announced abruptly. Then he set about the business of packing things away.

'Pardon?' said Temenos.

'I told you my name... You asked, so I told you. My name is Telson.'

'I thought that was what you said. It is just that — just that...'

'You know me?'

'Yes, I know you,' Lord-Lady Temenos admitted..

39

THE CANTICLE OF DISCLOSURE

The three men packed and prepared the horses. They gave Temenos some water. The Palatines ignored her. Telson gave her a casual look now-and-then. When everything was collected for the trip, they left their overnight camp.

They rode in line. With a guard in front, and the torturer behind. The course alternated between smooth going under-hoof and uneven lawns. Temenos strained hard to keep a-hold of the young Hound. Her arms hugged him tight.

For more than an hour, neither spoke. Then Temenos whispered in his ear: 'How did you guess?'

There was no response.

After a fleeting period, he spoke, 'It was not a guess, ma'am. I put in days, hours, and years of research... I have been studying, analysing and crossing checking files and reports all my summers. That was my duty at the Abbey of Saint Hubertus. I have been a keen collector of facts. Once I gather facts, I make conclusions, that is my ministry—'

'And what conclusions did you make?' she asked.

'I know you are a travelling consul. I know you are a free agent. I know your job involves 'rescuing' foundlings and bringing them into the community...' Her arms held him tighter. 'But I had to ask myself how did you know about the secret of nine bells? That call you made from the tower, to convene Zadock. How did you know that? It is a clandestine call. A hidden code. Only known to Black Hounds. We only use it in the most extreme of circumstances. To warn of calamity. They handed the secret call down, mouth-to-mouth, by tradition. We have not used it for a hundred years. It is not something that is known to any others outside our fraternity... also, in the court, you claimed to be both man and woman — this led me to a conclusion.'

'Shall I tell you?' Temenos asked. But there was no answer. They rode in silence for a while longer.

'I am both man and the woman,' declared Temenos. 'It is true.' She allowed this to settle into the young Hound's mind. Then continued: 'My parents rejected me because of my curious nature. Because I was neither a boy-child nor a girl-child. They left me to die because they could not handle the fact that I was made different. They left me for taking... just like your parents left you. My crime, according to society, was that I was half-a-boy. Your crime, according to society, was that you were half-a-royal...' The young Hound named Telson made no comment about this crude attempt at a joke. 'But anyway, I was taken away by the monks. Just like you. A travelling consul picked me up. She took me to an Abbey. And there, monks fed me and cared for me. And it was there they educated me ...'

They continued to ride while Temenos collected her thoughts. Then she continued. 'They raised me as a Hound...'

With these words, Telson stopped. The guards paused. He wanted to hear her next words precisely, so he leaned back in his saddle.

'Yes, they took me taken to St Hubert's Abbey...' He felt her breath on his neck. 'But before I reached puberty, the masters at St Hubert's took me from that place. They found I was an intelligent student. Controllable and open-to-learning. But I knew I was about to be dismissed, though I did not why They took me to another place. At this other place, they taught me how to be a free agent. How to do their bidding readily. They taught me how to wander. They trained me in the skills that were required to contact other agents and be an agent handler. They told me I was soon to make my own way in the world. Basically, they trained me to recover foundlings. They taught me how to collect the orphans that are left by the waysides. It was me that rescued orphans and it was me that brought the children back to St Hubert's Abbey... But they did not want me to be part of their community. They said they would never invite me into it. I would never be allowed full membership of the fraternity. They told me I could never, legitimately, be a Black Hound. Can you guess why? It's because I was not a complete boy. That made me feel sad. I felt disoriented. I wanted to be tonsured... I wanted to be a real monk. But I was rebuffed because nature and Almighty God had made me both male-and-female—'

'So you became a Music Bearer?' Telson asked.

Temenos paused. She needed to explain: 'Neither male nor female am I. I am both. Lord and Lady. I am they....'

He shook his head. He tried to understand; the young Hound repeated her words, ' I am they?'

So she added, to clear things up: 'Neither am I Bearer nor Hound. I am both. I am they...'

He grunted his understanding.

'Once freed from the Hound masters — I promptly joined the hunt. I worked as they expected me to work... as a free agent... I quickly went in search of prey. In a few weeks I had sniffed-out my first target. I was a good sniffer. But when I grabbed him — he made an agreeable sound. He made a sound that I now recognise as harmony.' She hesitated at this stage— recalling her first experience of music. 'So, instead of retrieving my prey, without damage, to bring him back to my masters for penalty, I did something very strange. I stayed with this harmony giver. I learned the sounds he taught me. He showed me how to make the same sweet sounds. I joined him in song. You need to remember, I had just passed fifteen summers, so perhaps I was falling in love. It was a fantastic season for me. I had fallen headlong for this song-maker. And don't forget, it was after the community had rejected me. That young Music Bearer, well I admit it now, he was my first affection. His love is still inside me. His love endures, to give me hope and strength. I constantly think of him...' She paused and gave a short sob. 'When I released the Music Bearer, to let him back into the wild— I made a promise to myself that I would help other Music Bearers. So when a child has been left for me, left on the waysides to die, or be saved— I choose to consider whether the child would make be a good Music Bearer. Or, alternatively, a good Hound. Once I make my decision, I take the child to the appropriate place—'

'You make these decisions by yourself?'

'Yes, after examining many children, I have learned the signs of harmony. I call it harmonic root. I also learned the signs a babe might become a good hunter—'

'And I?' Telson asked.

At this point he bent his neck around. He strained to see her face. He tried to focus on her eyes so he could check her response. Tears welled in her eyes.

'You did not...' she whispered.

'I did not, what? I didn't have this mysterious harmony you speak of? Is that what you are saying? Is that why I was taken to the Hounds? Is that the reason I have been given this path? This ministry?' Telson nodded his head in understanding. It all dovetailed, it al became clear. He thought about the consequences of the decision she had made that fateful day — the day she had found the baby dressed in rags by an old farmhouse. After a while he commented, 'You were wrong to perpetuate such an evil system all these years—'

'No, I perpetuated no system... ' She explained. 'I just save foundlings. It was not up to me to decide their greater purpose.'

Telson shook his head. He did not seem satisfied with her explanation. And although he chose not to respond, he felt disappointed with her reply. He checked the bridle, then started off again.

'Don't you want to know where I found you?' she whispered.

'I already know,' the young Hound replied. 'I identified the records. I found records of my collection from the wayside, several years ago. I explored the contents of those reports. I ruminated on their meanings. You found me near the royal palace, didn't you?'

'It is true, Telson. You are the son of His Highness. You are the son of our Landgrave.'

He nodded but didn't respond.

'But now I will tell you something you did not guess at,' Temenos continued. 'I will tell you something that is not in your records...'

He waited.

'You have a sister, Telson... Yes, it is true. She is also of authentic royal blood. She is a true noble.'

Now that *was* an interesting fact. And it was a fact of which he was *not* aware.

'Your sister is older than you, by about one year. I took her from approximately the same place you were left. Her father abandoned her in the cold, to die. That's your father too, the Landgrave. I took her away. I found that God had blessed her with the harmonic root. So I took her to the Music Bearers. They raised and educated her.'

'Why would my father do such a thing? Why would he leave a healthy baby to die or be taken away?'

'Ask him that yourself...'

They continued their ride

'Where are we going?' asked Temenos.

'To Castle Acre...'

'Good, that is where your father is now. So you can ask him.'

∽

Before the end of their riding day, Telson stopped in the saddle to consider Temenos: 'If I release you, Sister, will you promise to retire to a distant convent? Will you promise to stay away from Music Bearers and Black Hounds forever? Because, if I ever seen again you, I swear I will come after you. I will hunt you down. And then I will kill you. Do I make myself clear? Can you make such a promise?'

'That was my plan, anyway, before the Hound, Zadock, turned-up,' she offered, with a smile. 'My strategy was altered by the unexpected arrival of Zadock upon these shores. Believe me, I give you my oath now — if you release me, you will never see nor hear from me again—'

'Very well,' Telson said. 'But there remains work for you to complete. I will decide upon the terms of your release once your duty is done.'

40

THE CANTICLE OF TONSURE

Just before the 'young Hound' named Telson had planned to ask permission to go to Castle Acre, to capture the Music Bearer with the high cheekbones (named Brother Chad) and several weeks before he had saved Lord-Lady Temenos from the smoky tower at Hoxne Priory, he had received an urgent message from Brother Cyrus, the Master of the Library of Violators Associates. This is the account of those events.

Telson had gone straight to see Brother Cyrus.

'Telson, I thought you might need to hear this right now... It is an assemblage of reports that are just being collected and evaluated...' Cyrus gave Telson a portfolio of papers. Then he continued, 'The independent flyer that you were asking about — that travelling special agent they call Temenos. We have caught her!'

'What?'

'That's right! Sister Temenos. One of the Bearer's most important travelling agents... She has been arrested. A trial has been organised. She will certainly be found guilty and will probably be executed. This is big news...'

Telson became irritated by this news. He could not help but let his emotions show. He threw the papers down in anger. Hundreds of hours wasted. Days-upon-days leafing through documents trying to establish a pattern. Months attempting to track her down. And now someone else got to her first... who?

'Not happy, Telson?' Cyrus smiled. 'She is a most dangerous agent, that one. It is going to be one of the biggest trials in history... You ought to be glad that we bagged her.'

Telson was not happy at all. He had needed to talk to her first — before they burned her at the stake. He'd always hoped he would get to her before anyone else. He felt she had the secret of his 'finding' locked in her heart. And he had honestly supposed he was the only Hound capable of hunting her down. He believed he was the only Hound skilful enough for such a challenge.

'Who took her? Who oversaw this hunt? Who bettered me?'

'Zadock.'

'Who?'

'Don't you know Zadock? He's our most effective music-finder. He's the most feared of all. A true legend. We have heard reports that he's slaughtered more than a dozen heretics during the last few months. If anyone was ever going to take out this cunning bird... then it was always to be Zadock — he's the best-of-the-best...'

'Where is the cunning bird little now? Is she still alive?'

'Yes, the process is yet to take place. The trial is to be held at an old Priory. I forget the name of the place. But all the details are in that package — the package you just threw on the floor ...'

Telson stooped to pick up the file. He had little time, by the sound of it, to get to her.

He needed to memorise the facts, then ask permission from the Formation Director to leave this place and travel to Castle Acre.

Of course, he would have to make a detour to the old Priory mentioned in the documents first, so he could talk to Sister Temenos. Maybe even rescue her, if such a thing was even possible. He earnestly needed to talk to her in private. But how long would it take him to travel to that place? He'd never, actually, been outside these walls! How long would it take to get the authority he needed to leave? Would he even get permission at all? This would prove to be a testing time. His thoughts spun around in his mind.

Telson reasoned he had only one chance to get permission from the Formation Director to travel to Castle Acre. He knew he was pushed for time.

So, next morning, he attended the Formation Director's Scribe. He asked permission for an audience with the Director. He was told to come back after vespers, the last evening prayers.

After vespers, and at the allotted time, Telson went to the Director's office and waited, rehearsing his lines. This was a moment, and a meeting. He needed to get right. He'd worked hard and had calculated with enduring patience to get to this moment. He really needed to get out of this place and put his 'skills' to practise.

Finally, the Director's Scribe peered out of the room and beckoned him in.

Telson had some expectations. He had already speculated that the 'Superior of Superiors' would be irritable and uncommunicative. He would, no doubt, stay by the fireplace while Telson presented his case.

Telson's expectations were shattered, though, when he entered the room.

As he walked in, trying to appear as confident, Telson knew intuitively that something was wrong. Very wrong! Why had the meeting been scheduled to be held just after vespers? Why was the Scribe inside the room? Had the man been 'briefing' the Director, perhaps unfairly? Why was the Director's office so brightly illuminated? Telson had memories of it being kept moderately dark during other visits. Typically, there was merely the flicker of firelight to help him see his way across the space. Yet, on this night, the place seemed aglow with light and brightness.

It was a large room; larger than perhaps he had perfectly appreciated before. For example, this was the first time he had noticed that they decorated the room with tapestries and ornately carved tables lined the walls. And upon these tables balanced candle-trees — all were alight, so the room smelled of beeswax and scented oils.

When he entered the light — Telson felt any boldness he once possessed, progressively leaving him. He felt unmistakably uncomfortable. What was going on?

There were other shapes in the room, too. He now understood it was not just the Director and his Scribe in the room. He sensed other presences as well. Then, abruptly, an appalling thought struck him... had the Formation Director died? Was this his wake? That might explain the candles and smell of incense. Telson felt genuinely tense.

He saw the Director's Scribe signalling him to come into the centre of the room. His eyes became blurred, by the smoke and burning incense. Telson had trouble concentrating. He had altogether forgotten the primary purpose of his visit; and tried to remind himself he was here to ask permission to travel to Castle Acre. He saw a figure wearing ornate vestments, and wondered, with a fleeting notion, if that person in vestments was the priest providing *viaticum*, the last rites, to the Superior of Superiors.

But then, when he studied the figure more closely, Telson realised the character was not a stranger, but in fact was the Director himself. They had dressed him in his full liturgical garments. In his garb, he seemed completely different. More powerful, more youthful. Actually, a striking figure.

Well, that is a blessed relief, thought Telson. Then he scanned the room to see if he could recognise any other figures. But, as he recognised each face through the smoke, he felt progressively uncomfortable again.

The first face he acknowledged was that of his old Director of Study, the one that he had maliciously and falsely accused of furtively storing bread and cheese in his room. Why was he here? Telson had hoped he would never see that man again.

He looked along the line of faces — all were beaming at him. He recognised his Tipstaves, those he trusted in his library. And he recognised his friend Brother Cyrus from the Library of Violators Associates. He also saw some monks he had trained with and recognised those that had gained advancement over him. He knew their names and faces, but never got to know any of them well.

And there, at the end of the line, was the Master of the Library of Transgressors. The man he had dislodged and displaced through his nefarious doings. The man who had been to work with the pigs. Would Telson's guilty secrets come out tonight? Had the hour of his reckoning arrived?

Then another thought, more bizarre than the first one, struck him. Was he dead? Was this his final judgement? Was he at the entrance of heaven, or of hell?

But the 'Superior of Superiors' looked tenderly upon him and spoke soft words in a gentle tone. 'Brother Telson. Tonight we celebrate the marking of your formal entry into our community. It is a sacred rite instituted by The Church and we view it as honourable...' He looked kindly at Telson. 'Young man, tonight the shearing of your hair and the investment of your surplice will be the outward signs that we receive you into our clerical order. When you become fully tonsured, you become a full member of our family. You will share all our privileges and all our obligations. Tonight, if you agree, you will become a full member of our holy clerical order. Are you prepared?'

Telson couldn't find his voice. So just nodded.

'Telson, you have learned the basics of our faith, and have studied well. At this point, you will receive the Crown of St. John. We will shave a crescent of hair from your head. Afterwards, you will receive blessing and investiture.'

Once these formal words had been spoken, he invited Telson to come forward, where they had placed a kneeler. The Director's scribe held a large and a sharp looking knife. Telson watched warily as he turned the blade in the candlelight. Then Telson stared around at the circle of faces. All eyes gazed at him. For the first time in his life, he absolutely realised the seriousness of this ritual.

He had learned about 'tonsuring' from an early age. he had planned and longed for it for many years. But now, here he was, it was actually happening. And it seemed unusually powerful. Because it was the ultimate act of trust. He entrusted his life to these people — the same people he had mistreated, disrespected, and had plotted against in recent months.

He considered every person in this room to be a true enemy. His only friend here was Brother Cyrus. But to be honest, he didn't much trust him either. Telson felt sure that even Cyrus would double-cross him, if he needed to, without a second thought.

Yet now he had been asked to kneel before a man brandishing a murderous weapon. To bow his head while enemies looked on. Yes, it was a moment of sacred trust. The sense of holiness had not escaped him. He crossed himself and got to his knees. Telson bowed his head. Then waited for the blade.

After a few lines of Latin, mumbled by the Formation Director, he felt a warm trickle on his forehead. The liquid run lazily down his forehead. Was it blood? It glistened as it leaked across his eyebrows. No, it was not blood. It was oil. Anointing and soothing. Then he heard the faintest scrape. The sound was almost invisible. Assuredly, the deed was painless. The crown had been given. He was now at one with the community. A full member.

He felt the Director's hands laying cordially upon his skull. Hot and skinny. And he said more prayers. Then, at last, Telson was invited to stand. He had tears in his eyes. And abruptly felt thoroughly exhausted. Worn out by the sheer intensity of all the mixed emotions that welled inside of him. He gulped for air as the small congregation clapped. They clapped for him.

After this brief ceremony, the Director's Scribe brought out Telson's proper vestments. He would only wear them on high-days or for audiences with the Abbot or Pope. They would not replace his everyday habit. But on this holy tonight he would wear them. To try them out.

Then they invited him to have wine and desserts. Wine and desserts? After vespers? A sin, undoubtedly? But not tonight. Because this was a special night. A fuss was being made.

After desserts, the Scribe went over to him and whispered something into his ear.

'When you are ready, Telson, it is customary to kiss each one of your brothers here. To thank them for their participation. Each one of them has worked earnestly to get you here.. to help you arrive where you find yourself today.'

Telson nodded understanding, although he was not completely sure what the Scribe meant by such words. He felt apprehensive —

talking to the people gathered here at this place seemed odd. He had wronged them all.

But the Scribe smiled and nodded and pointed to the first person to be thanked: Telson's original Director of Study. The old teacher who Telson thought was 'an old fool.' He had planted evidence in his room. To gain promotion and recognition.

Telson approached the old man. It surprised him to see that the old man smiled warmly. Telson suddenly felt an uncontrollable sense of sorrow and guilt. His emotion spilled out into one huge sob. As Telson's eyes filled with tears, actual tears, not forged or phony, Telson acknowledged they were tears of acquittal.

'I'm sorry, Master. I'm genuinely sorry...' The apology spilled out. Telson did not mean to confess. But he could not keep the pain in any longer. In fact, he wanted to be on his knees again. To properly confess. For what he had done to this man. He wanted to ask for a blessing and absolution. From the man he had double-crossed and cheated.

'Never mind, brother. It does not matter at all. This is the way of the Hound. You performed well. We expected these things from you. We are proud of what you have achieved,' the old man told him.

Telson stared, with a questioning look in his eyes. The old man moved forward to kiss him on both cheeks. Telson returned the gesture.

Then he moved to the old Master of the Known Transgressors Library. The man that he had replaced, and who had been criticised when set-up, by Telson, about a missing file.

'I'm sorry, Master. For what I did to you,' Telson bowed his head in shame.

'I expected it of you, brother...' The Library Master said. 'You have the cunning instinct of a Hound. You have done many deceitful things. That makes you what you are. You are a hunter and a thinker. This is what we wanted of you. We are proud of what you have become. We are proud of your advancement.' They exchanged kisses.

Telson went down the line of all the people he once thought were his enemies — thanking each one. And asking for their forgiveness.

He exchanged kisses with them all as he passed. The last person he needed to speak to was the 'Superior of Superiors' himself.

'I have not earned this, Father. I have sinned and made mistakes along the way. Will you ever trust me again?'

The Superior of Superiors smiled. He had heard those same words before. Many times. From all the monks that had been newly tonsured.

'Tonight is a new beginning, Telson. Tonight you are re-born. Now you are a Hound. Now the tests will actually begin… All that has happened before is forgotten. Tonight, you are offered a fresh start. You have been taught well, my son, and you are ready for your first mission. When do you want to begin?'

'As soon as I can,' Telson said, tears still rolling down his cheeks.

'Do you not have something to ask of me?'

Telson had to think. Did he? Then realised what the Director meant. The focus of this meeting was presumed to be about gaining permission to travel to Castle Acre, although he had completely forgotten about it.

'Yes, Father. I seek permission to travel to Castle Acre. I think I can capture an important Music Bearer at that town. I've worked hard to track him down and I think I can accurately predict when he will arrive …'

'When do you need to go, Son?'

'Right away!'

'So be it.' The two men kissed.

The 'Superior of Superiors' gave Telson his final blessing.

41

THE CANTICLE OF THE HATCHING

They had sent the Landgravine word, from Atalanta, that the Music Bearer who they had been expecting — had arrived early into town.

This information was to be delivered as a handwritten note on a piece of paper. Atalanta had asked Melita to get the note delivered to the 'Prioress' who stayed covertly at the castle. Melita was delivered the message content, Atalanta read it aloud to her. Atalanta had long assumed, correctly, that Melita could not read. But before having the letter delivered into the Landgravine's hands, Melita had her 'tame' admirer check it over, to make sure the words in it were true. Her admirer loved to do these minor jobs for the charming Melita. The words seemed correct. So she delivered the note to her mistress.

The Landgravine received the message from Atalanta on the same day she was informed, by other agents, that a Black Hound had entered the town limits. How auspicious, she thought, that both Bearer and Hound should appear upon the same day! She decided she'd send word to this Hound, telling him he should attend her at once. Then, as planned, they would venture to the royal residence together. Where they would discover her husband in an evil act. With a Music Bearer. Of course, they would arrest her husband for heresy and because he'd be the company of a Music Bearer, they would try him for treason. Then he'd be executed. Dishonoured too. They'd delete his name from the chronicles. The Landgravine smiled when she thought about all this. So, she sent word to the freshly arrived Black Hound, telling him she needed to see him at once. She also sent a hand-written note to Melita and Atalanta. informing them they should arrange for the Music Bearer to take part in her plan tonight.

She instructed that the Music Bearer should visit the Landgrave one hour after sunset. It was important that this timekeeping was strictly observed. Then her husband would be captured in the act of wrongdoing.

A messenger informed Telson, the young Hound that arrived in the town, explaining that an important Prioress wanted to see him at once, in the town castle.

So Telson gathered his and headed for the stronghold. The young Hound ordered his hostage to remain hidden at the inn. Telson arrived at the castle and asked permission to see the false prioress.

∽

They brought the young Hound to her rooms in the castle. She sat upon a throne, wearing a cap and gown. Telson examined this 'Prioress' and after evaluating the woman, decided she was too plump and well-nourished to be a true nun.

She told him what she needed him to hear: 'It is good you are here brother...' she said. 'They tell me a person of noble birth lives up at the royal residence. I am told he is conspiring with heretics. A reliable source informed me of this. I was told this notable person will meet tonight, with a Bearer of Music...' She watched his eyes widen. 'If you go there, you will capture the heretic and the notable person in one go. How does that interest you?'

The young Hound rubbed his brow: 'How did you come by this information?' he asked.

'I have ears and eyes. I position them in high places. Here and around. Such things come to my attention. I thought it wise to tell you right away. So you can take appropriate action—'

'Do you know when and where this clandestine meeting will take place?' asked the young Hound.

'I do...' said the false prioress. 'I will go with you. I will show you the place and the person,' she offered.

That would be exceedingly irregular, Mother Superior. I prefer to act alone—'

'That is your right, I suppose. But do you want to ignore the wishes of a monastic superior?'

'No, but equally, I would not want harm to come to you, Reverend Mother. Though, if you insist on joining me on the hunt, I must allow it. Be aware, though, that I cannot guarantee your safety—'

'Good. So be it. I will join you on the chase...' She gave a teasing smile. 'I will meet you and your men at dusk. At the main entrance to the royal residence?'

'I will see you there,' Telson said. He knelt to kiss her ring. Then left to prepare.

~

Later that same day, the hand-written message from the Landgravine arrived for Melita and Atalanta, informing them they should arrange for the Music Bearer to take part in the plan tonight. The message instructed them to have their Music Bearer positioned at the correct place at precisely one hour after sunset.

Atalanta read the message to herself. Then re-read the words to Melita. But Atalanta failed to accurately translate the instructions. She changed the precise time of the act. She told Melita the words that explained they should get the Music Bearer into position... but misleadingly told her it would be midnight. Melita could not read words. They were meaningless to her, just squiggles on a sheet. Atalanta expected as much. And Melita didn't have time to get the words 'checked' by her admirer.

Melita was satisfied with these timings, anyhow, not because she trusted Atalanta but because the timings gave her a rare chance to bed His Royal Highness. Then, after making love, she'd tell him about the elaborate plan. The plan that an evil wife and her double-crossing maidservant had concocted. Then the royal gentleman would forever be in her debt, and they'd plan a future together. The evil Landgravine's plans would amount to nothing. In fact, they would arrest the stupid old mare for high treason and, at the very least, they'd incarcerate her in an institution for the rest of her days.

If all went well, thought Melita, she'd be the Queen at the end of all this… With these crazy thoughts in mind, Melita instructed Atalanta to collect the Music Bearer and have him secreted inside the royal residence.

She underlined the requirement that he should wait until the allotted time. Before making himself known.

After this, Melita freshened up, then put on her best silk dress.

She hurried off to see the Landgrave. This was going to be a night he'd never forget. She'd make sure of that!

∼

His Highness the Landgrave had been feeling completely refreshed since his stay at the Margrave's country residence. His days of hunting invigorated him. His nights of passion with Melita calmed him. The pain and suffering he'd lived through in recent months were almost forgotten. He felt unfettered and more alive than he felt in years. It was refreshing to be so far away from his annoying wife. She had been 'touched by the moonstone.' He was sure of it. She was totally unhinged. Soon, he'd plot a way of ridding himself from his mad wife, forever. He decided he would like to settle down with Melita, the servant girl. She made him feel whole again. She made him feel like the man he once was. She was the best thing that had happened to him.

So it overjoyed the Landgrave when Melita came to his room that evening wearing her best silk dress, the one he bought for her after their first night of passion. He was particularly happy when she slipped willingly into his sheets. She opened her legs for him. He reached in, his passions boiling. She was sweet and kind. She was a masterful love-maker too. He struggled, he cried, and he sighed. And he felt totally imprisoned by her love.

So enveloped by this passion was he that he did not hear the approach of a group that made their way to the royal apartment.

42

THE CANTICLE OF THE IGNOMINY

At the pre-arranged time, Her Highness the Landgravine, posing as a Prioress, met with the young Hound Telson.

This was at the main entrance to the royal residence. It was a little after sunset.

The young Hound had his Palatine guards with him. There was also a female with them. An older woman.

'Who is this?' asked the false-Prioress.

'She is my advisor, Reverend Mother. She is here to help. If she can—'

The Landgravine glanced at the woman. She checked her over. Another witness to my husband's act of betrayal will not hurt, she thought.

After a while, the little party made their way on foot to the royal residence. They left their horses and a carriage at the entrance, so as not to attract more attention than was entirely necessary. Telson ventured ahead. He led the way.

The young Hound arrived at the main entrance before anyone. His fanged cross shone in the torchlight. The guards at the door recognised his emblem at once. They understood the consequences if they strayed.

'I'm on official business...' Telson told them. 'Open up and then direct me to the royal apartment at once. This is a matter of the utmost seriousness. If you alert anyone to my presence, I shall consider you to be an enemy of the State and will have you arrested.'

He pointed to his men — the two dangerous looking Palatines. The torturer twisted his scourge and licked his lips. Two women accompanied the Hound. Both women came dressed as nuns. Both peered down, their faces shielded by hoods, so the royal guards could see neither properly . The guards opened the doors to the royal residence.

As the party turned a corridor, they heard a sound ring out. It was a peculiar noise. Something that none of them had ever heard before. The noise was discordant and rough. It sounded like strident strings being thrashed against prison bars very loudly.

'What is that?' Telson asked. He saw a shadowy figure by a wall. A cowering character hidden by a niche.

'Take him. Bring him to me,' Telson instructed his Palatine guards.

A guard moved promptly. He captured the figure. The person wore a hooded cloak that altogether hid his face. In his hands was a detestable thing. He held a musical implement. A tool fashioned to make music. The person clasped this foul apparatus. Telson guessed it was a phorminx.

'This is not right,' the false-Prioress said out loud. Her plan had gone wrong. The Music Bearer was required to be found with her husband in his bedchamber. Not out in the corridor. The plan was meant to play out so they would find together him with the Music Bearer. So her husband could be accused of sin and collusion.

Stupid girl, said the Landgravine. She had made a hash of a brilliantly detailed plan. It had taken weeks to piece *this* together. Yet her meticulous plot had fallen apart.

The strange figure clasped the musical instrument by its neck. Telson went to him and pulled down his hood. The young Hound revealed a youthful face. 'This is not the Music Bearer I seek—' he said, with confidence and authority. 'See — he does not have the high cheekbones. I seek the true Music Bearer, not this stripling imposter.' He held the cheeks of the young man steadfastly in his hands. He pointed the face towards his guards. So they might see, by light of the candle, that this young lad was not the man they looked for.

'Play it,' Telson demanded. 'Play the wicked thing!'

The figure seemed uncomfortable. He shifted on the soles of his bare feet. There was a flash of dismay in his eyes.

'Play it,' repeated Telson.

The youth did not move.

'Play the damn thing ...'

But the youth could not play the phorminx. He cut his hand across the strings. He sent out another harsh sound. The sound was absolutely not musical. The sound was tuneless.

'Hear that?' Telson said. 'He is not a Bearer of Music. They lied us to... They set us up to fail—'

He gave the 'Prioress' a reproachful stare. It was she that led them to this place. She that had lied to them. She had gathered them under false pretences. The young Hound's guards now looked at her in an ill-natured manner.

'But, but...' the woman began to babble. The noble lady tried to think things through. Who was the lad with the instrument? Why was he not capable of playing the awful thing? She could not explain any of it. So instead, she did what she showed up at the Palace to do, anyway. She marched straight into the royal bedroom. I can salvage something from this, she muttered under her breath.

She flung open the doors of the royal bedchamber. She let herself in.

The false-Prioress entered the room. She recovered her full majestic authority. She adopted her legitimate ways. She became the Landgravine and threw-off the falsehood of the guise she'd taken. She stood erect and proud. Her husband would vouch for her, she presumed. He'd explain who she really was. The young Hound followed her into the chamber, telling the guards to stay with the false Music Bearer.

They entered a sumptuous, well-lit apartment. The room had been adorned with wonderful features. Hangings lined the walls and expensive carpets scattered the floor. There was no one to be seen.

The Landgravine crossed the main room and walked to the opposite side. She headed for a large, padded bed. The bed reeked of expensive perfumes and had been furnished with the most exquisitely embroidered curtains. She drew back the curtains to reveal the Landgrave.

He was in post-coital embrace. With a young woman. An undressed young woman.

The Landgravine screamed. His Highness practically jumped out of his skin.

The young Hound viewed past the screens. He peered through the curtains towards a man he recognised to be the Landgrave. The minor kinglet was in bed with a whore. So what? It was the type of behaviour you'd expected from an aristocrat. They all did it. Why did she make such a fuss?

But, of course, her highness the Landgravine made a fuss because she had finally discovered the secret affair. Her husband, and her most-trusted servant, were lovers. She felt a sickness. It consumed her. Her stomach felt as if it were on fire. She thought that blood would pump through her head and make it explode.

'How could you do this to me Melita?' the Landgravine cried.

Meanwhile, the Landgrave sought to collect his blankets around him. He attempted to cover himself up. The minor royal endeavoured to protect what little nobility and probity he had left.

Melita sobbed. It was a tactic that worked well in these kinds of sticky situations. That misleading little wretch, she thought. *That little bitch Atalanta.* She had double-crossed everyone.

Telson decided he'd had enough of the drama. The situation was fast descending into absurdity. Temenos, stood behind him, her face hidden beneath a hood — but she was asked to join the young Hound by the bedside of the kinglet and his female companion.

The two wayward lovers seemed ridiculously vulnerable. They sat up in their feather bed, with barely a stitch to cover their nakedness. With the humiliated cuckquean looking on. And all this was being observed by a man of the cloth — a cleric, no less — with a nun.

The humorous aspect never entered the mind of Telson. He was a serious man. He was not accustomed to mirth. What he saw before him was a dirty old rascal in bed with a whore. He abhorred the scene, of course. Because adultery was a sin. But this man's past infidelities created the true bitterness he felt inside his beating heart. Because, you see, Telson had been left on the by-way, as a foundling, by this man, and left there because of his deeds. This old rogue was to blame for everything. The hatred that Telson felt run deep. It flooded through his young veins.

But the true sin that the old fool had committed was the abandonment of his first child, the true heir to the throne, the Landgravine's daughter. He had abandoned her wilfully.

Lord-Lady Temenos had told Telson everything, after he'd rescued her from the burning tower. His half-sister had been abandoned. The kinglet had abandoned her simply because she was female. She had been forsaken — cast aside — because the Landgrave wanted a son. He was a callous, insensitive, selfish old man. He called himself a ruler, but actually he was an egocentric bully. And a womaniser.

'Tell them what you told me—' Telson said.

Temenos gazed at the young Hound.

'Tell them about my sister —'

The Lord-Lady looked around at those gathered by the bedside. The broken queen — dressed in a theatrical costume, pretending to be a prioress. She ought to be ashamed of herself for this charade. But her heart was broken, her mind was utterly destroyed.

Then she looked at the bald old womaniser in bed — with his yellow skin. His nobbled knees stuck from the bedclothes. His repulsive little gut gurgled. She noted his ugly, protruding chin. She saw deep into his watery eyes. And she scanned his grey body hair and repellent saggy skin. What a fool, she thought.

Then she looked at the slut in bed with him. This floozy had spent an entire lifetime whoring. Clawing her way to the top. Just to get to this moment in history. Hadn't she done well to get the old goat? Maybe. Maybe not.

Finally, Temenos looked at the young Hound, Telson. Would he release her once she had performed this melodramatic task? Or would she remain his captive? Where did she go from here?

Temenos spoke. 'I am the Lord-Lady Temenos,' she announced. 'You may have never heard of me. I will explain who I am. I am a travelling consul for the Music Bearers...'

All eyes were upon her.

'The task they presented me, and it has been my holy ministry for years, was to collect foundling children that their parents had abandoned. Children that needed urgent adoption and care because their parents were dead or unknown. I took the children, the orphans, and I brought them to cloistered communities. And, in those secret communities, the fraternal brotherhoods cared for the babes — and the orphans grew-up and were fed and educated. There is hope that one day, each-and-every child will contribute to our world... Telson — the Black Hound who stands here — is one of my waifs. I am proud of him. His parents neglected him — he became left outside a stranger's home to die. I gathered him into my bosom, and I took him to the Abbey of St. Hubert. Where he developed into the striking man, you see today.'

They all stared at the young Hound.

'Telson is your son,' she added.

Temenos said this with unexpected frankness. She pointed at the Landgrave in an accusatory fashion. He gasped in response.

'But that's not all... One summer, before I collected Telson, your son, from near your Palace grounds, they informed me of another child who was also rejected... I was told they also left this child for the 'taking.' When I arrived, I found the baby to be fit and healthy. In fact, she was an intelligent child. She revealed signs of what we call the 'harmonic root.' She was well-equipped to be a musician and a Music Bearer. That abandoned girl was your daughter.'

Once more, Temenos pointed at the Landgrave as she uttered the accusing words.

Temenos heard the Landgravine sob at the shock disclosure. The anguished mother fell to her knees and let out a long groan of pain.

Temenos continued, 'I took that girl to the Music Bearers — she took the name Atalanta. She will be a travelling-consul herself one day. Perhaps she will take over my ministry once I am gone.'

The name Atalanta registered with the Landgravine.

Even through her sobs of pain, the name pierced her heart — like an arrow.

The Landgravine realised — in that moment — the true nature of these revelations. Because, through her own duplicitous and misleading actions, she had abducted — taken hostage — her own daughter. A daughter she thought was lost forever. And a daughter who was her only true love.

Abruptly the Landgravine felt more anxious than she felt before. Even now, as these things were revealed, she knew her evil machinations might lead to her daughter's death. The Landgravine peered all around. Where was Atalanta anyway? Why was she not here with the false Music Bearer? Had she somehow escaped?

Temenos concluded her accusations. So glanced at Telson, who gestured she may leave the royal bed chamber, though he lingered by the bed.

Once outside the chamber, Temenos instructed the Palatine guards to free the boy. They looked at her — puzzled — then stared into the open bedchamber, to get the order authorised by their boss. Telson nodded agreement. He made a sweeping motion with his hands, indicating the boy should be released. Telson was sombre and serious-minded, so they didn't want to disturb him any more than they needed. The Palatine guards took away the phorminx and told the boy to run off.

He fled the building at once.

The boy ran back to an old cabin in the grounds. There he met Atalanta, the neglected daughter of the Landgrave. She had waited for him. She gave him a huge kiss.

But there was no time for Jamin to tell his story. It had been a close-run thing. He almost lost his head. He would have time to tell his story yet... in the many nights they'd have together... the many night yet to come. Now, though, they had to depart this place. So, the pair made off in the night. Atalanta and Jamin together. They did not look back. They walked forward with courage. To explore a new future.

THE EPILOGUE

In the region of England where these events took place, people still say they frequently feel the disturbing presence of a black hound, a ghostly dog, which follows them, especially when they are on solitary journeys. Occasionally they imagine that the shadowy hound tracks them. It is said, by observers, that this otherworldly creature particularly hates music. So the people of the region caution visitors not to sing or play any musical instrument as they traverse the lonely tracks and by-ways of Suffolk.

Is the supernatural dog an imagined thing? Some speculate the ghost-dog is an omen of death. It is a popular myth.

In 1557, in the parish of Bungay, Suffolk, a black hound raged around the church of Saint Mary during a religious service. The beast attacked several members of the congregation. Supposedly, it went mad during the singing of hymns. Many reliable eyewitnesses attested to the event occurring and thought music caused it to react so furiously.

Of course, you might fairly think that what eyewitnesses saw that day was a quite unremarkable wild dog that had unwittingly invaded the church building and was then sent livid by a turmoil of unfamiliar sounds and smells. You're doubtless right! Who can argue with that logic? But, since then, an image of the Black Hound is incorporated into the official coat-of-arms for Bungay. See it for yourself. Is this phantasmal dog a folk-memory of the Black Hound named Zadock?

∼

Atalanta and Jamin, the son of the hawk-master, fled together to the free city of Vindolanda.

There, in the North, they started a new life.

The Sisters of Mercy took the Landgravine away. She lived-out her remaining days in a dark cell.

The young Hound named Telson arrested Melita and His Highness, the Landgrave. After their arrest, they disappeared. There has been much speculation about their fate. But it is likely they were both secretly garrotted by Palatine guards, and their bodies quietly burned.

The half-brother of the Landgrave, the Margrave, was established in his place — and became viceroy to the kingdom.

Cinnamon, who had prepared to be a consul for the Music Bearers — departed into the sunset. But she was happy with how things turned out because she was at last affianced to the man she loved. The Last Music Bearer.

DIABOLUS IN MUSICA?

Diabolus in Musica?

Is there a devil in music?

Could music ever be forbidden?

Polyphony was viewed as controversial in church music during medieval times, when the church occupied a centralized position in society. The authorities thought that polyphony obscured the sacred words and used uncomfortable chords.

Girolamo Savonarola, the Dominican dictator of Florence, 1494-1498, instituted an extreme puritanical campaign and he "banned" music in his city-state.

The church of Rome declared all theatrical music to be immoral in the early 18th century and this included famous baroque arias by Handel, Alessandro Scarlatti, and Antonio Caldara. Grammy award-winning opera singer Cecilia Bartoli released an album of this "forbidden" music, Opera Proibita, in 2005.

As recently as the beginning of the 20th century, Pope Pius X between 1903 and 1914 imposed a restriction on the use of certain wind instruments, including the saxophone.

Under the Lord Protector of England, during the Long Parliament of 1640-1660 (also known as the Puritan era), the state prohibited playing, practicing, and listening to music.

During the reign of the Taliban government in Afghanistan, between 1996 and 2001, music was banned. The Taliban broke their instruments and punished those who played music. Afghan musicians buried their instruments or fled to neighbouring countries. Those who remained in their homeland continued to earn a dangerous living, operating as touring minstrels. The music ban was resumed in 2021 with the return of the Islamic Emirate.

The Afghanistan National Music Institute, Kabul's first and only music academy, an internationally renowned school that teaches Afghan and Western music, operated a much-celebrated all-female ensemble from 2010 and right up until the fall of Kabul to the Taliban, in 2021. Fortunately, all the music students were evacuated to safety and found refuge in Portugal. Many of the evacuated students left their parents and loved ones to their fate and were told to bring very few belongings. Most left their instruments behind.

In Iran, all music must be approved by the Ministry of Culture and Islamic Guidance.

Pussy Riot gained worldwide notoriety when five members of the punk rock collective held a performance inside Moscow's Cathedral of Christ the Saviour, in February 2012. The group's actions were condemned as sacrilegious by the Orthodox clergy and the gig was eventually stopped by church security officials. The musicians said their protest was directed at the leaders of the Orthodox Church who supported Putin during his election campaign.

ABOUT THE AUTHOR

Neil Mach was born and raised in Surrey, England

He lives with his wife Sue in a small bungalow on the riverbank at Staines, near Windsor

He has two daughters, Tanna and Perdie

#neilmach

*For the Music Bearers of the world.
May they continue to bring us harmony...*

UNTITLED

A handy Music Bearer's glossary is available here: https://lastmusicbearer.wordpress.com

You can tweet to the Music Bearer's here: https://twitter.com/MusicBearer

You can get the author's Newsletter here: https://neilmach.me/

You can follow the author on Twitter here: https://twitter.com/neilmach

The author invites you to make friends here: https://www.facebook.com/author.neilmach

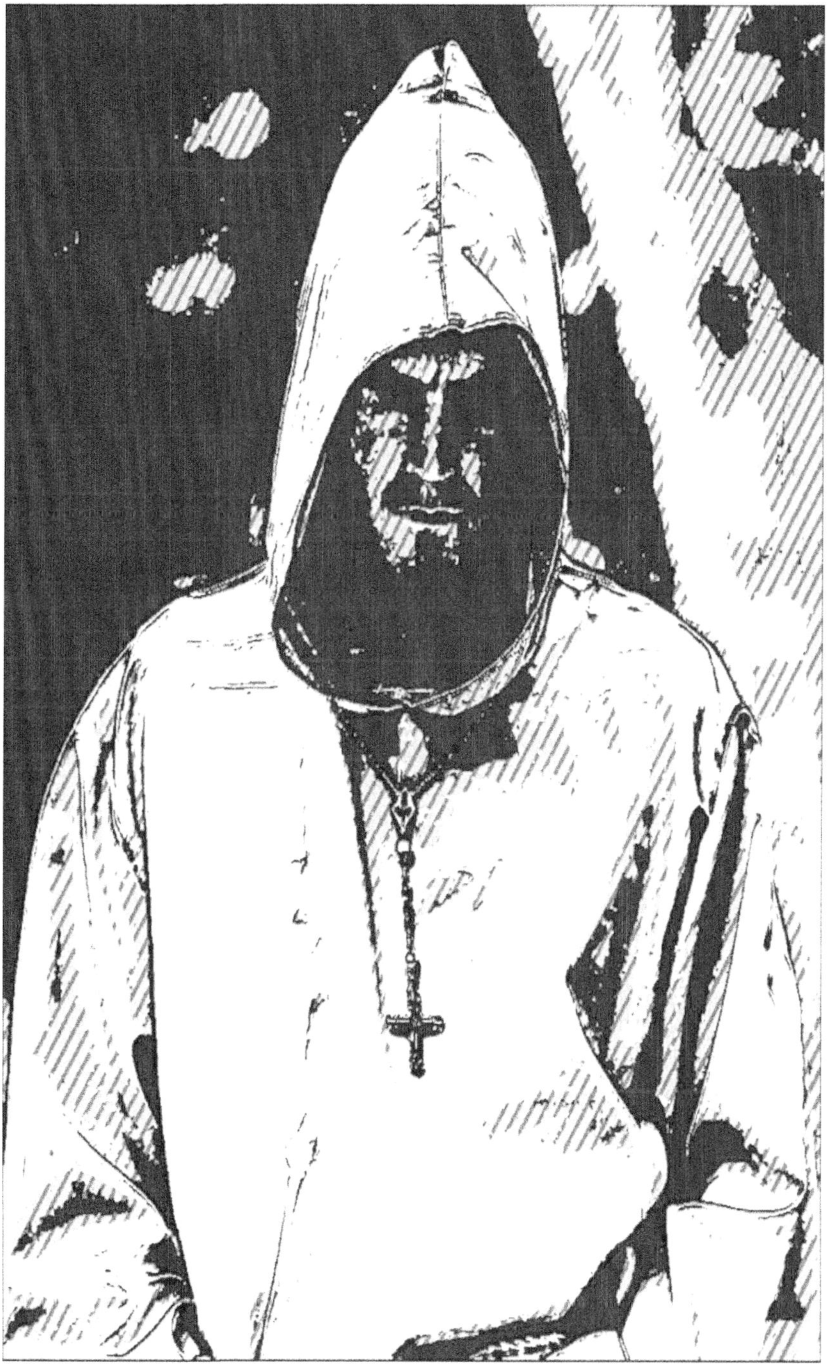

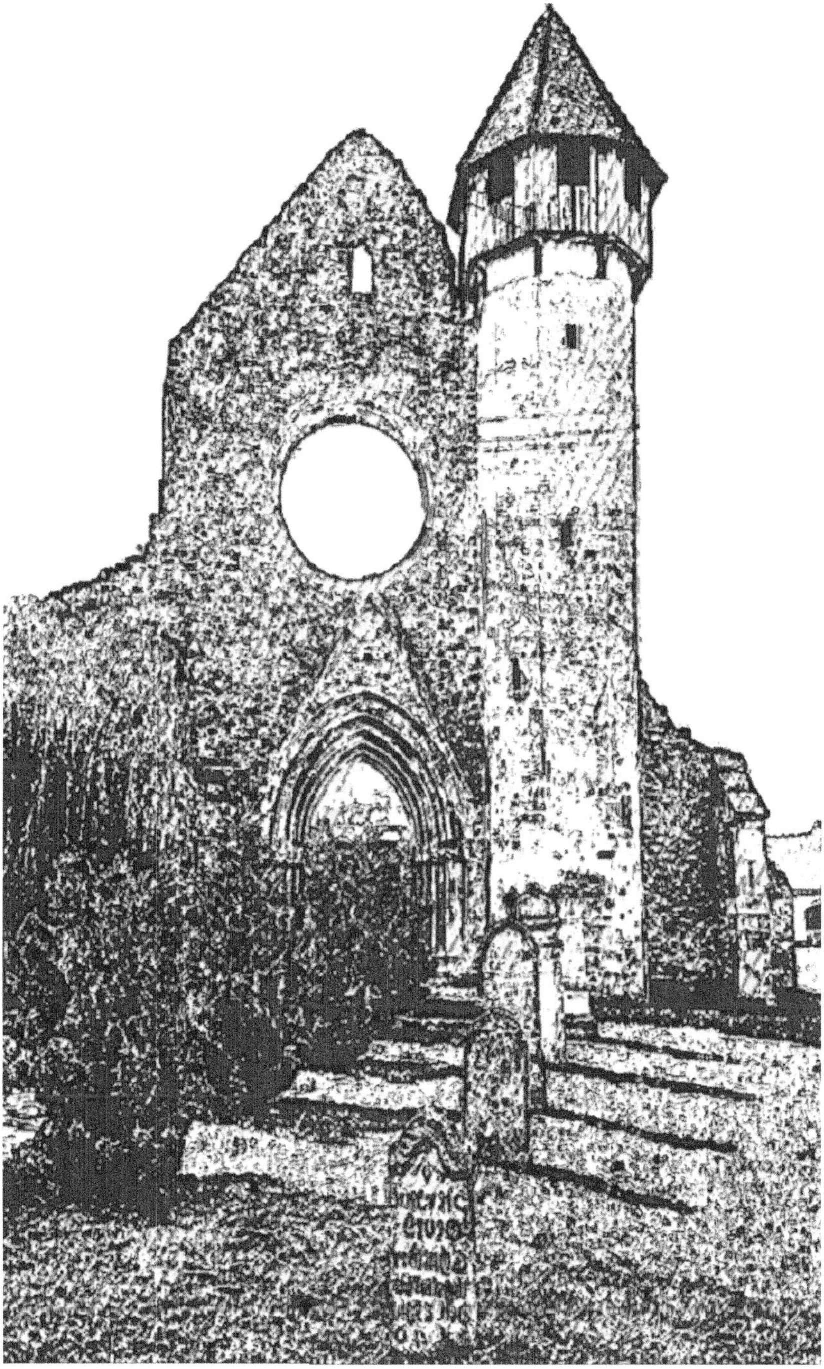

Printed in Great Britain
by Amazon

20767297R00149